BACKSTABBERS

BACKSTABBERS

Rahsaan Ali

www.urbanbooks.net

Urban Books
1199 Straight Path
West Babylon, NY 11704

ISBN- 13: 978-1-60162-160-3
ISBN- 10: 1-60162-160-4

First Printing May 2009
Printed in the United States of America

10 9 8 7 6 5 4 3 2 1

Distributed by Kensington Publishing Corp.
Submit Wholesale Orders to:
Kensington Publishing Corp.
C/O Penguin Group (USA) Inc.
Attention: Order Processing
405 Murray Hill Parkway
East Rutherford, NJ 07073-2316
Phone: 1-800-526-0275
Fax: 1-800-227-9604

PROLOGUE

*B*LAM!
*B*BLAM!
Brrrraaduup!
Brrrraaduup!

Tracy Kane never knew what hit him because he never
saw it coming. His merciless violator had filled him with
more lead than the reservoir water of New Jersey. Feet
scattered everywhere as frantic, terrorized screams of distress cried out into the night. He choked on his own blood
as he struggled to exhale. The threads that had once sewn
the essence of his spirit separated like double-stitched
clothing, and his torn soul quickly unfastened.

Tracy faintly heard a voice say, "Uh-uh, dawg. Let it go.
You a rider, right? Right, nigga?" Then his eyes fluttered
and focused slightly as the assailant's voice softly echoed
in his head, and everything faded to black.

CHAPTER ONE

TRACY KANE

"Yeah, nigga, tell me this ain't some real fly shit." Tracy sprang off the diving board of the indoor pool on the bottom deck of the American Cruise Lines ship.

Cameras clicked and quickly flashed, catching each frame of his acrobatic capability as he shot up in the air like a bullet from a .45 automatic. As he began his descent, he tucked and spun, straightened out his entire body, and sliced through the heated water. Then he quickly resurfaced after touching the floor, and climbed out of the pool.

"Yo, that's it, guys," Boochie, the photographer, said to his crew. "That's a wrap. I think your boy Christian gonna be happy with this, man. These looking tight." Boochie looked on the display screen on the back of his camera. "It only took like twenty takes," he sarcastically said. He tossed Tracy a towel.

"Yeah. Them shits will work because I'm done for the day, know what I'm saying? If dude call you, you tell him I'm retired for the evening."

"Whatever, man. I get paid, regardless. You coming to the dining hall party tonight?"

Tracy shook his head. "Naw. I got a date this evening. Talk to you in the morning when the ship pull in."

Mostly everyone in the swimming pool area was a model for some type of clothing line or magazine cover. Coincidentally, a popular magazine called *Twenty Going On Thirty* was throwing a party on the same day of Tracy's shoot.

Tracy didn't like them people from over there. They were straight haters and breeders of jealousy. It was an insult to him that they even had the audacity to invite him, seeing that he worked for a rival clothing company. He was a Christian Elijah model for life and wasn't shit going to change about that.

Tracy was Christian Elijah's top face, but he was an asshole. He was never on time and came to work when he wanted to. But that was his style, always resistant to the rules. His employer tolerated the bullshit because what Tracy brought to the table sold the clothes. He was the object of the Christian Elijah culture, the family, the fashion, the ravenously lavish and materialistic statement of masculinity. The modern-day conceited nigga with a fetish for chilled bottles of vanity locked deep within a bucket of ice.

To say he was arrogant would be an understatement. He was cocky as shit, and it showed by his nasty attitude. A smooth swagger in still motion was his theme, and money was the only thing on his mind. And if someone didn't like the way he carried himself, he'd cut 'em off.

Tracy loved the camera, and the camera loved him back. And when he wasn't busy playing "Pretty Boy Floyd" for Christian Elijah or posting up inside the pages of some inner city hip-hop magazine, he was fucking every woman he could get his hands on.

* * *

CEO Christian Elijah began, "Look, Trace—"

"Naw, you look, man." Tracy sat up in the bed in his room. "I'm out here as a favor to you. I don't have to be here. Shit!" He stood and walked to the window of his room. With the exception of the red lights blinking on the antennas of passing ships sailing off in the distance, it was pitch-black outside.

"Just shut the fuck up and listen! When you get off the ship tomorrow, I want you to come straight to my house. There'll be a car waiting for you when you pull in."

Tracy turned off the power on his phone. Some young lady Tracy had scooped up earlier in the week asked, "Is everything all right, daddy?"

"Hell yeah, everything's all right. Everything all right with you?"

"Damn. Your attitude is mad bogus." The young lady sat up in the bed, holding the sheets over her bare breasts. "What's your problem?"

"Know what? You're my problem. Company's over." Tracy stepped into his boxers. "What?"

"I don't feel like company anymore."

Tracy's stare was so direct, she quickly dressed herself and collected her morning things out of the bathroom.

"Peace," he said, lying across the bed, as she stormed out and slammed the door behind her.

CHAPTER TWO

TRACY KANE

As Tracy stepped inside the black Continental car that Christian assured him would be there when he got off the ship, the driver placed his Louis Vuitton baggage into the car trunk then got behind the wheel.

Three and a half hours later they were pulling into the circular driveway of Christian's house out in New Jersey's exclusive Cherry Hill Township.

Tracy walked up the five steps leading to the front door, which opened just as his finger extended to ring the bell.

Christian was a real thin man, walnut-complexioned and well conditioned. (His nails were manicured and evenly polished on both hands.) Forty-three and living real comfortably, his name was being worn across the T-shirts of thugs, and perfectly hand-crafted pairs of silk panties worn by the ladies. He'd started the business by doing some intricate hustling then borrowing the rest of the money from his friend Blue, who had everything on lock—the block, the life, and close ties with a corrupt police sergeant named Frank Ronald.

Frank had officers under him that were just as dirty, and he'd taken a special interest in a young officer fresh out of the academy. Slowly, with the assistance of other officers, the inexperienced officer, Dennis Frogger, from Yonkers, New York, was lured into the corruption.

Blue paid out a handsome sum of money to Sergeant Frank Ronald to alert him when it was time to close up shop. Meanwhile, the sergeant kept the competition off the street, using his officers to falsely arrest them, especially by planting drugs on them.

It was a time when everybody was making money and the only clean cop was a dead cop. If there were law-abiding officers working the shift where Blue's workers sold his product, Frank would let him know. Blue, in turn, would give the sergeant tips that led to arrests and convictions of competing dealers.

Officer Dennis Frogger quickly became enveloped with the idea of receiving a bonus every day. Sergeant Frank Ronald even had Frogger do a couple of pickups from Blue personally, and that's when he first met Christian.

Christian had worked with Blue on several occasions. He'd do a li'l something here, a li'l something there, and Blue would serve him a nice payday.

In fact, they'd been best friends at one time, but after fifteen years of friendship, Blue soon learned that their relationship wasn't as tight as he thought, even though he'd held Christian's pockets down with whatever he needed when he needed it. Christian was even there for the birth of Blue's first child, but it wasn't worth shit, because Christian only cared about Christian. And even though he wasn't the big man Blue was, Blue treated him as such.

Christian earned his biggest payoff when Blue had hired

him to kill a troublemaker named Stacy Kane. She and many others were tired of all the drugs in the community and complained every day to the commissioner, to City Hall, and gathered the community to protest every Saturday in the park in front of her building. The protests not only made the police look like they weren't doing their job, which reflected badly on Sergeant Frank Ronald, but they also disrupted the constant flow of Blue's hourly revenue.

But Stacy Kane had a son to raise, and she wasn't going to let the streets take him away. But the streets took her instead.

Christian was arrested shortly thereafter, and it wasn't long before the murder was connected back to Blue. Christian had snitched, and the key to Blue's cell was tossed out into the middle of the Pacific Ocean. Christian served no time at all because his confession got a conviction. And that right there put Sergeant Frank Ronald where he wanted to be.

Christian stole whatever monies he and Blue had accrued, and disappeared to an undisclosed location, where he stayed on the low with his lavish lifestyle. Every once in a while, he would throw Blue's wife and two young children, Cedric and Mia, some money, but then he suddenly stopped. When he heard they were dead broke, he laughed.

With the money he'd stolen from Blue, he started up his Christian Elijah clothing line, a venture he and Blue had once discussed starting up, with Blue fronting the money.

Blue would've had Christian killed, except that he thought it would have led back to him. But he wouldn't have been able to find Christian anyway. He'd been set up by a lot of people, and one way or the other, everybody was going to pay.

"Come on in," Christian said. "I'm out on the balcony. You want a drink or something?"

"I'm good." Tracy followed him up the stairs and out to the balcony.

"Sit down, man. What's the problem, huh? You not happy here or something?"

Tracy removed his red fitted cap and scratched his head. "Naw, man. Everything's everything."

"Well, something's got to be the matter. You're talking all reckless on the phone. I'm hearing your name come up in a lot of conversations. You telling other niggas things you should be telling me. They're not the ones paying you, I'm paying you." Christian patted his bare chest through the slit of his orange button-down. "You the only one that's been complaining. I hope I don't need to start worrying about you. I got a lot of shit going and don't need muthafuckas all up in my business." He pointed toward the city. "See what I'm saying? I don't need it."

"Yo, it's like this." Tracy clasped his hands together. "Yeah, you right, I shoulda been talking to you. Only, you don't answer the phone when you know a nigga calling for his dough. But then you turn around and always want a nigga to be on time? I love doing this shit, but if I ain't feeling right about something, I'ma speak on it."

"You still crying about that three thousand dollars. Here"—Christian reached into his pocket then pulled out a clip with a thin stack of neatly folded money—"I just took this out the bank this morning. This is eight thousand dollars," he said, tossing it on the table. "Don't let me hear no more shit, man. We men, so act like we are. Got some shit on your mind, you say it to me."

The balcony door slid open, and Trinity, Christian's nineteen-year-old daughter, walked out in a black sports bra and pink wife-beater. Mahogany-complexioned, she was 5 foot 7, athletically toned, and had a dimpled smile that could light up the northeast corner of a Mason's darkest secret.

"Hi, Daddy." Trinity kissed her father's cheek with her glossy, sensuous lips. "What's up, Tracy?"

"What up? How you?" Tracy responded.

"You know me, just school and work. Right, Daddy?" Trinity rubbed her father's head.

"You already know what it is—One decline in your grades and I'll take those car keys from you."

"Yeah, yeah. Anyway, so what you been up to, playa?" she asked Tracy.

"Same thing. Work is work."

"True that. Well, I got phone calls to make. I'm out." Trinity went back inside the house.

"That's my heart right there. She's my everything."

"So, yo," Tracy said, interrupting the sentimental soliloquy, "I'm about to be out too. We finished, right?"

"We are done. One more thing before you leave."

"What's that?" Tracy lifted himself out of the chair, both hands on its arms.

"Don't forget, we have a contract."

CHAPTER THREE

TRACY KANE

Tracy dropped a bowl of ice cubes into the blender that sat on a blue marble countertop inside his kitchen. Cajun battered shrimp generously seasoned with granulated garlic, cayenne pepper, and salt fried in a stainless steel pan atop the white Kenmore stove. This was the second time he had to refill the snack tray for his Saturday night poker game. Three of his main men from Christian Elijah, Shane, Cadillac, and Marcel, the other models that added to the mystique of "the Culture," were at his place, drinking Hennessy and soda.

"Soup's on, niggas. Shut up beefing," Tracy said as he walked through the double swinging doors. "Y'all about ready to come up off some more of that paper?" He placed the silver tray in the middle of the table.

Shane looked at the pile of chips on Tracy's side. "I'm about done. Y'all tapped me out."

"Yeah. I know you is, nigga. You be fuckin' wit' the Trace. You can't stencil this, nigga."

The men all laughed then began picking from the Louisiana-style snack.

"Yo, you straighten that drama out with Christian?" Marcel asked.

"We came to some conclusions, know what I'm saying? So shit is a'ight for the time being." Tracy popped a shrimp in his mouth.

Marcel continued, "You need to chill, son. You're in a real good position right now. Better than any of us. You got the longest contract and shit. Fuck, man, stop tripping."

"It's like this, man. Right now, Tracy Kane is very popular. I mean, I'm really what it is. Ya feel me? Dude better come correct, or I go elsewhere."

"Do what your instincts tell ya, playa." Cadillac sparked a cigarette. "We all in this together. Same shit happening to you could happen to us."

Tracy waved off Cadillac's interjection. "So, anyway . . . what's up with you, Shane? I hear you finally gonna go 'head and marry that bitch."

"Watch your mouth, man."

"Aw, come on, you know that's how I talk. My bad, a'ight? So you're tying the knot, huh?"

"No doubt. Real talk, and I ain't even being a bitch about it. I love her."

"That's what's up. I guess this calls for a celebration." Tracy walked to his room and returned with a small purple pouch. He poured a small mound of "willie" on the table. "Gentlemen, get your straws ready."

They quickly inhaled the illicit madness up through their nostrils, which resulted in a series of sporadic coughs, sneezes, and minor choking.

"Oh shit!" Marcel shook his head, trying to compose himself. "Yo, that's some fire."

Cadillac rubbed his nose. "Literally."

"I'm tweaking. Word. My dude, this is straight flames," Shane said.

Tracy laughed. "Told y'all. Only the best for my niggas."

"Yeah." Cadillac pounded the table with his fist. "You definitely gots to get me some of this here."

"No, my brother. You gots to get your own." Tracy laughed. "You gots to get your own," he repeated, laughing harder.

Cadillac laughed too. "You's a funny muthafucka."

"To my dude, Shane," Cadillac said, and they all raised their glasses in the air.

"You my nigga, you know that," Tracy said. "God bless you and yours. Cheers."

"Cheers," they all said.

CHAPTER FOUR

CHRISTIAN ELIJAH

Christian was in his eighth-floor office in New Jersey. He said into the phone, "Listen to me. I give you guys good business, exceptional fuckin' deals, and you're going to tell me you're pulling out? Why? You can't discuss that right now? Who the fuck do you think you're talking to? Hello? Hello? Son of a bitch!" He slammed the phone down and called through the intercom. "Alexis."

"Yes, Mister Elijah?"

"Get my lawyer on the phone."

"Right away, sir."

"I don't need this shit."

Christian walked over to the sink on the other side of the room and turned the water on. He placed his hands under the running water then splashed it on his face. He looked up into the mirror on the wall. Huge, hefty bags of deprivation hung under his tiresome eyes. Always on top of his business, he'd only been averaging about four hours of sleep a day.

His clothing line had begun generating huge amounts of money three years ago, but the clothes were selling because of Tracy's appearance. He was like the hip-hop model craze, his grey-brown eyes luring the hearts of women. Yeah, Christian could've found somebody else, but why try? He was doing a fine enough job jerking the shit out of Tracy.

Christian had bigger and better plans in the works, which he was going to discuss at a two o'clock business meeting with an African guy named Akinsanya, the friend of a friend, who was supplying the five boroughs of New York with foreign vendors who sold bootleg name-brand clothing.

"Mister Elijah, your two p.m. appointment is here," Alexis said.

Bzzzz! The door opened.

Akinsanya, dressed in a yellow linen short-sleeve shirt and a pair of matching pants, a sixteen-inch Italian gold chain hanging from his neck as if he were some expensive slave, and a row of permanent gold covering the top row of his teeth, walked into the room. He was very dark, and his skin was smooth. And the expression on his face was serious as black-on-black crime.

Christian watched Akinsanya as he stood looking around, seemingly impressed by the stylishly decorated office.

"Mister Elijah, *as-Salamu alaikum.*" Akinsanya extended his hand as he walked toward Christian's desk.

Christian met him halfway across his oak desk with a mutual handshake. "Akinsanya, right?"

"Yes, that is my name."

"You mind if I ask what that means?"

"In my country, it means bravery brings revenge."

"That's funny." Christian laughed then sat back in his chair. "That's real funny. I was just going to tell you the same thing before you walked in."

"I do not understand, Mister Elijah."

"You don't understand, huh? Then I guess we have nothing else to discuss. I'm sorry that I wasted your time."

"Americans . . ." Akinsanya shook his head from side to side.

After he turned and walked away, he heard the click of a trigger being pulled back. He stopped in his tracks and slowly turned around, his hands by his side. "What this is?"

"Selling my clothes bootleg—You know what happens to niggas like you in this city for doing shit like that? Robbing a muthafucka? Selling my name and I don't benefit from it? Huh?" Christian, his .38 aimed at Akinsanya's forehead, tilted his head to the side and slowly walked toward him. "Seems unrealistic, don't it? You come out thinking you're going to have a good day then life throws you a bullet—*Pow*," he whispered, taking a step back.

Suddenly the office door burst open, and three goons with size on them ran in and took Akinsanya to the floor with an enormous thud.

"That's him, the muthafucka that been stealing from me. Fuck him up!"

"Wait!" Akinsanya yelled.

"Oh, you ready to understand now? Pick his ass up and put him in the chair," Christian said to the thugs. "You making me lose money, playa. Now you gonna start paying me back. You're going to cease and desist selling my shit. Where the warehouse they making them at?"

"I cannot say."

"You better say something, unless you want that asswhupping."

"I will have to let you conference with my brother. We will set a meeting."

"So now you're saying your brother running things?

A'ight. Get him on the phone." Christian tossed him the cordless.

"Assante," he said to his brother after contacting him. "No, things are not well . . . Yes, I am here with him now . . . Yes, brother." Akinsanya passed the phone to Christian.

"Hello," Christian said. "Oh yeah, I'm ready to meet with your ass soon as possible."

CHAPTER FIVE

TRACY KANE

Tracy was out meeting with the so-called rival company, trying to negotiate a better deal for himself. It wasn't the first time he'd met with them. He'd always turned the money down because the contract they were offering was always bullshit. He really didn't know what he wanted to do, with so many people in his ear talking this, that, and the third. One minute, he was a thug in fly clothes that didn't let anybody bad-mouth Christian's company. The next, he was telling people that his contract was bullshit and that Christian had been robbing him blind.

Tracy and Michelle Renee, CEO of *Twenty Going On Thirty* magazine, sat on the roof of her Upper East Side Manhattan suite on the tenth floor, from where they could see tall, mirrored buildings scrape the sky and reflect multiple views of the evening moon hovering above.

Michelle said, "This is what is, Tracy."

"I don't see why I gotta change for anybody. I'm me. I ain't out here acting like something I'm not."

"That's what the problem is, darling." Michelle sipped her glass of water. "The reason why you're still where you're at is because you haven't yet learned how to leave the hood in the hood. In other words, you don't have to act like a nigger all the time, fighting in the club, riding as a passenger in a stolen car. You're not making a rap album, boo. You're just a model."

"My inside business is just what it is—my fuckin' business."

"I think you're becoming much too full of yourself, babe. This shit can be over for you just as quick as it started. You just happen to be what's in this season. What about next season? Seasons change, and once you lose your publicity, the public will toss your black ass out. See, what you seem to keep forgetting is, you need the publicity. The publicity doesn't need you, sweetheart."

"Apparently, it does. Ain't that why I'm here? Pardon me one sec." Tracy flipped the lid on his Nextel. "Yo . . . no doubt, no doubt . . . I'm in a li'l meeting right now, but I'ma holla."

"So what do you think about the terms of my contract?" Michelle asked, a little irritated with his arrogance.

"Know what? I'ma get back to you on that."

"You do that." Michelle slid him a manila envelope. "Here's a little incentive to help you think on it a little more."

Tracy and Cadillac were walking down 34th Street in Manhattan toward 8th Avenue to the convenience booth around the corner, so Cadillac could get some cigarettes.

The African bootlegger next to the booth shouted, "Christian Elijah tees and pants! Twenty dollars for two tees!"

Cadillac turned to Tracy as they approached the man. "What that muthafucka just said?"

"Ay, yo," Tracy said, picking up the pace in his step.

"What's up, brother?" the man said. "I got that Christian Elijah. For you, two tees and two pants for forty-five. All these other muthafuckas sell for fifty or more. Come on, I give good hookup." He pulled a large box from under his foldup picnic table.

"You're going to give me a hookup? Gimme this shit." Tracy dumped the box of clothes on the ground and flipped the man's table over. "You don't sell this muthafuckin' shit out here."

"What are you doing?" The man grabbed a bat and ran around the table.

Before the man could use it, Cadillac grabbed it from him, and Tracy punched him upside the head, knocking him down on a pile of clothes, sunglasses, and umbrellas.

"Stay down. If I come through here again and see you out here selling our shit, you'll get the same shit again, bitch." Tracy kicked what was left inside the box over to him.

A crowd began to form around the scene, and cars, taxis, then a police vehicle pulled over to the side and jammed up the traffic. As Cadillac and Tracy began quick-stepping from the scene, two black officers emerged from the squad car.

"Hey, you," one of the officers yelled, running up, his hand on the handle of his Glock.

Tracy turned around. "Yo, what's up, man? Something we did wrong, officer?"

"What happened back there?"

Tracy asked the officer, "Did you talk to him?"

"Don't worry about all of that. I'm talking to you right now."

The other officer stepped up and pointed his thumb at Tracy. "Witnesses say it was this guy."

"You better start talking," the first officer said.

Tracy looked at the officer's nameplate. "I didn't get your name."

"Officer Owens, and this is my partner, Officer Thomas. Now speak."

"That nigga down there bootlegging my clothes, so I flipped his shit over and put him on his ass."

"You can't take the law into your own hands, sir," Officer Thomas said. "If he wants to press charges, we're going to have to arrest you."

"Man, this is bullshit." Tracy waved his hand in front of Officer Thomas's face. "That man ain't got no business out here selling our shit."

"Do me a favor, my man—Keep your hands by your side and out of my face."

Tracy dropped his hand. "So what? See if he wanna press charges. Make sure you arrest him too for pulling out a bat on us. The witnesses didn't tell you that, huh?"

Cadillac, overshadowing the officers with his 6 foot 5 frame, smoothly said, "Know what, brothers . . . how can we make this go away? I mean, we, me and him, is two busy men that got shit to do, just like you do. So why not make your job a little easier and get a bonus for it?" He pulled a nice little knot from the right pocket of his jacket.

"You trying to bribe us, sir?" Officer Owens asked Cadillac. "You think that, because you called me *brother*, I give a shit about your bribe? Man, put your fuckin' hands behind your back." The officer walked up on him.

"Stay right where you're at," Officer Thomas said to Tracy.

Cadillac pushed the 5 foot 3 Owens. "Yo, you not arrestin' me."

Thomas, swinging his gun back and forth from Tracy to Cadillac, barked, "Get on the fuckin' ground now!"

"We need backup!" Owens shouted into his radio.

"Backup? Man, you's a bitch!" Cadillac placed his hands behind his head.

Officer Owens quickly stood up and pointed his gun at Cadillac, while Officer Thomas placed his gun back in its holster and held Tracy's wrists together to lock the cuffs around them.

Tracy wiggled in Officer Thomas's grasp. "Yo, you doin' that shit too tight."

Officer Owens cautiously walked up to Cadillac and placed him in cuffs.

"Just chill, Trace. They ain't got shit."

Officer Owens looked at Officer Thomas. "Oh? Assaulting an officer ain't shit? We'll see."

"Yo, I'm not going to tell you again. You grippin' me too tight." Tracy spun around and clocked Thomas in the jaw.

More squad cars pulled to the scene, and an army of officers ran up the steps and out of Penn Station terminal. In fact, they came from every angle.

"I told you the shit was too tight." Tracy rubbed his wrists as he looked around at the odds against him. He was surrounded by eight officers, who slowly walked toward him.

Cadillac was taken down by officers more his size, while the others punished Tracy for striking out against a fellow officer.

Thomas and Owens stood back and almost regretted calling for backup as they witnessed their white counterparts take pride in handing a beat-down to another nigger.

CHAPTER SIX

TRACY KANE

"This is Angela Pileggi of Channel Zero news. Good evening to you. I'm standing here on Thirty-fourth Street and Eighth Avenue at Penn Station, a scene that appears to be yet another major strike at home for the NYPD. It all happened about five-thirty this evening when witnesses say Christian Elijah model, Tracy Kane, struck a man and flipped his table over in a fit of rage for selling bootleg T-shirts of the very company he models for. Tracy and fellow model, Kirk Cadillac Brown, became aggressive toward two investigating officers, which led to a melee, the results of which you see behind me." Angela moved to hold the mike up to one witness.

"It was straight bonkers," the witness said.

"It was foul," a young lady said, passengers rushing to board the express train bumping her.

An elderly lady carrying some Duane Reade bags said, "It's not right. The police do and get away with whatever they want. My grandchildren is more scared of the police than they is of the dealers and thugs in the lobby of my building. They beat on that boy like he was an animal, and two black officers stood by and watched. Hmm . . . they oughta be ashamed of themselves, and that's all I have to say about that." The lady then hobbled through the doors of the station and down an escalator.

The camera swung back to Angela.

"All of the officers, including Officers Owens and Thomas, are suspended with pay, while there is an investigation into whether or not there was a violation of the civil rights of the two models. I'm Angela Pileggi, reporting live from Penn Station. Back to you, Jim."

Tracy clicked off the television that sat up on a shelf attached to the yellow hospital wall. His right cheek was swollen, his lips busted, his ankle sprained, and his head was pounding.

The hospital room door opened, and Christian walked in wearing a blue corduroy blazer and jeans.

He walked right up to the bed and grabbed Tracy by his chin to observe his condition. "You lucky that damage ain't permanent, or else you'd be looking for work somewhere else. Your little partner in crime got his fingers broke. What the fuck was y'all thinking? That name belongs to me. You don't got to be out there fighting for nothing unless I say so. You listening to me, Trace? You're out there acting a fool for nothing. That's *my* name, nigga!"

"Man, fuck that! It's your name, but it got my face. I made that name what it is. You just happened to be born with it. I'm not about to start acting any different than how I always been. The street ain't never left me and I ain't leavin' it. I see somebody playin' me then I'm going to handle that. I'm sayin' though . . . if you feelin' salty about it, you can always get rid of a nigga."

"You can pull all the stupid acts you want. That shit don't move me. I got something that'll make you stop acting like a bitch when you get out. Just in case you wondering why your silly ass ain't cuffed to that bedrail, my lawyer worked something out. Your bail was set and paid without you having to do a second locked up."

"Where's Cadillac?" Tracy grimaced in pain.

"Caddyshack is home tending to his wounds."

"They fucked him up real good, huh? Faggot-ass 'po'-nine.' "

"Not bad as you. Stop acting up, Trace. You might think you being real, but you're really just putting my company in a bad light. If the days start getting dark for me, where you think that's going to leave you? Think about that."

"Oh yeah? A'ight. I'm getting tired." Tracy rolled over in the bed and turned his back on Christian. "If everything go all right, I'll be out of here in the morning. Them bitch asses is already trying to make a deal with me."

"Who?"

"The police department . . . talking about, they're willing to drop the charges, if I drop the charges."

"You need to listen to them. I got some good shit going, and I don't need them muthafuckas following you around everywhere so they can see what I'm doing." Christian walked out of the room.

Three days later Tracy was released from the hospital. Cadillac and Marcel walked through the hospital doors supporting Tracy's balance as he limped out on crutches. He refused to be rolled out on a wheelchair in front of all the media standing outside, awaiting his statement.

Shane pulled as close to the curb as possible and sat double-parked in front of the medical establishment in a blue Expedition, *Sexy 1* on the front and back license plates, and his windows rolled all the way down.

A reporter shouted, "Mister Kane, do you feel that you've had your civil rights violated?"

"What you think? Look at me." Tracy nodded down at his leg. "Hell yeah, my civil rights been violated. The police don't ever beat down a white man like this. Only thing they forgot to do was shoot me in the back and say they heard I had a gun."

"So, are you saying that you will be filing a lawsuit?" another reporter yelled.

Tracy stared into the camera. "I didn't say anything. One thing is for certain, though. These police is gonna learn that they can't be just beating up on every nigga they see. Or one of these days a real fed up nigga is going to retaliate. Maybe go around and start sniping cops in front of their own house, just like they do to niggas in the hood. The police are out of control. They tried to make a statistic outta me, but a change is gonna come."

A third reporter asked, "Is that a threat, Mister Kane?"

"Yeah," he said, after thinking about it. "Yeah. The shit is a threat." He covered the camera lens with his hand. "Interview over." He grabbed on to Marcel's shoulder.

Cadillac pushed Tracy in the backseat and hopped in beside him, and Marcel sat in the passenger seat. As they moved in slow motion through the congested traffic, nobody uttered a word until they crossed the 59th Street Bridge.

Marcel looked back at Tracy from the passenger seat. "I don't think that was a good look, man."

"What you talking about? I was telling the truth."

"Dude, you are not being serious about your career. Make me understand what you think you doing."

"I'm doing me," he said, cracking his window.

"What you gonna do, man?" Cadillac asked. "I'm dropping the charges. Shit, I already got my call. I won't have to do a day in jail. You gonna pursue it?"

"You damn right, nigga. I ain't about to let them play me."

Shane looked at Tracy through the rearview mirror. "You wildin' out."

Tracy was let off in front of his condo. He denied his friends' assistance and used his crutches to get inside the lobby. He took the elevator to his floor and walked to his door.

Something above the peephole caught his eye—a note: *KEEP YOUR BIG MOUTH SHUT, NIGGER.* He crumpled up the note and laughed out loud.

CHAPTER SEVEN

TRACY KANE

Tracy was standing on the long line at Borders bookstore to pick up a couple of the latest magazines he was posted in. He used his crutches to walk over to a Starbucks store on the other side of the building. He grabbed a hazelnut smoothie and headed back.

When he returned, a stocky, baldheaded man with a stern face stood patiently waiting for the line to move.

"Ahem!" Tracy cleared his throat.

The man turned around. "Oh, pardon me, man. I didn't realize you'd been standing here before. Here you go, brother," he said, moving so Tracy could get back into his spot.

Tracy pounded the man's fist. "Good looking, man."

The man looked at Tracy's crutches and face. "Looks like somebody was mad at you."

"What's it to you? Look, you did your merry-go-round good deed for the day already. Don't go and start tryin'-a make conversation with me, okay, *Akbar*?" he said, picking up on the man's religion.

"Solasse."

"What?"

"The name's *Solasse*, not Akbar. I'm just being friendly, man. No offense." The man held his hands up. "This line is ridiculous, right?"

"It's some real bullshit. I'm about to be out." Tracy placed the magazines back on the rack.

"Tracy Kane," the man said, flipping through a magazine in his hands. He compared the picture in the magazine to the person standing before him. "You look a little bit different in person."

"The NYPD will do that to ya. A'ight, partna, be easy."

"Say, before you leave, do you think I could get an autograph?"

CHAPTER EIGHT

CHRISTIAN

Christian met with up with Assante at a public library out in Manhattan. Both teams had goons on standby outside in the pouring rain. Both of their drivers parked on opposite sides of the street from one another.Up the cement row of stairs, Christian stopped and stared through the double glass doors before him. Thirty feet away sat a very tall Assante, equally dark in complexion as his younger brother, Akinsanya.

Assante looked up from the book he'd been skimming through and nodded his head as a well-dressed Christian Elijah casually walked inside the literary sanctuary.

They met in the middle of the floor then walked to the nearby elevator, which they rode to the second floor in complete silence. The doors hummed as they opened, and the two men exited. They walked down the aisle of the music section, where they both took a seat.

Assante stretched his long legs and stared Christian in the eyes.

"So, what are doing here? Do you have something for me?" Christian asked in a low tone.

"What I have for you is a proposition. It will make up for the disrespect you have shown me and my brother."

"A proposition? The disrespect I've shown you and your brother? Let me make something clear to you, Assante. You're the one bootlegging my shit, which is illegal by city law and street law. I contemplated having you beat down something good, but that wouldn't get my money back. Taking you to court would. I mean, where the fuck do you get off thinking you could get away with this shit?"

"Shhh." Assante put his finger to his lips. "A place of quiet, right? This country is about free enterprise. I come here six years ago. I make a good living. I send money home every month to my wife and ten children. It isn't about robbery, it is about survival. Back home we are not allowed to care for our families. The economic system is a setup. Structured."

"That has absolutely nothing to do with me. I don't care to hear that shit. The way I see it, you only have two options—court, or we work something out. Something where you show me your past records of what you made selling my name."

"How will you repay me for what your friend Tracy did to my brother in Manhattan?"

"I could give a shit . . . really."

"Then I must say that I am saddened by this meeting. I thought maybe we could come to an understanding, but you are not negotiable. Believe me when I say, it is not all for nothing. I will be straight with you, if you will listen."

"I'm fuming over here, man. My time is precious. Hurry up and speak."

"Okay, let me show you something." Assante reached down for his black duffle bag and pulled out an unauthentic black Christian Elijah T-shirt. He straightened out the wrinkles then laid it flat out on the table. He then sat back in his seat.

"What? Are you trying to be funny or something?"

"What I have brought with me is a revolution. This right here supports it." Assante tapped on the shirt.

"What the hell are you talking about?"

"Your name. It has become very big over the past three years. I have to watch this, or I won't know what is—how do you all say?—hot. I have to follow what is hot."

"I'm not fuckin' understanding, and I'm pretty much finished listening."

"Wait." Assante handed him the shirt. "Turn it inside out."

Christian snatched the shirt from him and reversed it. He looked it up and down and still had no idea what Assante was talking about.

"You don't see?"

"No, I don't see," Christian said, mocking Assante's accent.

"Look!" Assante pointed to some white stitching under the inner sleeve of the shirt. "Do you see it?"

Christian read off the shirt. "Seven-seven-twenty? What in the fuck are you doing to my clothes? What is this?"

"Look closer. It is money, Mister Elijah, money in the bank. More money for you, more money for me."

"How? Because I'ma tell you something. I'm really not feeling why I'm still sitting here."

"The date, Mister Elijah, seven-seven-twenty, it will make you rich, richer than you have ever dreamed."

"Keep going," Christian said, spinning his hand.

"Oh. It is so deep, so very deep, Mister Elijah." Assante slid his chair closer to Christian and crossed his legs. "Your clothes help supply the funds to support artillery that comes from home. You see, the more guns in the street, the more money is obtained. The more money obtained, the more I can continue sending money back home. The more I can bring my brothers and sisters here."

"What does that have to do with seven-sevem-twenty? Come on, Assante, work with me here."

"It is what I planned to say next. We have not long to go before two thousand twenty arrives. The plan is already set."

"What plan, Assante?"

"I am tired, Christian. We are all tired. The police. At home they are such a problem. Here also. My people come here, and—*BANG!*—the police shoot them dead because they do not speak the American language."

"Is there a point to all of this? Better yet, when you getting to the part where I make all of this money?"

"I shall cut you in and repay what I owe. But I will let you know now. The people wearing these shirts are part of a movement here, to collide with police, if they must. Two thousand twenty, Mister Elijah, is when our movement will simultaneously clash with these so-called agents of death. Either which way, you do not lose. That is my offer."

"You're going to sit here and make me an offer for you to make money off my creation? I think not."

"Ah, but I believe so. You see, Mister Elijah, I am very well connected. Having friends in high places will keep you afloat. I know about you. I really, really know about you."

"What? You threatening me now?"

"Why with you must everything be a quarrel, Mister Elijah? What I know of you could be damaging. It could bring you down. You'll soon see that you've dug yourself so far into a hole, you will find yourself in China by the morning. Would you now like me to tell you what I know? Or do you wish to quarrel some more?"

"All right. What you know?"

"For now, I will just say, think back to that thing that happened with you and an incident in Brooklyn. You do not remember? Let me refresh your memory. The woman you killed was not a good thing. You are under a very huge microscope."

"I don't know what you're talking about."

"I cannot make it much more simple. You murdered a federal informant. From what I understand, she was highly regarded by everyone. I know where the gun is at you killed her with, and a witness. It was most recently brought to my attention for a very hefty purchase. So, as I said earlier, I know you." Assante handed Christian an envelope.

Christian pulled a photograph from the envelope, momentarily studied it, and instantly became infuriated. "Where'd you get this from? Who'd you get it from?"

"You remember now?"

Christian stared down at the photograph he'd dropped on the table. A dead woman's body lay sprawled out on the hood of a silver BMW.

Assante grinned. "You may keep the photo. I have plenty."

"You're extorting me."

"Is it extortion, Mister Elijah?"

"How do I know this ain't all one big-ass setup? I heard stories about governmental agencies trying to set niggas up when they become successful. So how I know you not one of them?"

"You do not, but is it worth second-guessing? This is a revolution." Assante stood and extended his hand to Christian.

CHAPTER NINE

TRACY KANE

Boochie was photographing Tracy sitting atop a motorbike. He said, "Turn just a little to the left, *T*."

Other models revved up their bikes behind him with one hand, holding black helmets in the other, dust kicking up from the back tires of the bikes. They all perspired as the bright sun bore down on them.

"Trinity, I need you over here," Boochie said to Christian's daughter.

Tracy turned around and gave her a wink, and Trinity smiled as she slowly walked through the western-styled dust screen.

"I want you to sit in front of Tracy and kind of tilt your head back into his shoulder. Put your hands on the bars, and, Tracy, you wrap your hands on top of hers. Don't forget to rev the bike, y'all." Boochie positioned himself on one knee. "Perfect. But I want to take just one more shot," he said, clicking Tracy and Trinity in a compromising position. "That's hot. Y'all just lit this shit up. All right, everybody," Boochie said, "it's quitting time."

Trinity wiped a little perspiration off her forehead. "Oh God, it's so hot out here."

"You black," Tracy told her. "This should be your type of weather."

She snickered. "And what are you?"

"*Underpaid.* Shit, I ain't never told a lie." Tracy stepped off the bike. "Who you came with? Boochie?"

"Yeah. I got a flat tire on my car, so he gave me a ride."

"Is he taking you back, or do you need a ride?"

"You offering?"

"Come on." Tracy smiled and turned to walk toward his car.

"Why you always gotta act so nasty to people, Tracy?" Trinity asked as he dipped in and out of traffic on the fast-moving parkway. "I mean, why you always got to act like—"

"Like what? Such an asshole? Say what you mean."

"Not quite the word I was going to say, but yes. Why you try to push everybody so far away?"

"Truthfully, I ain't got no time for nobody trying to get close to me. I just do my job then go home." Tracy sped past a black Lexus.

"I think you's a good dude. No matter what you might think, my father is not trying to play you. He talks about you all the time. It's you who made him blow up, so why would he try to play you?"

"There are a lot of things that you just wouldn't understand, Trinity. This business is hectic. Everybody wanna be down with you, always offering a better deal than the previous. People are always standing in my face every day waiting on a handout. I'm getting tired of the shit." Tracy honked his horn at a slow-moving Suburban in front of him. "I swear, man, these niggas get these new trucks and drive 'em like they tanks or something." He shouted at the driver, "Drive, muthafucka!" He pressed down on his horn again, veering to the right then back in front of the truck.

Trinity turned around and looked through the back window. "You really need to check your temper."

"I just can't stand non-driving niggas, you know what I'm saying?"

"What's the problem, Tracy? Where is all of the anger coming from?"

"That's just me. You know that. It ain't like you don't know me. It's how I do." Tracy grilled the driver in the Jaguar beside them. "What the fuck is you looking at, man?" he said to the white man.

"You're going to die young if you keep acting like this— I'm nineteen and you're twenty-five—Why I gotta be telling you this?"

"Actually, you don't got to be telling me nothing. I'm a grown-ass man. No disrespect, Trinity, but it is what it is."

Even before Tracy got on, he'd always had a fucked-up attitude. He'd be the first to tell you, though, that it had nothing to do with the fact that his father used to beat the shit out of him for every little thing he did. Or that, when he was just nine, his mother, a community activist, had been shot dead in the streets by an unknown assailant.

Tracy had started hanging around a real bad crowd after that and had to do whatever it took to eat. After a while he began to realize that even the dudes in the street that he called family soon would turn on him. He wasn't a sucker by far, as many may have thought, but because of his good looks, he always had to defend his character. He began seeing it for what it was. People he considered friends weren't trustworthy. They were jealous. He was considered a pretty boy, and pretty boys always got all the women.

So he kept on thumping and thumping, until the fateful day that Christian Elijah came along and saved his life.

Much as Trinity detested Tracy's arrogance, at the same

time, it turned her on. It turned her on even more, knowing that he was a pretty boy with heart. He was conceited, confident, and apathetic, and to her that shit was kind of sexy. She'd had a crush on him ever since she was sixteen. A woman now, she was truly down for whatever. She gave off love signals to him every now and again, but, for the most part, played it low-key.

"You are so rude. I don't know how the chickens you deal with can stand you."

"Just look at me." Tracy peeked in the rearview mirror and smiled. "Do it look like they got a choice?"

"Oh God. You are so in love with yourself. You don't need no woman."

"You right. They need me," Tracy said, pulling in Christian's driveway. "Looks like Christian ain't home yet." He looked at the empty parking spot then back at Trinity.

Trinity turned to him, quickly locked her mouth around his, and thrust her tongue down his throat. Then, just as quickly, she pulled away. "Gotta go." She smiled as she trotted up the walkway to her house.

CHAPTER TEN

TRACY KANE

"Tell me why Trinity kissed me today," Tracy said to Shane as they sat inside the VIP section of the Twenty/Thirty club sipping on a five-hundred-dollar bottle of champagne. It was the last day Shane was to be a free man. He was getting married in less than a month, and Tracy was making sure he enjoyed his last days as a playa.

"Don't do it to yourself, Trace. Let that one go."

"I'm way ahead of you."

"Word, yo. Christian don't play that shit when it come to his daughter."

Tracy smirked. "The thought never even crossed my mind."

"I'm serious, man."

"I heard you. We ain't talking about that no more. You ready to make it happen, nigga? You really ready?" Tracy poured himself a glass of champagne.

"I never been more ready for anything in my life. My money's right. We got a fly-ass rent-a-house out in St. Albans, Queens. I'm living."

Cadillac said, "You sure is, bitch," as he and Marcel approached the VIP.

"Y'all finally made it," Tracy said. "Well, get your asses on up here." He tossed them both cigars as they walked up the five burgundy-carpeted steps.

The men all exchanged pounds, hugs, and then Cadillac and Marcel took their seats.

"Did you get a letter today?" Cadillac asked Tracy. "I did. They want to settle out of court."

"Who?"

"Who you think? The NYPD. I'm going to settle and take the money." Cadillac lit his cigar.

"You gonna settle out of court? How's that gonna make me look? How it gonna make you look?"

"Look, man, I thought long and hard about this, and at the end of the day, none of this would've ever happened if you didn't punch dude in the face. What the fuck was you thinking, man? I got a career to think about. I can't go pulling no radical accusations about some damn-near unjustifiable shit."

"You seen my eye lately, nigga?" Tracy pointed at the bruise around it. "What in the fuck you think look justified about this? You sound like you Uncle Tom-ing."

"Me? What about you, nigga? You out here purposely making a fool outta yourself, like you tryin'-a get a recording deal or something. You gonna keep acting the fuck up and somebody gonna pop your silly ass. I'm only telling you this because I love you like a brother. I'm out of it, though."

"You out of it? I'm not even surprised."

"What's that supposed to mean?"

Tracy comfortably leaned back in his chair and smiled. "It don't mean nothing, playa. Do what you do, how you do it."

"Hey, y'all, this my day, right? I mean, this is a celebra-

tion for me, so let's stop fuckin' around and celebrate."
Shane refilled all the glasses.

"Get drunk, daddy," Cadillac said. "This is just the beginning."

"I'm going to take a piss," Tracy said. "Be right back."

Tracy came back to the table of four and caught eyes with the fifth element added to the private venue. It was Shane's fiancée, Star. She was slender with a narrow facial structure. Her skin was light, her lips were thin, and her hair, cut a little past her ears, and the ends sharply spiked, was jet-black and straight. She was sipping on a Corona with a lime twist and all hugged up on her soon-to-be husband.

Star laughed along with the fellas as Cadillac attempted to perform his impression of Denzel Washington.

An intense expression on his face, Cadillac licked his lips, and puckered them slightly. "Are you saying I'm crazy, nigga? No. No. You said that I'm crazy? Isn't that what you just told me?" he said, pointing intensely. "That I'm crazy? Naw, I ain't crazy. You're all crazy." He nodded his head up and down. "Yeah, that's right. This whole city is crazy, this world is crazy, this whole goddamn universe is crazy." He licked his lips. "Yeah . . . uh-huh." He licked his lips again and puckered them.

Star looked up and caught eyes with Tracy. She smiled as he stepped back up to the private booth. "Tracy Kane, it's such a pleasure to finally meet you. I've heard nothing but good things." She looked at Shane.

"Good things? Good things from who? This guy over here?" Tracy pushed Shane's shoulder.

"That'd be the one." Star looked down at his crutches. "How's everything going for you?"

"Hey, it's all good. Enough about me, though. You really gonna marry this dude?" Tracy smiled into her light brown eyes.

"Follow the trend." Star kissed Shane on the lips. "I'm going to make him a good wife."

"Tracy is nowhere near thinking about marrying anybody. Real playas never marry. Ain't that there right, boy?" Marcel sipped his champagne.

"That's right. No marriage for me." Tracy looked around at the many available gorgeous women frolicking around the club. "So I guess this is it? That final step?"

"Forever, my dude." Shane kissed Star's hand.

"Aw, man, can't y'all save that for the honeymoon?" Cadillac started refilling all the glasses on the table.

"Tell me, Tracy," Star began, "why did it take us so long to meet? I would think, with all you guys all being so close, I'd have met you when I met these knuckleheads."

"I'm a lot busier than these part-timers. Comes with the looks."

"Hope I'm not interrupting anything," Solasse said. He was the man who Tracy had met inside Borders bookstore. Solasse stood at the foot of the stairs.

"Who the fuck is you?" Cadillac said.

"Oh, pardon me." Solasse extended his hand to everyone. "I'm Solasse. Tracy? I met you the other day inside Borders bookstore." He smiled. "Remember?"

"He must be one of the perks that come with the looks," Shane joked, his arm wrapped around Star's shoulder.

"What's up, man? What you doing up in here? This ain't your kinda scene." Tracy stared at Solasse.

"I'm here with the wife. You know you got to take them out every once and again."

"Naw, I wouldn't know about that. Anyway, I'm chilling right now. Good seeing you again though. Peace, Akbar," he said, swaying his attention back to the table.

"All right, man. Y'all be easy and have a wonderful night." Solasse turned to walk away.

"Hold on," Marcel said. "Any new friend of Tracy's is a new friend of ours. You said you was with the wife, right?"

"Yeah. She's down over by the bar."

"Since my man here is getting married in a couple of days and you already married, you may as well join us. It's a celebration."

"No, thank you. I'll let you all do your own thing. Just wanted to shout out. Nice meeting you all. And congratulations, you two." Solasse walked off toward the bathroom.

Tracy gave Marcel a look.

"What, man?" Marcel bit off the butt of his cigar. "It's a party, right?"

"That's what it looks like, but ain't nobody invite me," Christian said as he climbed the steps, three women stepping behind him. He was wearing a white linen outfit and a pair of expensive white shoes with three-inch black heels. "Any room for four more?" He smiled as he joined them on the circular-shaped tan leather couch. "Your eye looks a lot better, man," he said to Tracy. "I guess that's what happens when you don't see a nigga in a minute. Where you been hiding yourself? I've been calling." Then he said to his small entourage, "Why don't you ladies run and get some drinks for us?"

The three women all wore sleek, sexy, black Spandex that tightly stretched and caressed around the back and melted down to their well-fed calves. They wore half-cut black tees with the inscription *C.E. 7-7-20* intricately triple-stitched into the front of their shirts.

"Hey, woman." Christian put his hand on Star's leg. "You better take good care of my dude. He's a good man. Keep 'im pretty and don't go scratching up his face." Smiling, he pulled out a white folded envelope from his brown bag and put it on the table. "That's a li'l something toward y'all nest egg."

"So what's with the new tees them bitches wearing?"

"Trace, my lady, man," Shane said, reminding him to mind his manners.

"Pardon me, Star. That's just how I be talkin' sometimes. I don't mean nothing by it."

"That don't affect me none. That's the difference between me and them out there." Star pointed to the crowd of scantily dressed women dancing on the floor. "That word in no way, shape, or form could ever apply to me." She massaged her temples. "Baby, I'm getting tired. I think I'll go home."

"You want me to come with you?"

"No. I'm just going to leave. Have fun with your boys, baby. I'll see you at home. My girls is probably waiting for me in front of the house anyway."

"You sure?"

"I'm good." Star stood up.

"All right, then. Gimme a kiss."

"Uh-uh." Star placed her finger on his lips. "The next time we kiss is when we become Mr. and Mrs. Shane Richardson. Gentlemen, and Tracy"—She rolled her eyes— "I'll see you all tomorrow." Then she said to Shane, "Walk me to my car, babe."

Shane rose from the table, his glare all over Tracy's face. He then took his lady by the hand and took her toward the exit, through the path made by dancing feet.

All the men present stared at Tracy, who poured himself another drink and leaned back. "What y'all looking at me for?" he asked. "What I do?"

Christian said, "You don't know how to have some respect when a woman around?"

"Oh, leave me the hell alone. The bitch said it didn't affect her. Y'all niggas is way too sensitive. *Sheesh!*"

CHAPTER ELEVEN

TRACY KANE

Five months after Shane's wedding, Christian Elijah unveiled his new clothing line for the following summer. Tracy, Marcel, and Cadillac rocked the future apparel on a hip-hop show geared to young adults. The men boldly walked up and down the runway of a mid-town Manhattan auditorium.

After the crowd stopped cheering, the men all took a seat, and from the left of the stage, Assante and Akinsanya walked out and stood on opposite sides of Christian.

"What's up, New York? How y'all feeling today?" Christian smiled as he pulled up his white tweed derby from over his eyes. "First, I'd like to give mad love to y'all out there for putting Christian Elijah on the map. Thanks to all the rappers who rock my clothes in their videos. Thanks to all the models that make my clothes what they are. And if you think what you're wearing right now is hot, what y'all think about the new style? That's right, C.E. 7-7-20, that new Christian Elijah Culture.

"Make sure you support this and be part of something, part of a movement. Stop spending your money on clothes made by people that didn't have you in mind when they designed them. Collaborate"—He looked back at the host of the show—"They're telling me to hurry this up, y'all. These African gentlemen here are my new investors, Assante and Akinsanya. Collaboration, y'all," he reminded the audience. "Together we've created a marketable concept to blow those imitators out the water. We've got men's and women's suits on the way real soon, y'all. It's getting big. Also, be on the lookout for Assante and Akinsanya's winter wear clothing line, Militia 7. Thanks for having us on your show, Parker, and much love to New York City's best hip-hop show." Christian held out the microphone to the audience.

They shouted, "TBA!" (typical black audience)

After the unveiling, Christian and company all rode out to Assante's house to have a sit-down. A sit-down that would forever change all their lives.

Some of Africa's most prominent figures proudly stood, forever immortalized, within the golden-framed trims of the portraits on the walls of his foyer, his country's flag acting as curtains that hung from the ceiling to the floor over the entrance into the living room. Two silver stands filled with rock incense burned slowly, like the slow-lit fuse that ignited the Watts riots in California in the summer of 1965.

When the men stopped to look at the portraits, Assante said, "Let us move forward."

"This some hot shit, man," Tracy said. "Marble floors and shit."

Before they entered into the living room, Assante had asked the men to remove their shoes, for his carpet was blessed, in the name of Allah.

They walked into the living room, the carpet cool and soft as Mary J. Blige singing "My Life" on a cloud. A white leather couch curved and touched base with the partially mirrored walls, and was spaced between each cushion, for purposes of reclining. Black drapes covered the enormous bay window, and ivory plants hung around the frame.

A 70-inch flat-screen television anchored off the wall displayed images of Ethiopia's doomed infants. Babies cried out and clenched their bony fists in agonizing pain, flies covering their bodies and dancing on their open eyes, sometimes settling on their dry lips. Mothers, their dehydrated breasts looking like raisins in the sun, and incapable of nourishing a child's life, cried out helplessly and looked up to Allah, their eyes rolled to the tops of their heads, saliva seeping from the corners of their mouths.

The focus of the report posed the question, How could our president spend trillions of dollars on an orchestrated war, trying to "civilize" some nation, but totally ignore starvation in other countries? And does it really make sense?

"Please, sit down," Akinsanya said.

"Yes, everyone, sit." Assante walked over to his bar in an extended room. "Gentlemen, what can I offer you?" he asked, pulling down the glasses.

They all shouted out their orders.

"Let me start this." Christian looked at Assante then the others. "This the dude that been doing all the bootlegging. You already know that. Now you just need to know why he not fucked up." He looked at Assante again. "No disrespect. There's some shit this man got going that we in now. I took the liberty of speaking for you because I know y'all niggas like getting that paper, right?

Tracy, Marcel, and Cadillac looked at one another in bewilderment.

Cadillac said, "Ay, man, why don't you just say what's

on your mind, cat? I don't understand all that subliminal, metaphorical shit."

"Please, please, this is not what we are here for. Tracy, I want you to know that it was my brother, our brother"—Assante swayed his hand back and forth between himself and Akinsanya—"That was unnecessary, what you did to that man in Manhattan. How do you plan to rectify that?"

"Just like I do every day—with my hand on my dick!" Cadillac said with a serious face. "Speak your speak, man. I got things to do today." He leaned forward off the couch. "If you're waiting on some sort of apology, or for me to bow down, well then I'ma have to tell you right now, *Prince Akeem*, it's gonna be a long night."

"That is fine. America has done nothing positive for you." Assante bowed to him. "Breathe, my brother."

"What y'all talking about?" Marcel asked. "Christian, I'm about to break."

"Squash this shit with this nigga so we can get this going, Trace," Christian said. "Assante been bootlegging the clothes to send money back overseas to buy guns, all kinds of guns. Some is to be sold in the street. And there ain't nothing but money in store for us, you hear me?"

Cadillac wanted in, it seemed. "What's the seven-sevem-twenty all about?"

"The day, seven-seven-twenty." Assante sipped his drink.

"So, so, just tell me if I'm bugging," Marcel said. "How am I supposed to prosper off of this? If I'ma lose paper, then you can just rip our contract and I'll be out, Christian. How the fuck I look, getting caught up in some gun-running scheme? Who does that?"

"Shut the fuck up and just listen! Now, what you talking about being out? Ain't nobody *being out* this shit. When y'all fuckas going to get it through your heads? I own y'all. You are bound by contract, niggas, that's right. So just listen. Go on, Assante."

Assante went on to explain to the trio his diabolical plot to give the police a little payback. He told them that he'd taken the Christian Elijah Culture name and branded it in the hearts of his supporters as a movement on the police. Every Saturday, rain or shine, he and about one hundred other brothers would meet in the woods upstate and train. These men were from different states and would take what they learned up here in New York back to wherever they resided. Take it back to the brothers, angered by and fed up with all the police brutality, and their blatant hate and disrespect. The strenuous sessions were physically intense, but necessary, in order for everything to go exactly according to plan. A plan to, once and for all, put these cracker-ass police in their final resting place. July 7, 2020. Just imagine. The city would never be the same.

Unbeknownst to Christian, Assante had an even bigger motive for designing such a ruthless plot.

"My brothers, as you already know, the country and city you live in do not like you. If they could send you back to where you came from, you'd already be there. I come here and it is all bullshit. I have now come to understand what the American dream is—To see every nigger in the world dead or made a slave again. I can't make a living in my country, so I come here with my brother to survive. I have a family to feed. The war going on in my country is the same war here where you live. It is not. Hell is where wars without warrant kill innocent women and children. I come here and the police shoot African immigrants down and walk away free men. No more. How can I bring my family here if I cannot make money and ensure their safety from the same force running rampant in my country?"

Tracy said, "Assante, what the fuck is you talking about? Because I'm lost like a muthafucka."

"I'm talking about doing to them what they do to us. As

of now I buy guns from overseas based on the sales of Christian's clothes on the street. There are five other states behind me. Christian Elijah is the best-selling name everywhere. I use the profits to feed families, and they in turn help out other families. The bigger portion of the money is used to buy more guns. I have brothers ready in D.C., Baltimore, Seattle, California, and Texas."

Cadillac cut in with, "For what, man? Where am I hearing the part about the money?"

"The guns. We move a lot of them. You help unload the shipments and sell to the places and people I direct you to."

"Hold up, man," Marcel said. "All this talk about shipments, guns, revolution and poverty, where you going with all this, Assante?"

Christian said to Assante, "Get to the point."

"That is the point."

"Your big money scheme is to kill as many police as you can?" Tracy asked. "Oh, yeah. I can see where you think that shit is a great plan and all, but what about retaliation?"

"One hundred armed men in each state, and rising, feeling the same pain as you and I, will be sure to avenge us, if necessary. They all represent the Christian Elijah Culture and are willing to die for the cause. Our families must be protected by any and all means. A message must be sent."

Marcel shook his head. "That shit sounds crazy, and I ain't with it. I'll go elsewhere. You're talking some crazy shit. Christian, how you let this silly nigga talk you into some bullshit like this?"

"The money. It works out for all of us. I mean, it ain't like he not telling the truth about the other shit. I said it before. Why should the white muthafuckas be able to sell their clothes to us but never intend for us to wear them?

Then, like assholes, we go out here and buy boots with imprints of trees on them. The fuck you think that really means, huh? He lynching y'all pockets. That man gotta be laughing his ass off."

"I don't think it's a good move. You gonna fuck your own shit up." Marcel looked at Tracy and Cadillac. "Why don't y'all talk some sense into this man?"

"Man, after getting my ass whupped on by them white boys, and thinking back on how they handled my mom's murder, the shit's a splendid idea. Count me in," Tracy said.

Cadillac agreed. "Sorry, Marcel, the shit does make sense."

"Y'all crazy."

Tracy then asked, "So, Assante, when do I get my first check?"

CHAPTER TWELVE

TRINITY

Trinity stepped into the running water of the shower in her bedroom. She closed her eyes and let the jet-powered stream of water run down her body. Her feet waded in the ankle-deep oasis produced by the forceful water escaping from the wide-mouthed brass faucet sticking out of the peach-tiled wall. The bathroom filled with steam, and its mist dimmed the row of bulbs installed above the floor-length mirror.

Imagining herself standing under a heated waterfall on a deserted island, the quiet darkness of an open-mouthed cave behind her, she released her ponytail and let it fall down to her shoulders. Then she reached up for the window ledge and grabbed her bottle of coconut body wash. She massaged its rich, tropical exoticness over her entire body and sighed after the dripping suds settled on her wings of love. Behind schedule, she rushed her waterfall rinse.

Trinity hated being late, something her father had instilled in her.

Especially when it came to her period. It saved her from the trials and tribulations that came with being an unwed mother impregnated by an unfit father. But it also deprived her. It deprived her, because she eagerly wanted to indulge in a little long-overdue experimentation in the study of physical interaction, but anytime she came close to doing something, she always saw her father's face. She respected and loved him too much to ever defy the laws of the house.

Christian had been raising Trinity on his own ever since she was two years old. Her mother, Erica, had run off with her new boyfriend to God knows where and was only heard from whenever she sent a postcard to them, no return address. But it meant nothing to the two of them. Far as they were concerned, she was just a faded memory. So fuck her.

Growing up, Trinity never needed for anything, because Christian gave her everything. He couldn't teach her how to be a woman, but he did teach her to carry herself like one. A pretty perceptive young woman, she learned everything else on her own. But as long as she lived in Christian's house, she was either going to attend school, work, or both. He did allow her to model for extra money, and the last of her energies was committed to sharing her poetry at The Spot, an underground location in Bellport, Long Island.

As Trinity rushed up the stairs into the large room of poets she'd befriended over the past six months and some new ones looking to vent their anger, the emcee waved her backstage.

"You almost missed your spot," he said, peeking through the curtains of the stage. "Everything all right?"

Trinity pulled out a notebook from her purse. "It's all good. How's it going tonight?"

The emcee nodded his head as a baldheaded man wearing glasses smiled and walked by them. "A lot of new performers."

"New one, huh?"

"Yep. Let me get out there." The emcee pulled his head back through the curtains. "Ladies and *gentle*, coming to the stage, this brother's deep. Show some love for Solasse." He stepped backstage as Solasse took the floor.

The audience applauded for him then simultaneously simmered down as they took their seats, spotlight on Solasse. He coolly took hold of the microphone and journeyed verbally through the realm of poetic puzzles, collecting pieces of a dream, to complete a reality.

And, just like that, he was done.

The audience cheered and threw up a black fist.

Going backstage, he walked by a smiling Trinity, who patted his shoulder. "Real powerful," she said to the emcee. "He's good."

"Yeah. He definitely got to come back. I'm going to holla at him after the show. You ready?" he said, rushing back out to the stage. "Coming to the stage, give a big round of applause for our baby sister, Trinity Elijah."

She received mad love because she was nice with the words every time she blessed the mike. She was always a little shy when she first walked out on stage, but after a couple minutes or so, she'd be just fine.

"How y'all doing tonight? I'm a little behind schedule, so y'all gonna have to forgive me. A sister gotta pay the bills."

A lady shouted out from the audience, "It's all right, sister girl!"

"Thank you." She chuckled. "This is called 'Real Shit.'"

"A'ight now!" another lady said.

And a man yelled out over the applauding crowd, "Get it, ma!"

"Look at me," she said, extending her arms. "Look at me," she repeated, catching her flow:

"I'm free
Or am I really
Lord, Will I ever know liberty
Can I be a green bitch, hold a torch in my hand
Stand in the water, the masquerade, concealing my
black ass
Misconceptions of elections, segregated in certain
sections
We're the unaccountable minority, majority with no
protection
Not by any means are we safe in our own streets
The nuclear arms is in the hood, George
Why you overseas
The police, it's crazy
They arrest us like cardiovascular, inner city massacre
Free South Africa. Sarafinaaaa." She sang, *"Free South*
Africa.
It's all a setup, like presidential assassinations
Guns, politics, genocidal mutilation
We/ all/ live/ in/ a/ rhythm/ nation
A drug-addicted nation, the C.I.A. in LA, teaching how
to kill an entire generation"

Trinity bent over and inhaled deeply. "Whew!" She laughed as she straightened up, perspiration dripping down her forehead.

The audience cheered and stood as she recomposed herself.

" 'Real Shit.' Are y'all feelin' me? 'Real Shit.' Here's more:

We be talking about a revolution
A change is gonna come

Yet we're still fighting for reparations
paying to learn their education
My crying heart bleeds like menstruation
It floods the grasslands of our brothers lost in the war
Which war? Any war . . . Our war . . . This war
A nigga versus a nigger.

"WE ARE AT WAR!" she yelled, sticking up a black fist.

A brother and a sister forgetting that they're siblings
Forgetting simple forgiveness,
Forgetting they're just children
Forgetting there's no conclusion after the blood spills on
the ceiling.

" 'Real Shit,' y'all."

The emcee said, "You bad, girl."

Tears in her eyes, Trinity took a bow to a huge standing ovation and walked backstage to an applauding crowd of fellow poets.

Solasse stood apart from them clapping his hands slowly. "That was real powerful, Trinity."

"Glad you liked it, but you wasn't no slouch yourself. I never saw you here before. Where you from?"

They walked over to the bar. "Seltzer water, Monty," she said to the bartender.

"I'll have the same."

"You don't drink?" Trinity asked, almost impressed.

Solasse dipped a lime in his seltzer after Monty brought back the drink. "I lost my wife to that self-destructive way of living."

"Oh, so you used to be married?" Trinity looked down at his finger.

"Yes. I've moved on, though. Found a woman better for me and my newfound way of life."

"Wow. I'm sure she's proud of you."

"Who? My ex or my new wife?"

"Both." Trinity chuckled. "Your present woman, silly."

"Oh, Marisol? She's wonderful. She's like every single thing I've ever wanted in a woman." Solasse tilted his head to the floor.

"Not to be rude or nothing like that, but where's she at? I mean, why she not here supporting her man?"

"She works nights."

"What she do for a living?"

"She works for the state."

"True."

Solasse spotted the name Elijah tatted on the left side of her neck. "Say, you wouldn't happen to be the same Elijah as in Christian Elijah?"

"Why you ask?" she snapped.

"Just because of the last name. Didn't know you were going to get all offended."

"Naw, it's cool. Yeah, Christian's my dad."

"I thought you looked familiar. You've been in a couple of his magazines. You take some very beautiful pictures."

"Thank you, Solasse. Well, I'm about to get ready to get out of here. I got work in the morning."

"Hey," he called to her as she walked away, "are you going to be here next Friday?"

"No doubt. You'll see me. I may be a li'l late, but you will see a sister."

Trinity walked into the dark parking lot in back of the club and deactivated her car alarm as she approached it. She stepped inside the eggshell white Lexus and started it up. She pushed a CD into the player then adjusted the volume control. Beautiful blue lights brilliantly lit up the vehicle's tan leather interior. As the motor hummed quietly, she rolled down the tinted windows.

Trinity bopped her head and sang to the queen of neo-soul, Jill Scott.

"Trinity, hold up," a voice from behind her called, and the person came running to the car.

"What the fuck?" she blurted out, about to shift the car into reverse.

"It's me. Chill out," Solasse said, standing away from the car.

"What the fuck is you doing?" Trinity slowly said, anger in her voice. "Are you freaking crazy or something?"

"I was just trying to catch you before you drove off."

"What for?" She revved up the car's engine.

"You dropped your wallet in the staircase." Solasse smiled and handed it to her through the window.

"Yo, I'm so sorry," she said, taking the wallet from his hand. "You scared the shit outta me."

"We all make mistakes. No need for an apology." Solasse smiled. "See you next Friday?" he asked, walking over to his Isuzu Trooper.

"Next Friday," she replied with a smile, driving off.

CHAPTER THIRTEEN

TRACY KANE

"Naw. That's bullshit," Tracy blurted out after seeing the article about his dispute with the police. "I never put a hand on any of them cops." He was sitting on the couch in his living room and complaining over the phone to Christian.

"You see that, man?" Christian calmly said. "Didn't I tell you it was going to lead to this? But do you listen? Naw. You just do what the fuck Tracy wanna do. You got Cadillac tied all up in this shit. Drop the charges before shit get worse for you and definitely worse for me. Now I'm the one who bailed you out of jail. I think I deserve some fuckin' ode of thanks. You feel what I'm saying? You wanted out, and I got you out. You gotta pay that back, homeboy. You can start by not bringing a lot of shit to my business. I spoke with the lawyer and he said it'd be your best bet. You'd get five years probation. You'd have to give a public apology to the NYPD, and that's it. Then you can stay stuck in this contract with me until your hardhead ass pay off your debt. Ya feel me, Tupac?" Christian hung up on him.

Tracy looked down at the phone, turned its power off. He sank down into the soft cushion of the couch and frowned.

The phone rang again. On the fourth ring, he answered, "Tracy."

"Tracy, this is Dave Horwitz. Christian's attorney. I regret to inform you that I will no longer be representing you in your civil suit."

"So what you saying?"

"I'm saying that I'll have to give Christian back his check. I can't represent you. Good luck, Mister Kane. I truly do apologize."

No doubt this was the doings of Christian. Tracy knew it. All Christian was concerned with was making sure nobody found out he was investing money in anarchy. Tracy wasn't stupid though. If Christian was going to flake him, then he was going to flake him back. Yeah. He'd play the whole game with him, Kunta, and Kinte. Then he'd fuck them all.

"Grimy is . . . is grimy back?" Tracy slowly nodded his head up and down while plotting.

A disturbing knock at the front door broke him out of his trance. He thought about throwing on a shirt and sweats before he answered it but instead grabbed his .45 from under the couch. He hadn't invited anyone over, and no one had said anything about coming over. He didn't like that kind of inconsideration, just showing up and shit, like a muthafucka don't have shit to do but pop the fuck up unannounced. Kind of like police raids.

"Yeah. Who is it?" Tracy peeked through the curtain of the living room window. Between the recent drama with the police and the anonymous threats he'd been getting in the mail, he was on edge.

"I think you'll wanna talk to me," the stranger said from the other side of the door.

"Yeah? Why would I wanna talk to you?" he asked, his gun cocked.

"What you're in there doing behind that door right now, let me tell ya right now, buddy, I don't think that'd be a good idea. You got enough problems with the police as it is. Why don't you go ahead and look through your peephole? You'll see my badge. I just want to come inside and talk about some things with you, is all."

Tracy looked through the peephole at the detective. "Me and you don't have nothing to talk about."

"Tell me something. You been getting a lot of mail lately?"

"Why? I don't gotta be talking to your ass. Get away from my door before I call the police."

"Call the police?" The man laughed. "What the hell do you think I am? You better start understanding how this here works. If any of those officers get indicted or lose their job behind your bullshit, well, that could be a lot of trouble for you. I'm just trying to give you a heads-up, kid. At the end of the day, you still resisted arrest. You broke the law."

"I hope I see ya in court, detective. I don't need no special favors."

Tracy creeped toward the window to peek out into the parking lot in time to see two unmarked cars quickly speed off. He ran to the other window in the living room and saw the two cars run a red light in congested traffic. "Fuck y'all bitches!" He laughed as he put away his gun.

He picked up the phone and dialed. "Hey, Michelle? Michelle? It's Trace. You around?" he said to her voicemail. "Yo, Michelle, you home?"

Michelle finally answered, "What's the matter with you, hollerin' like you crazy? Are you bleeding or something?"

"Funny. So check it . . . I wanted to know if I could swing by. I wanna kick it about that business."

"That's what's up, because I'm tired of waiting on you. Soon there won't be any more slots to fit you into. I'm trying to help you, *broth*."

"Yeah. Everybody trying to help out Pretty Boy Tracy Kane."

"You know what, Tracy . . . you could walk away from all this anytime you want to. I ain't seen you move a notch. You sneaking here and there, doing all this on-the-low shit. No disrespect, playa, but you need to step up to the plate and stop acting like a bitch. That's not trying to talk to you slick or nothing like that. What time did you want to stop by, darling?"

The phone dangled from Tracy's hand as he went momentarily comatose on another of Michelle's famous I'm-just-keeping-it-real speeches.

"Hello? Hello? Tracy?"

Michelle answered the door in a pink and white Juicy Couture sweat suit and white fluffy slippers. It had just started to rain as she opened the door for Tracy, who walked inside with his head down, and his eyes covered with the brim of a dark blue fitted.

"Come on in, playa. Why you disrespecting my home?"

"What you talking about, man? I ain't did nothing."

"The hat. Give me your coat too, so I can hang it up in the closet."

Michelle liked giving orders. She didn't do six years at Howard University for nothing. She had her shit together and felt educated enough to spread some of it on those who didn't care to hear it. She was the kind of person that liked imposing her will on you, taking command of every situation and handling it accordingly. That's why she was so successful.

"My God, you is a beast, baby." Tracy followed her into the kitchen.

"I like formality. So what are you going to do, man? You for us or against us?"

"I'm gonna fall back for a minute, know what I'm saying? Christian got me tied into some shit that'll mess me up good if I fuck around."

"Oh, I'm sorry." Michelle pulled a bowl of chopped celery out of the refrigerator. "I thought I was talking to Tracy Kane, bad boy of the modeling world. Mister, I don't give an *F*. I thought you did what you wanted. What you doing here, if not for business? Isn't that why you said you were coming by? Now you don't want to do business?"

"I do. I really do, but my shit is real deep right now. I got court coming up next week. I don't even know if I'm going to jail or not. The shit is fuckin' with me. I'm feeling like my back's up against the wall."

"You did it to yourself. You are aware of that, right? I hope you learned something from all this."

"Only thing I learned from all of this is, ain't nothing sweet."

Michelle dipped a half-cut piece of celery into a snack-size peanut-butter container. "You should've already known that. At the end of the day, though, it's your life. Nobody can walk the path you make for yourself but you."

"Go 'head, Confucius. Look, I don't need anybody preaching to me, especially no woman. Tracy Kane gonna be a'ight." He slapped on his chest. "Oh well, fuck it," he said, standing up from the bar stool at the kitchen's island. "Like I said, yo, I'ma fall back. See what I'm saying? Good luck in all your future endeavors and shit. That's what I came to talk about."

"I trust you'll have my five-thousand-dollar incentive I gave you back to my office first thing in the morning," she calmly said, chewing slowly.

"You know what . . . I'm not giving shit back. What you gonna do?"

"Get out of my house! You not giving it back?" She chuckled. "That's fine, Tracy. You hold on to it," she said, and closed the door behind him.

Outside the door Tracy looked to the left then to the right before walking down the steps.

"Welcome back, nigga," Tracy said, standing on the porch of Shane and Star's temporary rented home in St. Albans, Queens. "You wasn't playing, dude. You really did move into 'Cracker Estates.'" He looked around at the hedges and well-manicured lawns up and down the block. "You look like you put on a few." He playfully tapped Shane's slightly bulging stomach.

"We been eating fast food ever since we been back. With all this unpacking and shit, there ain't time to cook."

"I hear ya. So you speak to any of the fellas yet? Christ-ian?"

"I ain't spoke to nobody since I been back from my hon-eymoon. Hold up, I'm lying. I did speak to Cadillac yester-day morning. Why? What's up? Y'all still beefing?"

Tracy swatted at the air. "Man, nobody beefing."

"So what's up then, nigga?"

Tracy followed him into the guestroom and plopped down on the couch. He moved a couple of boxes out of his way, to extend his legs. Then he explained the whole bootleg operation story to Shane.

"That shit don't surprise me none. See, I know that dude just a little bit better than you do. He can be a bit of a spontaneous muthafucka. If he thinks there's a way he can get more paper, he'll do whatever it is he has to do. You rolling with that program?"

"Hell yeah. That'll at least make up for the money he

been jerking me on. Now he talking about how I owe him for bailing me out of jail."

"But you didn't even go to jail. Not yet anyway. What's he talking about?"

"I'm recorded in the system but didn't have to go through the system. Don't ask me how he did it, because I don't know, but whatever he did, you see I'm standing here."

"You going ahead with the case?"

"Why everybody asking me that? These niggas beat my ass. Why should they get away with that? All I told the officer was that the cuffs were too tight, and then he and his partner start spazzing."

"Yeah. But it's just you and Cadillac's word against the NYPD. You know how that shit usually turn out."

"Doesn't even matter, *B*. I got the marks and bruises to prove it."

"All right. Only Trace knows what's best for Trace." Shane extended his hand to Tracy for some dap.

"That's right. Not like faggot-ass Cadillac. He bitched up on me."

"You wrong, man. That dude gotta live his life as he see fit. Don't be like that."

"Whatever. Anyway, what you think about that Christian thing?"

"If he call me in on it, I'm with it. Bills got to be paid, and wifey gots to stay happy."

"You whipped, nigga."

"Baby," Star called out, "I'm about to leave for the store." She entered the guestroom. "Oh. Hey, Tracy. I didn't know you were here. You have to excuse the mess. You know we just moved in." She shifted around a couple of boxes.

"Naw. It's a'ight. I was just about to breeze on up out of here anyway." Tracy stepped aside so Shane could lead the way to the front door. "Get at me if Christian call you on that, a'ight?"

"Yo, seriously, you be easy, man," he said, pounding him and giving him a hood hug.

As Tracy pulled into the parking space of his condo, squad cars and a lead detective car surrounded him, red and blue lights blinking. He turned his car off and threw his keys out the open window.

A husky white detective walked up with four officers behind him. "Get out the car now!" he yelled.

"I tell you what, you open the door and I'll keep my hands outside of the window. I don't want nobody thinking I'm holding a brush that looks like a gun." Tracy stuck his hands out of the window.

"Just get the hell out, smart ass!" the detective said.

Detective Dennis Frogger snatched the door of Tracy's car open with one hand and jerked him out by the arm with the other. The officers quickly cuffed Tracy then stood away.

Detective Frogger wrapped his hands around his waist and walked to the front of Tracy's car. He then placed the palms of his hands on the hood. "Goddamn it!" He quickly retracted his hands and pounded the hood with his fist. "This hood is hot as hell. Maybe it's because of driving away so fast from a COP KILLING," he yelled into Tracy's ear.

"A cop killing? Man, I just came back from my dude's house. You talking about some cop killing. Y'all niggas kill me. Search the car, *B*."

"Search this dick," Dennis yelled out to no officer in particular. "You got any guns, drugs, or anything like that in the car?"

"Man, go and search. Ain't shit in here."

"Where're you coming from?"

"I already told you, man, my dude's house."

"What you mean, your dude's house? You mean, like your boyfriend? Your lover?"

"How about your mother, man?"

"How about my mother." Frogger chuckled. "How about *your* mother?" He gave him a quick jab to the abdomen after pulling him from the open door of the car.

Tracy held his stomach. "This here is bullshit. I don't know nothing about no dead cop."

"Then it's just by coincidence that that dead cop just happens to be one of the officers you was going to testify against?"

"I don't know nothing about that, man," he said, now struggling with silver bracelets cuffed tightly behind his back.

"What's the matter, Tracy? Are the shits too tight?" Frogger laughed. "Do you remember that? I told you the shits was too tight," he said, mocking Tracy's defense for striking an officer.

"Fuck you!" Tracy spat on Frogger's shirt.

Det. Frogger grabbed him by the collar and gave him a little shaking. "Fuck around!" he said, damn near kissing Tracy's cheek.

"Y'all just trying to pin some shit on me because your people was in the wrong and they're fuckin' going down. That's right. Y'all not getting away with murder this time."

"You believe this prick? You know why they call me Detective Frogger?" He pressed Tracy up against the car. "Because I'm used to hopping on lots and lots of niggers' asses."

"Everything's clear in here, sir," one of the officers said from the passenger side of Tracy's car.

Det. Frogger frowned then searched the car himself but still came up with exactly what the others did. Nothing. He paced back and forth.

An embarrassed Tracy leaned back on his hood, as his neighbors stood on their balconies and peeked through their blinds.

The detective stopped in his tracks and pointed his finger directly into Tracy's face. "That was my friend, you little fuck! I'm taking you in for questioning. Somebody put this piece of shit in a car besides mine. I can't stand the smell of a lying nigger sitting behind me while I'm driving."

Tracy sat cuffed to a metal ring built into a table in the interrogation room of the police station. With the shade up on the window of the wooden door, over which a gated clock with no hands hung, he watched as the mean-mugged officers served him up hostile looks. The windows of the room were barred, and the fading light green paint on the walls gave way to patches of plaster.

"You just can't seem to stay out of trouble, can you?" Dennis tucked his swinging badge into his shirt. "Now you're going to tell me what I want to know."

"How I'm supposed to tell you what I don't know?"

The captain entered the room. "Have you taken any pictures of his face, detective?"

"No, sir."

"Detective," he said, closing the blinds on the door, "get a camera and take pictures of this man's face. I don't need any more bad publicity for this department."

"Tracy Kane, huh? I'm Captain Frank Ronald. You know, Tracy, it'd be in your favor to start talking. I may be able to do something for you, depending on your level of cooperation. Accidents happen. Court is coming up for you. You had to be just a little nervous. He was sort of an asshole. Tempers flare. Things are said. Just a rookie, you know. How am I supposed to explain that to his wife and newborn child?"

"I don't know what the fuck you gonna say. There's nothing for me to cooperate with. I didn't do shit."

Another detective poked his head through the door. "Captain, we recovered a gun." Captain Ronald turned to Tracy and smiled. "Anything you'd like to work out before we run your prints against the ones on that gun, son?"

"Run 'em. Run them shits." Tracy laughed. "This is some real bullshit for y'all to be doing. I wasn't even nowhere near where ol' boy got put down. What the fuck would I shoot him for anyway? Killing a cop? Come on, man, y'all just making it worse on yourselves. How you think it's gonna look when I go to court and the jury finds out I've been harassed?"

"Wise up," the captain said. "Who do you think an all-white jury is going to believe? My officers say you put your hands on them first. They're allowed to defend themselves. You put your hands on my officers, and they will retaliate accordingly. As you see, there are a lot of angry faces in here this evening. It doesn't have to be that way, though." He sat on the edge of the desk.

Det. Frogger re-entered the room with a Polaroid camera and a frown. "Fuck! Fuck! Fuck!" He slammed the door shut.

"What happened?" Captain Ronald asked.

"Fuck!" Det. Frogger pounded his fist on the table under Tracy's face. "You're one lucky son of a bitch. It's not him." He released Tracy from the cuffs. "It's not fuckin' him, Captain. Goddamn!"

"See, y'all got real problems headed your way." Tracy rubbed his sore wrists.

"Were your cuffs too tight?" Captain Ronald asked with sarcasm.

"I'm fine." Tracy beamed back the same laser-eyed stare Frogger was giving him.

Dennis stepped toward Tracy. "You got a fuckin' staring problem or something? You fuck!"

"Uh, it's Captain Ronald, right? Ain't there a law about animals in a public building? You wanna get your pit bull over here on a leash?"

"You're free to go, Tracy," Captain Ronald said. "Keep your nose clean. I'll be watching."

As Tracy exited the interrogation room, a sea of dark blue–suited sharks with badges exposed their sharp teeth at him. They angrily departed, standing shoulder to shoulder in commemoration of their murdered colleague.

Captain Ronald and Detective Frogger stood at the office door to secure Tracy's safety as he departed. Dennis banged on the doorframe.

Tracy turned around when he got to the stairs and gave the detective a wink and a corner-of-the-mouth smirk.

CHAPTER FOURTEEN

THE CULTURE

"Black to the bone, my home is your home
So welcome to the Terrordome . . . "

Public Enemy

The early morning sun slowly rose over the large row of renovated warehouses deep in the factory-established section of little-known West New York, which sat obliquely opposite West 59th Street not far from Manhattan Island and the Hudson River.

Four white vans towed behind a blue Eddie Bauer limousine, driven by Assante's personal chauffeur. The vehicles stopped a little ways down from the distant view.

Six motorized garages of the once-deserted warehouses simultaneously opened. One of the garages contained well over thirty men, each putting together and cleaning a deadly arsenal of weapons. Some guns were held in the air and aimed at imaginary targets. Each man wore green Christian Elijah jumpsuits and black low-cut steel-toe boots. Gigantic fans catty-cornered in all the warehouses' walls whirred loudly, significantly dropping the overbearing heat and humidity within them.

Three men from each of the vans behind the limousine got out and opened the back doors and immediately began transferring boxes into the houses of weaponry from the vans, stocked from floor to ceiling, silently passing messages back and forth between them as they diligently scurried to and fro like ants in the Amazon.

Assante, Akinsanya, Christian, Tracy, Shane, and Cadillac all sat in the back of the luxurious chariot before exiting. Assante took the lead, and Christian walked up and side-stepped next to him.

"Come," Assante said, proceeding toward the garage.

"Now that's what I'm talking about." Tracy smiled, turning his fitted backwards.

"Damn, man!" Christian said. "I didn't know it was like this."

They all stopped six feet in front of the entrance.

"That is a fuckin' army, man."

Cadillac looked at one of the tables full of gats. "Yo, this is crazy. Look at all them guns. That's some ol' Rambo shit."

"Damn, that's a lot of niggas," Shane said, observing the row of men. "A lot of 'em. Feel like I'm at the ten-million-man march." He chuckled.

"They are just peas in a pot of many. There are warehouses just like this one all throughout the States," Assante responded.

"Yo, I ain't even gonna front, Assante," Tracy told him. "I really thought you was bullshitting about all this, but you really ready to go to war, huh?"

"The time has come. How long will you live in a country under the white man, who says you have opportunities, then pulls the rug out from under you every time you try to stand on your own two feet? That's what happens in a Third World country, but this? This racist country you live in, that we live in, the so-called greatest country in the world, does not take responsibility.

"They say if you do not like it here then go back to Africa. Well, I am from there, and unfortunately, it is no place I want to ever return. At least not until I seek out and annihilate the source of my country's conspired demise."

Cadillac sang as if he were in a congregation at church. "*Well . . .*"

"We are not doing this out of spite," Akinsanya said. "Someone has to pay. We do not need their money, to truly ever feel free. It is their blood we require. It is the only thing that will make all right."

"I have something else to show you."

Assante walked into warehouse C 49. They walked past all the men, who gave nods of acknowledgment then went right back to work. All the way at the very end was a steel door guarded by two men.

Assante asked the guard to his left, "Sakou, how is he?"

"He is waiting for you," Sakou said.

The guard on the right unlatched the long bar that secured the iron door and pulled it open. Assante and the others walked inside, and Akinsanya pushed the door closed.

The walls of the room were made of thick concrete, and the floor was a mixture of gravel, dirt, and broken glass. A hanging lamp shone down upon a badly bruised boy in his late teens sitting on a metal foldup chair.

"Get up," Assante said to the teenager.

Wearing one of their shirts, stained with dirt and his own blood, he stood up and faced Assante. "Come on, Assante, man. I didn't mean to do it," the boy said, spitting up blood.

"Shut up! Just shut up!" Assante punched the boy in the face then slapped him several times. "Akinsanya." He nodded his brother over to the boy.

Akinsanya pulled a ten-inch-thick metal rod from his belt holder and swung it into the boy's knees. When he fell to the floor and curled up, Akinsanya hit him again, drawing elastic-like strands of saliva between the boy's upper and lower lips, as he cried out in agony.

Assante yelled down to the boy, pointing down to him, "What are the rules? What are the rules?" When he didn't respond, Assante signaled his brother to whack his knees again. "What are the rules?"

Assante grabbed him around the throat and began shaking him off his feet, which dangled three inches from the ground, then dropped him. "Stand up!"

The battered teenager rose weakly, obviously fearful for his life at this point.

"The police have found the gun you used to shoot the officer. They blamed that man there for your foolishness." Assante pointed to Tracy.

"Okay, okay," he said, his hands up. "Let me go to the police and turn myself in. Please."

"You do not tell me what you will do. *I* tell you what to do. The police are now scouring the city for a cop killer. You are interfering with Christian's business and my plans. It is a shame."

"Man, oh, you think I'd say something about you if I get locked up? I swear, I wouldn't say nothing, man. I swear." Bits and pieces of his life flashed before his eyes.

"Shhhhh," Assante said. "You know the consequences of your actions end today. Take him," he told his brother. "Tracy, go with him. He is the flaw that will alter the action of this entire movement."

"No, Assante, please. Don't do this," the boy yelled as the gigantic Akinsanya dragged him out by the back of his neck, slamming his head into the steel door before opening it, then pushing him out into the dirt-filled lot out back.

Akinsanya aimed his gun at the boy's forehead.

"No!" The boy held his hands in front of his face.

"A'ight. Hold up, man. Just hold up a second." Tracy grabbed Akinsanya by the arm. "If he wants to turn himself in, then why kill him?"

"Fool. Americans." Akinsanya shook his head. "He will try to make a deal. None of us can afford to stop now. This little ignoramus has started it."

"Why'd you do it, you?" Tracy said to the boy. "If it wasn't time yet, then why did you do it?"

"He was fuckin' with me, man. If I could take it back, I would."

Brrrraaduup! Brrrraaduup! Brrrraaduup!

Akinsanya let his semi-automatic weapon spit hollow tips that went through the boy's head and ligaments, sending him where all the foul niggas went.

Tracy looked at the boy's smoking, bullet-ridden body as he lay bleeding, dead with his eyes open. "He was saying something, man."

"He is of consequence no longer," Akinsanya said.

"But he was about to say something."

"Tell me, Tracy, what do you think you'd say if a gun was in your face? He shouldn't have moved without a given order from me or my brother."

"He was just a kid. No more than nineteen, twenty years old."

"He's lucky he has survived that long. The children back home die much earlier. Grab his feet. We will drop him in the hole over there beside the Payloader. Hurry." Akinsanya grabbed the boy's hands, and they swung the boy over the hole, counting to three.

"Think of it like this, brother," Akinsanya said to Tracy. "If it were not for him, you'd never be a suspect."

"So what you gonna do? Just leave him in the bottom of some ditch?"

"It will save the cost of his funeral expense for his mother." Akinsanya spat into the twelve-foot grave, on the boy's body. As he walked away, he said, "Traitor."

Tracy stood a while longer, staring at the young man who'd just been murdered in front of him.

"Come," Akinsanya said, never looking back.

Two days later Tracy had his first day in court. He arrogantly walked into the room of justice rocking a stocking cap, baggy jeans, and a pinstriped button-down. Almost the whole police station was sitting to Tracy's right, while his peoples sat in back of the courtroom. And the accused all sat on the long wooden bench, whispering to one another and their lawyers.

The huge-sized baldheaded court officer standing between the two benches said, "Remove your stocking cap. Please stand for the Honorable Lenny Weitz."

The judge said to the jurors and observers, "You may be seated. What am I looking at here?" He frowned, quickly searching through a mess of folders. He looked over the brim of his glasses at Tracy then at the police.

After a series of questions, cross-examinations, and character decimation between the defense and the prosecution, a verdict still had not yet been reached.

Tempers flared, as black jurors exchanged looks of disdain with the racist, brutish alliance of killers.

Tracy was beginning to wish he'd taken everyone's advice and just stepped.

"Mister Kane," began another prosecution lawyer for the officers when Tracy took the stand, "how are you today?"

The tension in the room was so hot, you could backstroke in the pool of perspiration falling off the faces of both sides. Including Tracy's.

"I'm fine. How are you?" Tracy responded with an attitude.

"Well, I have to say, Mister Kane, I'm a little hot under the collar." The lawyer tugged at the neck of his expensive tie. "I'm hot under the collar because I'm having a little trouble believing the story you've conjured up to justify your belligerent actions against sworn officers of the law. Have you ever been arrested before?" He looked through some papers in a folder he was holding. "And please keep in mind that you are under oath," he said, staring at Tracy through his crystal-blue devil eyes.

Tracy hesitated and looked around at the portraits up on the wall of a lying I-cannot-tell-a-lie George Washington; a kind, caring former slave-master, Abraham Lincoln; and the incomparable I-just-love-niggers Hillary Rodham Clinton, all collectively noted as the overseers, looking down and smiling at him. An American flag sitting to the left of the judge swayed in the light breeze coming in through two open windows on opposite sides of the room.

"Yeah, I been locked up before. Nothing big."

"Nothing big? Getting arrested is what you deem as nothing big? No further questions, Your Honor."

Tracy's new defense attorney, Common Harris, approached Tracy then turned to the jury. "Are we tired of this yet, people? Have we not yet become tired of this redundant scenario? This, this repetitious crossing of racial borderlines?"

"Objection, Your Honor. The defense is attempting to sway the verdict into the favor of the accused before questioning him."

"Sustained."

Tracy looked across the room at the prosecution. "Yeah. Whatever, man. You would say that."

Completely irritated with Tracy's nasty disposition, Judge Weitz asked, "Mister Kane, how are you feeling today?"

"I'm good, man. I'm just up in here trying to get some justice."

The judge pierced Tracy with a look. "May I ask why you're looking for justice?"

"Why does it matter to you how I'm feeling? Does it really make a difference? I mean, this country, this city, just be doin' what they want to, anyway. It don't matter what I say or do if some fool out getting his ass whupped by police. It can be on camera, and the police still get off. So, you wanna know how I'm feeling? To be quite honest, Your Honor, I'm feeling pretty fucked-up."

Some members of the jury roared in disbelief, while others yelled at officers standing by the doors of the court-room. Some officers looked to the judge for direction. Camera crews from Channel Zero and CIA (Caucasians In America) fought for position to record the events.

The judge's face turned red, and the wrinkles tightened with his dismayed frown. "Order in the court! Order in the court! Order in the court!" He banged his gavel over and over. "Mister Kane! I can hold you in contempt of court for that use of language in my courtroom." Judge Weitz lifted his thick black spectacles to the top of his head. "When you're in my courtroom, you will respect me, the jurors, visitors, or whoever else may drop by." He leaned over as close as he could get to Tracy's ear. "Is that under-stood, Mister Kane? Are we clear on that?"

"Yes, Your Honor, very clear," Tracy responded, looking straight ahead.

CHAPTER FIFTEEN

TRINITY

Trinity lay on the royal blue carpeted floor of her bedroom, exhausted from her daily routine of early morning crunches, her thighs throbbing and her stomach burning.

She sprang up without the use of her hands then quickly jogged in place, staying in sync with the song playing on her stereo. Bass bounced off the baby blue walls and shook the mirrors hanging off them. Her pretty breasts jumped up and down while securely cupped in the silky soft embrace of a pink lace brassiere.

Christian knocked on her bedroom door loudly, over the music. "Hey, Wonder Woman."

"Yeah? Hold up." Trinity turned down the music then cracked her door open slightly. "Hey, what's up?" She smiled. "Good morning."

"Good morning." Christian smiled back. "How can it be, when you blasting that loud-ass music this early in the morning?

She snickered. "I'm sorry. Did I wake you up?"

"Oh, you think it's funny, do ya? Listen, babe, I got some

bad news. I'm not going to be able to go to the house in Florida with you next week. I got some real important business I'm taking care of right now. I need to be here."

"Isn't that why you hire people? To handle them kinda affairs?"

"Sometimes you got to watch your own affairs. You see where I got us living now, baby. This"—He looked around—"All of this is from handling my affairs personally. You like where we living, right? The car you driving? Couldn't have any of that if I wasn't directly up to speed with each and everything that's going on. This is all for you. Everything."

"Okay. Do you need me to make you a cup of coffee or something?"

"I'm serious, Trinity."

"I know you are, but I really have to get ready for school."

"All right. I'll see you downstairs."

Trinity closed her door and turned the music up again before stepping off into the shower.

Solasse flagged down Trinity. "Over here." He was sitting on the outside deck of a seafood restaurant by the water out in New Jersey. He walked out to the entrance of the white picket fence and pushed it open.

As Trinity walked through the gate, a light wind lifted the back of her hair.

"How you doing?"

Solasse smiled and led the way back to their reserved table, where warm rolls in a small red plastic basket and Long Island ice teas awaited them on a white patio table with an umbrella implanted down its center. A mesh screen covered the deck's eating area, protecting its patrons from being viciously attacked by hungry gulls crowding the sea. Vacationing tourists standing on the top decks of cruising ships off in the distance waved excitedly at one another as they sailed by.

Trinity held on to her black skirt as she sat down. "This is nice."

"Yeah. I was going over some places online and ran into the website for this."

"A'ight, so what's up? You was talking about working on something together for the next jump-off?"

"Trinity, I think you have a lot of talent. Your words are strong. It comes from the heart." Solasse touched his own.

"That's what's up. We can do that. Got anything in mind?" Trinity asked, scanning the menu.

"We'll come up with something."

"Sure the wife won't mind?"

"Huh?"

"The wife, you know." She sang, *"Here comes the bride, all dressed in white."*

"Oh." Solasse chuckled. "I'm sure she'll be fine with it."

"Cool. I don't need to be having no issues with a chick thinking I'm trying to steal her man. But if you say it's a'ight, then I guess it is."

"It's a'ight." He laughed.

"You making fun of me?"

"No, I'm just kidding you. You ready to order?"

"Yep. You know I keeps it one hundred ev'y day, so let me get the shrimp basket, curly fry combo. Oh, see if they got some Louisiana hot sauce for me, please."

"You're cute." Solasse smiled. He looked around for a waiter.

"So, Solasse, tell me a li'l something more about yourself."

He chuckled. "I can only tell you what you ask. I can't afford to be incriminating myself."

"Okay. Where'd you grow up at? And how long are you here? Why am I the only one you felt the need to do this with?"

"Whoa!" Solasse held up his hands. "Did I say or do something wrong?"

"Naw. I'm just saying, answer a few questions. I like to know who I deal with."

"You do know me. We perform at the same spot. My face has been seen there talking to you."

"Look, Solasse, don't try to beat me in my head. I'm only here because we all have a mutual cause. Far as people seeing us speaking at the spot, doesn't mean nothing. You could be a coldblooded killer, for all I know."

"Then why are you here?"

"For the free meal, and it's a public place. Besides, I keeps something real special deep down in the belly of my significant other." Trinity patted her black Kate Spade purse.

"Well, I don't wants no trouble, boss. I grew up in Nuremberg, Germany."

Trinity raised her brows. "Army brat?"

"Army brat. My father was a sergeant."

"How long was you there for?"

"Until I was about seven. After that we was just all over the place. My mother got tired of it and just one day up and left. She didn't leave a note, a message, or nothing. She just made moves and got in the wind."

"Oh. That's so sad." Trinity peeped the tears of his heartbeat as they dropped into a pool of fucked-up memories.

"Everything happens for a reason."

"Hi. Welcome to Sea Basket. My name is Tonya, and I'll be your waitress this afternoon," the enthusiastic, happy-go-lucky white girl said. "Are you guys ready to order?"

"Hi." Trinity asked Solasse, "You ready?"

"Go on."

"Let me get the shrimp basket and fries combo. You guys serve curly fries here? It don't matter. Any kinda fries and a nice-sized pitcher of water. Put mad ice in it please."

The waitress looked at Solasse. "And you, sir?"

"I'll take the number four special."

"Okay." Tonya quickly wrote both their orders down on the pages of a small black pad. "All right." She smiled. "That'll be about twenty minutes. Anything else I can do for you while you wait? We serve all kinds of tropical mixed drinks."

"We're fine. Thanks a lot, Tonya."

Trinity laughed after she walked away. "Damn, her ass is happy."

"Does she have a reason not to be? She white. Even her worst day is a good day."

"She probably got herself a li'l something-something before she came in. I don't know about all that stuff you talking."

"Trinity, come on. If you was white, don't you think you'd have every reason to be happy? You ever see how they walk around just smiling the hell away . . . almost as if they know something we don't?"

"What you mean? Like a conspiracy?"

"No. Like factuality! They're living the way they want to live, even those run-of-the-mill, trailer-trash misfits. Born with silver spoons in their mouths, but steady trying to eat ice cream with a knife. We're not born with that silver spoon. You're one of the few exceptions."

"So what? You going to blame me for smiling," she said in all seriousness. "I say like this—I wasn't born into this, and my pops bust his ass to get where he at, feel me? See, you can't just go around pointing fingers when you don't know somebody. On another note, and pardon my

French, playa, but I'm happy and feel blessed to be in the position I'm in right now. I'm a smiling bitch ev'y day, and I know some shit they don't know either."

"Goddamn!" Solasse playfully jumped out of his seat. "You're vocal. I respect that. So, just out of curiosity, Trinity, what'd you mean when you said you know things they don't?"

CHAPTER SIXTEEN

CHRISTIAN

♪ I took quarter water, sold it in a bottle for two bucks
And Coca-Cola came and bought it for billions,
What the fuck ♪

—CURTIS

Christian began opening up new stores in different states. He'd planned on being a big name, but he had no idea it'd happen so suddenly.

Everybody was happy. Young black teenagers were getting jobs in his stores and warehouses, whether it was young women answering phones or interns looking for a permanent position. All were required to wear a Culture shirt every day. His money had become long, and with money came power. Power to do, say whatever, and go wherever he wanted to.

The phones rang off the hooks as he sat at his desk in his new Manhattan office.

"Mister Elijah, the brothers are here. They're outside waiting in the car."

"Yeah. Thanks a lot, Crystal. I was on my way out anyway. If my daughter calls, tell her I'll be in a meeting all day."

Crystal, Christian's new secretary, entered his office

and closed the door behind her. "Does that mean I won't see you tonight?"

Butter-cream complexioned and high-cheekboned, Crystal had grey eyes, and a perfectly shaped nose with small brown freckles sprinkled on it. Her blonde-rinsed hair was long and split off into pigtails, just one of the many requirements Christian demanded of the women working for him, in and outside of the building. He loved pigtails on a woman and automatically took to her the day she was interviewed. I guess you can kind of say she impressed him, "in a Monica Lewinsky sort of way." And it'd been on ever since, at least in her eighteen-year-old mind.

"Probably not," he said, grabbing a folder off the desk.

"Tomorrow night, maybe?"

"Crystal, stop it, all right. What you're talking about right now isn't important."

"It's not?" Crystal grabbed his crotch and looked seductively up into his eyes. "It's not?" she repeated, massaging it, kissing his chin.

"It's not." Christian pushed her hand away and walked out of the office, leaving Crystal standing there, and slowly closed the door after him.

"Yeah, yeah, I'ma be gone all day, Tracy." Christian stepped into the back of Assante's black chauffeur-driven Lincoln Continental Town Car. "Yeah. Peace." He slipped the phone down into his jacket pocket. "Gentlemen, what's good?"

"It is going very good," Assante replied. "But there is something further to discuss."

"Anything, man. Go on. I'm all ears."

"We need more room for our artillery."

"Why is that a problem? You're supposed to have your half of the deal completely covered. I'm doing my part by acting as your front. You don't want to fuck with me, Assante."

"I believe it should not be a problem, because we're placing the guns in your warehouses. The extras, well, I've come up with something for that also."

"Not that I'm even hearing you right now, but what's the extended plan?"

"Hide them in the churches. I'm sure the ministry will be more than happy to receive an enormous donation without the congregation knowing who it came from."

"Your mind works sick. You're crazy."

"Did I forget to mention, there's a huge incentive for your approval right now? Akinsanya, *toon hom die* briefcase." (Pass me the briefcase.)

Akinsanya reached around to the front passenger seat and pulled back a brown briefcase. He placed it upon his lap, turned it around, and popped it open. Just as Assante promised, money was neatly stacked by the thousands.

Christian quickly snatched out the first stack he saw.

"There is money to be made, Mister Elijah. What else do you have, if not for money? I know your kind. No disrespect intended, but you are like the hyena of the prairie land, vicious and always hungry for more, no matter how much you've already consumed. Are you tired of being full yet, Mister Elijah?"

Christian sat back looking at the briefcase, and the long perspective of things, and concluded that he wanted all of the food. He wanted to devour every morsel life had to offer him. "No, no, I'm not," he said, dropping the money back inside the case. He took the briefcase off Akinsanya's lap and closed it.

The two brothers looked at one another and smiled.

"I just think the whole shit is a li'l extreme, Assante," Christian explained to him as the two sat in lounge chairs on the roof of one of the warehouses out in West New York.

"Look around you, Christian. What do we really own? What do we have? We have to fight for what belongs to us, and if people must die, then so it must be. This is a kill-to-gain game. They have been playing it on us for many years. In six more months all of New York and Jersey will be flooded with guns. See who the police will fuck with then."

"Wouldn't that be defeating the purpose? I mean, you flood the hood with guns, then the assholes you trying to help start shooting each other instead of the police. Then what? What the fuck would all of this have been for, Assante? I mean, when I say it like that, it do start to sound a li'l retarded, doesn't it?"

"What do you know? You've been brainwashed into thinking you've been living in a free world. Everybody wants to think that the slavery of the old was the worst thing that ever happened. Which is true. But now it is even worse, because the spirit of the old-time slave exists within the average nigger today."

"I don't get it. None of your bullshit is making any sense. What do you mean, old-time slave, the average nigger? What the fuck are you talking about, man? I thought you was doing this so we could get paid and you could get your peoples straight."

"Everyone out there deserves to be able to defend themselves. Agreed?"

"Yeah."

"So then what is the problem?"

"The problem is, the Culture is about revolution. You talking about genocide, homicide, and suicide, my man."

"Don't act like the Culture stands for anything positive. The Culture is about power and money. We have followers, Christian. Your name is iconic. We can one day control shit as long as we have the kids, an entire generation of name-brand freaks. Do you not see the financial gain in that, Mister Elijah?"

An incoming delivery ship's foghorn sounded off so loudly, it appeared to shake the full moon suspended above the edge of the ocean. Striped bass off in the distance quickly danced up into the night sky, momentarily posing within the beams of the moonlight, then sliced back through the pool of liquid ice.

Workers from the fabric building ran outside and crowded the deck, and Assante's men arrived soon after.

"It is so beautiful." Assante laughed. "Everyone is working together. It is how we shall win. I am very happy about this." He picked up a pair of binoculars to get a closer look. He blinked both eyes before placing the viewer to them. The meter on the bottom of the screen inside the binoculars zipped back and forth and beeped before zooming in on the Jersey scene.

As the workers transferred crates from the ships to the vans and to the warehouse, Assante laughed. "Excellent. Excellent."

Christian stood behind him, watching and wondering if the money was really worth it.

"Mister Elijah, is something the matter?" Assante lowered the binoculars and turned to him.

"Naw," he said, staring up at him. "Naw. Ain't nothing the matter."

"Very well then," Assante said, looking back to the warehouses.

It was three in the morning when Christian pulled up into the driveway of his home. He accidentally pushed against the car's horn as he got out. He closed the door then quickly spun around, gun in hand, after hearing footsteps approaching.

"That's real stupid, Crystal," Christian said, after making her face out in the dark. "You trying to get yourself popped? What you think you doing?" He placed his gun back into its holster.

"You're crazy," she said, realizing she could've just been shot.

"It's three in the morning. What you doing here? You can't keep doing this."

"Can I come in? I been waiting out here for you since ten o'clock. Can I get some dick please, or are you going to shut me down like how you did earlier?" Crystal about-faced and walked toward the front door.

"Look, I'm tired. I don't got no time for the shit right now."

"You know, you been acting real shitty to people lately, Christian. Especially to me."

"This is where you get off." Christian stopped her at the door before she could walk in behind him. "I gotta be up in three hours to get to Tracy's court appearance today. You can't stay the night. I need my rest. I'll talk to you in the morning at work. You need something for your purse?" He reached down into his man bag.

"Forget you, Christian. I don't need anything. I just wanted to chill with you. I miss you."

"All right." He closed the door on her.

"Fuck you!" she yelled, banging the door before walking down the steps.

A pair of headlights pulled up into the driveway next to Christian's car. Crystal couldn't make the vehicle out at first because of the shadows cast by the fresh green leaves of summer sprouting out of the tall oak trees lining both sides of his driveway. She slowly walked down to the last step and stood there.

Trinity walked up, her hand on her bag. "Can I help you?"

"Trinity, right?" Crystal asked with attitude.

"Do I know you?"

"No, I'm a friend of your father's. I work with him out at the office in Manhattan."

"A'ight." Trinity still held the gun lightly through the purse. "So what you doing standing outside?"

"Oh, I was just about to leave. I saw your headlights coming up and was just looking out."

"That's what's up. What's your name? So I can be sure to tell my pops that you were out here on the job, looking out after he closed the door," she cattily said.

"Oh, it's Crystal. You looked real cute in last month's edition of your dad's magazine."

Feeling more relaxed, Trinity released her hold on the weapon. "Which one was that, hon?"

"The one with Tracy Kane. Mm-hmm, girl, y'all look real good together. Kind of like a mini-version of me and your father."

"Is that right?" Trinity smiled. She placed her hand back on her bag.

The porch light came on, and its flooding light washed away the shadows that had taken up temporary residence upon the blacktop driveway. Small crystals embedded deep within it sparkled around Trinity's sandaled feet.

Christian pushed the door open and leaned out. "What the fuck you still doing here, Crystal? Get inside, Trinity. It's almost four in the morning."

"I'm coming. I was just out here kicking it with your li'l friend. She was holding down the fort for you while you were sleeping. She a soldier, daddy." Trinity walked past her.

"Awww." Crystal smiled. "She's so cute, Christian."

"I got your cute, bitch," Trinity said, turning around.

"You better get your ass off my property right now."

"Stop tripping. It's been a long night. I'm out anyway.

See you in the morning," Crystal said, stretching and yawning.

"Damn, that girl is crazy." Christian closed the door.

"You know how to pick 'em, Daddy. She got some issues."

"I got some issues too. Where you been at? You ain't called or nothing. You know I get worried when you do that."

"Be easy. I'm not going to let anything happen to me. Dad, you got to stop worrying so much. I'm going to be twenty years old in a couple of months. I'll always be your little girl, just not your baby girl, okay."

"That shit ain't going to work, Trinity. I'm your father and I love you more than anything. You always going to be my baby girl, whether you like it or not."

Trinity hugged him. "That's why I love you, Pops."

"A hell of a time for a heart-to-heart." Christian chuckled. "Just remember one thing for me," he said, holding her by the shoulders. "It's just me and you against the world, only me and you. All them other characters don't mean shit to me."

"I feel you, and I promise to call if I'm going to be late from now on, a'ight."

"That's all I ask."

CHAPTER SEVENTEEN

TRACY

The verdict was in. Tracy was found not guilty on all charges, except for resisting arrest. The case would've been completely over, if not for the surprise witness that came forward with a cell phone video of the incident between Tracy and the police. After a much more thorough investigation by Internal Affairs, it turned out that each one of the officers involved in the visit had a history of using excessive force, lying, and one even had a case pending over an alleged rape charge when he was a deputy in upstate New York.

Tracy's lawyer saw money in this and coaxed him into getting the case retried. The procedure was put into motion and set to begin a year from the day of the incident.

As days turned into weeks and weeks turned into months, Tracy began frequenting some of New York City's hottest radio stations to address police brutality, each interview more outrageous than the previous. His spontaneous outburst and hostility toward the police had quickly propelled him to the top of the FBI's list as a problem. He was becoming the same controversial mouthpiece his mother had once been, vehemently speaking out against illegal searches and promoting the right to bear arms in self-defense.

He sat in the recording studio in front of a microphone, wearing a set of headphones, with the beautiful Dominican princess, deejay Melissa Conterez. The station's producer sat in the window inside the control room and slowly counted them down from three on her fingers.

"Hey, what's up, New York? You're chilling out with your girl Melissa Conterez. Welcome to a very special edition of 'Foot Patrol.' We have supermodel Tracy Kane of the Christian Elijah clothing line sitting in with us this evening. He's going to talk about his arrest, his upcoming court case next year, and his possible departure from the Christian Elijah clothing line. You are listening to 91.45 Black Radio FM, where, if you just talking about it, then you ain't really doing nothing. We'll be right back after a short break."

Melissa pulled her headphones off and popped open a bottle of orange juice. "So, how you doing, man?" she said, rubbing Tracy's hand.

"I'm upset. It's like real crazy to me how knocking out a African nigga could lead up to all of this."

"You want to discuss that on air?"

"Naw. I can never let them see me sweat. My people believe in a dude, know what I'm saying? I'm letting niggas know just because I got an iller car than you or more paper don't make me any different than you. My car or my paper can't get me out of this. I gotta handle this shit head-on now, because I was disrespected. How I'ma be Tracy Kane if I back down from some racist police?"

"I'm saying, Tracy, were they being racists, or just abusing their power? Because there is a difference."

"Naw. Fuck that! Them dudes was expressing racial anger upon my body."

"Melissa," the producer said through the intercom, "we're about to go back on the air."

"Put your phones on, baby." Melissa winked at Tracy. "Hey, welcome back to 'Foot Patrol.' I'm sitting here with Tracy Kane. Most of you probably have already heard of his recent run-in with the beast. So, Tracy, after everything you've been through up to the present, how has this affected your everyday struggle?"

"What's up, New York? Yo, I'ma tell y'all like this. Getting violated by the police for any reason is a no-no. This is why *bleep* niggas be poppin' cops. It ain't really affected my life none though, except for the fact that now I gotta be watching my back all the *bleep* time. They be feelin' a way right now, y'all."

"So, what exactly is happening right now? The case is being retried? You know, a lot of people are wondering why you just didn't leave it alone after you got off with a slap on the wrist the first time. What do you say to those people?"

"I don't say nothing, man, because nobody know what I'm up against. They don't know the circumstances behind my *bleep*. The case is being tried because some Good Samaritan, quote unquote, came forward with a video from they cell of them pounding me out. An investigation was run on them and they all foul. One of them even got a pending rape charge going on upstate. These is the *bleep* cats the city want you to believe is gonna protect you? A *bleep* rapist?"

"Tell us what the Culture is doing. How has their support of you been?"

"Oh, that's been all lovely from day one. Word up."

"I hear you guys are planning a protest next month in Mother Harlem."

"Yeah, that's right. We gonna be right out there on 135th and Lenox Avenue."

"Tell our listeners what the protest is about."

"Well, it's gonna be a peaceful jump-off. We gonna be out there repping for every *bleep* ever shot by the police or disrespected. We not gonna take it anymore."

"I understand the Culture extends the borders of New York?"

"Word. We're all over the place. We'll all be marching at the same time."

"Sounds like that's going to be a beautiful day."

"Trust, it will be."

Tracy and Shane were on the second level of Menlo Park Mall in Edison, New Jersey, walking out of Foot Locker. They both stood outside the entrance of the department store, contemplating leaving the mall before the bigger rush started to arrive.

Tracy said to Shane, "A'ight. So you ready to be out? It's about to be four o'clock. I got things to do."

"Yeah. Let me go take a piss and we out. Stay right there, man."

"Where I'm going?"

"I know you. Some chick will walk by, and you'll follow suit, like you always do. Don't leave."

"A'ight, man." Tracy waved him off. "Just go do what you do."

After Shane headed for the men's bathroom, a loud, obnoxious group of four young men wearing baggy pants and oversized shirts that bottomed out of their oversized jackets walked past Tracy. Knowing how young boys was, Tracy stepped closer to the railing and leaned his back against it. Upon further observation, they didn't look so young after all. They were thirty-something-year-old grown men. Tracy coughed as they walked by and shook his head.

The man leading the pack stared down some white

shoppers then turned around and walked back toward Tracy, his men in tow. "Ay, yo, partna," he said.

"Keep that distance you got right there," Tracy said, pointing out more than his three feet of personal space. "What's good?" He dropped his bags to the floor. "You know me from somewhere?"

"Naw, you really, really don't. You don't want to know me."

"Nigga, what the fuck you want? I got it for you." Tracy took on a Brooklyn stance. "What, nigga?" he yelled, gathering the attention of frightened customers.

"Ain't you that Christian Elijah nigga, cocksucker bitch?"

Shane walked straight past Tracy and smacked the dude right across his face. His men hopped on Shane, but he swung his way out.

Tracy ran over and pulled the initiator off and threw him on the floor then hopped onto his chest and his face. "You don't know me, bitch!" he said, stomping his face.

The man, though badly stomped out, still managed to dig deep within his waistline and come up with the referee, so Tracy stepped back with his hands up, and all the fighting ceased.

One of the dudes said, "*D*, what you doing, man?" He pushed Shane aside.

Screams from the people up top signaled the people down under to look above and observe the potential murder scene.

"Be cool, Tracy," the man said. "See what I'm saying? This how you break up a fight—slapping the shit out of a nigga with your pistol."—He whacked Tracy across the face.

Tracy stood firm, holding his bruised face with a thug's caress. "I'm not gonna fall, man," he said, a tear in his eye.

"I don't want you to fall, bitch. You just listen up. There

are a lot of people watching your ass. You keep getting up on all them radio talk shows speaking that nonsense, you're going to have a real early funeral. Gentlemen— how do we say?—let's bounce."

The other two men released Shane from their grasp and pushed him next to Tracy.

"Show's over, folks," the initiator said. "Hey, Tracy, did you notice how no security or police came to your rescue? Just look at this place. Everybody's all excited and whatnot. Maybe it's because they thought I'd do this." The man lifted the gun to his head and pulled the trigger.

Tracy yelled out, "NO!"

The man laughed as the head of the gun lit a small flame. "Scared like a bitch. This one's fake. The one right there"—He pointed to his man—"that shit is real. You think about what I told you. Keep it up, and you won't have a friend in the world. Peace." The man threw up two fingers then twirled them in the air before his peoples about-faced and followed his exit.

"What the fuck just happened?" Shane said to Tracy, who was steaming and raging with utter embarrassment.

"I want something real nice," Tracy said to Assante in the back office of a car dealership out in the Bronx.

Tracy was looking for a new piece of protection to carry on his person. His .45 would stay in the condo under the couch, and this new one would become his enforcer.

Assante was willing to place something nice in Tracy's hand after hearing about the earlier events of the day. "I'll do that for you, but now you must do something for me. It is a small thing. Very minute."

"So, what's up?"

"Where is the other guy that was with all of you in the beginning?"

"Who? Marcel? He out. He's not trying to rock with this."

"That is not good. Is he a talker?"

"What you mean, a talker? Like a snitch and shit? Naw, not at all."

"It is interesting."

"You get up with Christian about this?"

"No, no. It has just been crossing my mind lately. It is nothing. Do not even bother remembering that I mentioned it. I'll have my brother meet with you later tonight, so he can give you yours. Tracy, listen closely . . . all things are running as planned. Do not become an enemy of mine and do not turn on me."

"You talking to Tracy Kane. I ain't no snitch. Shit, nigga, I was with this program from the beginning. Now everybody's getting paid. We're all in this together. Don't even trip. Fight the power, nigga." Tracy laughed as he walked out of the office.

"I need a break, Christian. There's too much going on in my life right now. My stress level is off the fuckin' meter right now. I got cops knocking on my door, people are walking up, talking to me out of nowhere, and I got a bitch-ass detective all up in my shit. And now this, a gun up in my face in the middle of the mall? Not good."

"Shane said the gun was a fake."

"Yeah, but the one his man had was real."

"Well, you don't really know that, Tracy. Did he shoot it off in the air? I mean, how y'all really know his shit wasn't the same?"

"Christian, what the fuck is you saying? Dude had a gun on us. I wasn't trying to find out if it was real or not."

"You need to get your mind right and stop trippin'. You're still alive to tell the story, right?"

"Fuck you, man! Fuck you!" Tracy said, staring him down.

"Naw. Fuck you! None of this would be happening to you right now if you weren't such a hothead. No one can ever get through to you. So, now, you just need to roll with the consequences. We don't have to like what you did, but you're part of the Culture, and we all got your back. By the way, Assante called and told me about a li'l something he got for you on standby. Better be careful, boy. Don't let that temper get you killed, nigga."

"Why he callin' you tellin' my business?"

"We're supposed to be selling the guns, not buying them!"

"This nigga. You got a shitload of guns in your house. How you gonna tell me I can't protect myself?"

"You can protect yourself, but you got to do your shit smarter."

"No. Somebody try to get at me, and I'ma get at him first. I'm not gonna let nobody catch me slipping."

"How can you, when you do so much slipping on your own? Tracy, you are an unappreciative muthafucka. I pulled your ass out the streets, jail, predicaments, and all types of other shit, and how you show me love back? By fuckin' me from behind. You know what I'm saying? You blow this shit for me and mess up my money"—He pointed a stiff finger at Tracy—"I don't even want to discuss it anymore," he said, waving it off. "Just get your shit right, man. Go out and have a drink or some shit."

"I don't know, man," Tracy said to Cadillac as they both pulled in front of Shane's home. "You ever felt like the world was caving in on you? I mean, like all the worst shit you could think of actually was happening to you?"

"You all right?"

"I'm still Tracy, but I'm feeling sort of nervous. I feel like I shouldn't have went any further than I did with the case."

"You're you, nigga. Ain't that what you always say? I think you just going through the motions. Everything you do is real, because it's coming from your heart. Isn't that one of your sayings? This is all you, all this right here." Cadillac opened his arms wide. "See, that's always been you. You just gotta be everywhere, all the time, just all over the place making noise. I gotta tell you, nigga, I love you like a brother and everything, but the shit you doing is not ill. Look at you, sitting there, scared for your life. You put us in the middle of a situation that led up to all this bullshit you in now.

"You putting Christian's name out there, telling people he's a thief. That's some real bitch-shit. I'ma tell you now—Christian's a crazy muthafucka. Don't sleep. At the end of the day what I'm trying to tell you is, Tracy, you doing a li'l bit too much. You need to be focused on the shit we got going, so you don't fuck shit up. You should go to that lawyer and tell him you forfeit. That's what I think you should do, and I ain't got no more to speak on it."

Every now and again, a nigga, on any given day, needed someone to tell them about themselves, somebody to bring them back down to earth and put them in their place. Today was Tracy's day to be given the truth, and Cadillac was that somebody.

Tracy stepped out of the car. "Ay, you ready to get up on in there, nigga? I'm starving."

"Yeah." Cadillac shook his head as he closed the door. "You's a wild boy, Tracy."

Tracy rang the bell to Shane's house.

"Who the hell is it?" Shane said from the other side of the door.

"Big Trace and Caddy," Tracy answered.

Shane opened the door. "What's good, fams?"

They walked inside and followed Shane into the guest-room, which was decorated now, touched by the hands of a woman's natural instincts for keen style. A seventy-two-inch flat-screen sat up on the brick wall, over the mantle of the decorative fireplace. Awards and plaques consumed the left and right sides of the five-foot-long slate, and the ten mini-speakers covering the walls thundered, shaking the water of a small fish tank with guppies that sat in the middle.

The kitchen identified itself immediately after Star opened the sliding door and the aroma of the best Southern fried chicken you ever smelled forced its way into their nostrils, making their stomachs growl with hunger. Not just any kind of hunger, but that I'm-hungry-for-some-fried-chicken, finger-licking, lip-smacking, banjo-playing, knee-slapping kind of nigger-hungry hunger.

"Uh-uh. I know y'all ain't got your shoes on my brand-new carpet. Fix the problem, Shane." Star folded her arms and looked at him.

"Oh damn, y'all, I forgot. You can't be in here with your shoes on because it's her brand-new carpet. My bad."

The men all complied.

Cadillac said, "Damn, Star! You get a li'l house on the hill and you act like you Martha Stewart."

"I *am* Martha Stewart," she said, showing off her stylishly decorated home.

"You crazy," he replied. "So where them fly-ass homies you said was supposed to be coming?"

"They're coming. What? You starving or something? Why you so quiet, Tracy? You haven't said a word since you been here."

"Yeah. What's the matter, my dude?" Shane asked.

"Nothing," Tracy said, shaking his head, snapping out of his funk. "Naw. I'm good. Shit, why y'all fuckin' with me?" He laughed. "Y'all like Tracy being the star of the party? Then let's get this party started right." He pulled out a stash of that goodie. "I know y'all holding, so let's all go on over there to that table." He walked over to the card table, alady set up with three new decks. "Come on," he said slowly. "Come on," he repeated, a pitch higher. "Tracy the natural born star is ready to get it in."

"Now that's the Tracy I know." *What an asshole.* Star walked away to the kitchen.

"You's a crazy muthafucka. You definitely missed your calling." Shane pointed at Tracy and smiled. "Ay, Star," he called out, "I'm sending Trace in for some more ice. You don't mind, do you?"

Tracy walked into the kitchen in time to see Star drop the last few pieces of chicken into the fryer.

"It's right on up there in the freezer," Star said, standing by the dishwasher.

Tracy rolled his eyes. "A'ight."

"You all right? You were looking kind of bothered out there."

"You talking to me? I'm good. Thanks for caring."

"I really don't, but I do have company coming through and don't need you bringing down the party mood while you're in a funk."

"I'm good."

"You sure? Because you don't look it."

"Why you care? I told you I'm good. I ain't going to mess up your li'l party mood, a'ight. Damn!"

"You have the worst attitude I've ever seen in a man. What's your problem?"

"I don't got a problem. You want me to have a problem? Because my attitude gets a lot worse than this."

"It's bullshit. Whatever's going on in your life that has you all messed up is on you. You can't bring that to the table you're eating at with everybody else. You either be a man and stand behind the choices you make in life, or you just stop complaining, because at the end of the day, Tracy, nobody really cares about what's negatively affect-ing you in life, if you bring it on yourself. I've been meaning to talk to you about this. I didn't give a shit, until you got my husband involved in that nonsense at the mall. You're a grown-ass man who likes trouble."

"That's what you think?"

"No. That's what I know. Just look how you messed up your own life and the people around you. You don't care about nobody but Tracy."

"You don't know me to call it."

"It shows. I don't care what you're going to do, but I'm not going to let you bring my husband down with you. If those other fools want to follow you down the drain, then that's on them, but you are not going to bring Shane down with you."

"Yeah, whatever. I'm outta here. You don't know how I grew up, the choices I had to make, the choices I gotta make each day just so I can live comfortable. You don't."

Shane hollered out over the music, "Hey, what's up with that ice?" Then he walked through the door of the kitchen. "Hey, you making the ice, man?" He looked at Tracy. "What's the holdup?"

"Nothing. Look, yo, I forgot I had a couple of things to do today. I'm about to break."

Shane grabbed the bucket of ice off the counter. "What? But the party is just getting started."

"Yeah. Maybe that's just what the problem is. This ain't gonna be the everybody-get-on-Tracy party, so I'm out."

As Tracy pushed through the kitchen door, Shane grabbed him by the arm. "Trace."

"Let him go," Star said. "You don't need that bullshit in your life."

"That bullshit?" Tracy stopped at the doorway. "You think my shit is bullshit, but Shane running guns is all good though, right? That shit is just fine, huh?"

Shane looked at him in anger. "Tracy."

"That's right. Everybody wanna look at me like I'm the

bad guy. I'm not the only one caught up in some felonious shit." Tracy stared at Star. "So what you got to say now?"

Star turned to Shane. "What's he talking about, Shane?"

By the time Tracy realized what had slipped out of his mouth, Shane's fist was already deep down inside of it, knocking him back through the door and onto the floor, where Cadillac and Star's company stood after they'd entered.

"Whoa! What's going on?" Cadillac scooped Tracy up under his arms and brought him to his feet.

Shane stormed through the door, whooping and hollering, Star doing the same behind his back.

"Get that rat-bitch-punk out of my house!" Shane took another swing at Tracy but missed and lost his balance.

Tracy slipped loose from Cadillac and caught Shane with a left while he was off-balance.

"Come on, y'all, we peoples here. This ain't no good look. What the hell is going on?" Cadillac used his huge size advantage to act as a brick wall between the two, holding them apart by their shirt collars as they tried to get at one another. "CHILL!" he yelled. "What's going on?"

Star walked by Shane and calmly said, "Cadillac."

"What's up, baby? I got it under control."

"We cool, right." Star touched his hand. "I mean, we family, right?"

"No question."

"Tracy told me y'all running guns. Is it true?"

Cadillac released Tracy and Shane and stood back and looked at Tracy. "What the fuck is on your mind, Tracy? You leaving doors open for us to get knocked or something?"

"It slipped," he nonchalantly responded.

"Nowadays, partna, it's been real hard trusting your li'l slip-ups. Real hard."

"That's what it is you doing now, Shane? Being a thug?

Selling guns? I didn't get married just so that I could go to bed with a life of crime."

"Star, we'll talk about this later. We have company." Shane nodded over to Star's group of astonished female friends.

"Word. Star, later," Cadillac said. "We'll put you on, I promise."

"You"—Shane pointed at Tracy—"you need to get the fuck out of my house. Fuckin' snitch!"

"That's the thing about keeping secrets from your wife, Shane," Tracy said on his way out the front door. Then he added, "Shit you do in the dark always comes to light," and slammed the door behind him.

CHAPTER EIGHTEEN

TRINITY

"I am the decider of my future, and the future is bright." Trinity inhaled deeply as she stared into the mirror of a private gym out in Brooklyn.

She was waiting on Christian. Today was their Saturday to exercise together. She was there an hour earlier than usual because she had some things to catch up on. She'd missed her workout last weekend because she was just too lazy to get up and go. That meant the day's workout schedule would call for a double of everything. She was up to it though; she liked staying fit and in shape. She refused to let her stomach hang down, unlike so many of those out-of-shape, calling-it-thick-when-it's-just-plain-old-nasty chicks.

She slowly squatted up and down, her hands wrapped around her waist, painfully enduring the fire that burned her abdominal region.

"Hey. You saving some of that for me?" Christian, sporting a wife-beater, entered the room with a duffle bag, a towel around his neck.

"There's plenty." She huffed as she rose out of a squat. "You can borrow some of mines from last weekend."

"I'm good. I got my own problems. What time you get here?" Christian placed his duffle bag on a blue vinyl bench.

"About eight-thirty."

"Shoulda woke me. I would've rode in with you."

Trinity chuckled. "You old men need your sleep."

"How many of your friends' fathers look in as good a shape as me? Shit, I get by on damn near an hour of sleep a day. I'ma be all right."

As he lifted two fifty-pound dumbbells from their rack, she teased, "You still a old man."

"Forget you, Trinity. I bet I'm not an old man when you need that car note paid, now am I?"

"You'll always be my old man."

"Cute. So what's on your agenda today?"

"Remember the dude I was telling you about from my poetry club?"

"I remember you saying something, but vaguely. What's up?"

"Him and me supposed to be getting up and putting our heads together today. We wanna put something together for the show. Matter of fact, we may even save it for Tracy's protest."

"I don't want you to go to that."

"Why not? Aren't you going?"

"Yeah. It's going to get dangerous. I know it is."

"And what's that supposed to mean?"

"It's supposed to mean, it's too dangerous, so I don't want you to be there."

"I can't do that, Daddy. My whole team is going. How's that going to look on me if I front? You know that ain't my style. You raised me to stand behind everything I believe in, right?"

"Yeah, but—"

"But nothing, Daddy . . . unless you changing your state of word." Trinity stood erect to stare at him.

"Nobody changing no word. I just don't want to see you get hurt."

"Come on, Daddy. You know you can't protect me forever. I'm too old for it, and so are you. You did a good job raising me and instilling the right values I needed to become a responsible woman. I'm not that scared little girl anymore. I'm good."

"Wow!" Christian smiled. "And what a woman you've become. Sometimes I forget that you're all grown up now. Remind me every now and again if I get too overprotective with it, okay," he said, taking her in his arms. "Still love me?"

Trinity kissed his cheek. "Never stopped. You're my first and only, boo."

"Still don't want you to go."

"Now isn't that just the sweetest sight." Crystal snapped a picture of the two with her digital camera.

"That's the crazy chick from the house."

Christian released Trinity. "How you get in here, Crystal? This is a private gym with a private session. You operating on my time."

"Hi, sweetheart," Crystal said to Trinity. "You're looking real exercisable today."

"Do me a favor in the very near future, ma," Trinity said.

"What's that, hon?"

"Don't call me *sweetheart*, like you know me, and don't be taking my picture without my permission. You don't know me like that."

"What are you doing here?" Christian demanded.

"The only time I get to see you nowadays is at the office. What's up with that? I gotta come all the way here to have a conversation with you? You won't even answer your phone. Do you ever check your voicemail?" Crystal took his picture again.

"Stop it!" He reached to grab the camera from her.

"You got some kind of nerve, Christian. You can't just fuck me, and try to treat me like I'm some kind of groupie."

"You disrespecting my father, with me standing right here, bitch? Don't you know that I will beat your ass?" Trinity tightened the laces on her sneakers.

"Chill, girl." Christian pulled Trinity back. "What do you want, Crystal? You're not supposed to be here. This session is on the clock."

"I'm not leaving until you talk to me." Crystal crossed her arms and gave Trinity the once-over. "What?"

Christian grabbed Crystal by the arm. "Let me talk to you outside."

CHAPTER NINETEEN

CHRISTIAN

Christian took Crystal to the parking lot of the gym. "I warned you about talking funny to my daughter. Secondly, this stops now. I'm way too important and busy to be playing this game. If you keep this up, I'll have to relieve you of your position at work. I don't want to, but I will, if you keep this shit up."

"What did I do? You're breaking up with me?" she asked, tears welling in her eyes.

"Crystal, we were never together. Did I ever tell you we were a couple? You seem to be under the impression that having a good time is the same thing as dating. It's not. There's dating, and then there's having a good time. I'm a muthafuckin' rich-ass clothes designer. Why would I want to be dating anyone that has less than me? Why? Because you suck my dick real well? You fuck whenever I want? You a dime a dozen, trust me. And I'm not even trying to be disrespectful to you or nothing, but the truth is the truth."

"You're a real ugly man, Christian. Your money is the

only thing that attracts women to you. If it wasn't for that, you wouldn't be shit."

"But the case is that—I *am* shit, and an entire city is attracted to me. You're a weasel, and you serve absolutely no purpose in my life. I'm not going to discuss this any further. We don't got no drama. But you really need to make a move. You interrupting me and my daughter's together-time."

"I swear, soon as y'all black men get on top, y'all all do the same thing."

"Instead of sitting around watching a man get his, get up and get your own. You talking about you swear. I swear, I ain't no round-trip plane ticket, muthafucka." Christian turned to walk away.

"You pompous piece of shit!"

Trinity walked into the parking lot, toward her car. "Hope I'm not interrupting anything."

"You're not. We was just about finished." Then Christian sternly asked, "Ain't that right, Crystal?"

"Yeah, a'ight," she answered between sniffles as she walked to her car.

"See you at work on Monday."

"Fuck you!" She gave him the finger. "It all comes back."

"Long as it don't got you with it when it does. You're fired. Try to show your broke ass something outside of hood life, and you want to show your ass. Like I owe you some shit? Back to the project rooftops you go. See how you like sleeping in the pigeon coops again." Christian headed toward the building. "What you waiting on, Trinity? Be out."

CHAPTER TWENTY

TRINITY

"So instead of performing it at The Spot, I thought we'd save it for the protest. Tracy has some strong support behind him, and he has all of us. It's going to be great," Trinity explained to Solasse inside a back office of The Spot. "Will you be bringing the wife?" She scribbled down some words on paper.

"Of course. She wouldn't miss it for the world."

"That's what's up. I'll finally get to meet her."

"Yes. I've told her all about the project. She's very anxious to meet you."

"That's a good thing."

"Trinity, can I kick it with you about something on more of a personal level? I mean, outside of business."

"What's on your mind?"

"Promise not to get offended?"

"Long as it ain't disrespectful."

"Never that. Just curious about a rumor I heard involving your dad and Tracy."

"Yeah?" Trinity looked up from the paper. "A rumor like what?"

"I don't really know how to say it without it coming off the wrong way."

"You know what I respect more than anything, Solasse?" Solasse raised his brows. "What's that?"

"I respect a man who's not afraid to say what's on his mind. All that other mess comes later. Say what you have to say, or drop it."

"I don't want to get information twisted, but I hear that your dad is involved in some illegal activities. I can't afford to be caught up in any negativity. I'm trying to keep my life on the right track."

"That's the thing about rumors, Solasse. It's just hearsay. Jealous people make shit up when things aren't cracking for them the way they'd like them to be. So they go and make up false accusations, hoping to bring a black man's success story to an early end. I'm shocked you'd even fall for that drama. My father would never do something to destroy his success. Can we change the subject please?"

"My intention wasn't to upset you. I just don't want to be near it."

"Where you hearing your information?"

"People talk."

"That's not going to fly with me. You say that my dad's name is being slandered, right? That also involves me. Who's the liar trying to destroy my dad's livelihood?"

"If I tell you, you have to promise not to say I told you."

"Fuck that!" Trinity said, flinging her pen to the floor. "You a man. Stand behind your words."

"One of the models from your father's company. I think his name's Marcel. My wife was at an industry recording party last week and overheard him telling someone how he was breaking away from your dad because he's selling guns with some Africans who are supposed to be his partners-slash-investors."

"Marcel? You buggin'. He'd never say anything bad about my father. Your wife is mistaken. Sorry. Is she a fan of Marcel's or something? How is she so sure it was him?"

Solasse held his hands up. "You're right, you're right. But I do trust my wife. She wouldn't tell me anything like that if she wasn't absolutely positive."

"Well, I'm telling you she's absolutely mistaken. Just to be on the safe side, though, I'll have my dad talk to Marcel. But if a rumor like that really existed, don't you think with all the publicity surrounding Tracy, something as damaging as that would have already come out?"

"I'm just telling you what I heard. We're friends, right? I'm just trying to put you on. You can still give your dad the heads-up, let him know, even if it is a lie."

Though it seemed that Trinity was taking these accusations lightly on the outside, inside she was fuming with rage. She didn't like anyone saying anything about her father. She knew of Marcel wanting to break away from Christian, but didn't know the circumstances behind it. But if it was Marcel talking that craziness, then he'd be dealt with.

"A'ight. Good looking out. I'm telling you, though, there's nothing to be worried about. My dad wouldn't put me in harm's way."

"Guess I don't have to worry then."

"You don't gots to worry about a thang," she said, and kissed her hand up to the ceiling.

"Calm down, Trinity," Christian said over the phone. "You know I'd never be caught up in anything like that. Selling guns? It's bullshit, and you know better than that. I'll have a talk with Marcel though. And you say the guy you met from your workshop's wife heard Marcel saying this personally? I want to meet him, because you don't even really know this dude."

"He's from the workshop. I don't see him making it up. That's not his swagger."

"Yeah? I'm going to get to the bottom of this. You ever meet his wife?"

"No."

"Trinity, I want to meet him. Invite him over for dinner."

"To the house?"

"Yeah. Soon as possible." Christian hung up.

Soon as Trinity hung up the phone, it rang again.

"Yep," she answered.

"Trin, it's Tracy. What's good?"

"What's up, poppa?"

"I'm good. Uh, I was wondering what you was fien'ing to get into this evening?"

"Nothing. Why?"

"I need somebody to kick it with, just to talk. You know what I'm saying?"

"I got you. Everything all right?"

"Not really. Stop by my rest about six. We'll order some pizza or some shit like that."

"A'ight. I gotta run to the mall for a minute and take care of a few things, but I'll see you. You need me to bring anything?"

"Just your ears."

"I don't know what to tell you, Tracy," Trinity said as they sat on the couch in his living room. "You can't turn back the hands of time, though, so you're just gonna have to roll with the punches. Everybody got your back."

"I'm not so sure about that one. Lately it's beginning to feel like everyone's turning on me."

"It just seems like that. This is a very tense situation for everybody. You're all over the news. My father's company is under the microscope because of that. People running around saying he's running some illegal gun operation with them African investors."

"What'd you just say?"

"You're all over the news."

"After that."

"The gunrunning thing?"

"Yeah. Where'd you hear that?"

"Why? You know something about it? Because your name's involved in it too."

"Naw. Who would say some shit like that?"

"There's a dude from my poetry workshop that said his wife heard Marcel at some industry party saying it to somebody. I'm thinking that this man's wife don't know Marcel from nowhere, so how could she make it up? Everybody knows Marcel's a model for my dad. Who would just make that up?"

"I don't know." Tracy got up to go to the kitchen. "You want something to drink?"

Trinity followed him. "Tracy, if you know something about this, you should tell me."

"It's the most ridiculous thing I've ever heard," he said, turning on the faucet. "You told your father about this?"

"Yeah. He's going to have a talk with Marcel about it."

"A talk about what?"

"That's what I want to know."

"I'll have to get at your dad later on. Right now, though, I could really use a friend. I can't even front, Trinity. I'm nervous than all fuck. Cops are stopping by here talking shit on the regular. Nobody wants me to talk about shit. Everything's my fault. What the hell am I gonna do?"

"Let me ask you something. Do you believe in what you doing? The whole protest thing and whatnot?"

"Hell yeah."

"Then nothing else matters," Trinity said, touching the side of his face. "It doesn't. Long as this"—She touched his heart—"long as this continues beating true, you'll be a'ight."

"You say it like you believe in a nigga or something." Tracy looked down into her eyes.

"I do believe in you. I always have. Even if everyone else thinks you an asshole."

"I don't know whether to be offended or thankful."

"I'd be thankful." Trinity pecked Tracy's lips

He pulled away. "You can't keep doing that. You my employer's daughter. It don't feel right."

"Stop fronting. I see you watching me. You be all over me whenever we do shoots together. It's a'ight to like what you see."

"To *see*, not *touch*."

"It's not about touching. I know you like me, Tracy. I like you too. I always have." Trinity touched the side of his face again. "I love you."

Tracy held her hand on his face. "Don't say that."

"I'm in your corner." She extended her neck to kiss him, but this time he didn't resist.

The warm, caring twist of her tongue parted his lips, and his mouth slowly opened and locked around hers. He placed his hands on her back then massaged the soft tissue surrounding the base of her spine.

Trinity's body stiffened in his arms, and her nipples became aroused, as their tongues rolled around in one another's mouths and their hands explored each other's bodies. "Where's your room?" she whispered.

* * *

Tracy momentarily contemplated the possible outcome of yet another of his spontaneous actions. "You sure you wanna do this? I mean, with you being, you know . . . "

"Your boss's daughter? I know what I want." And she kissed him again.

CHAPTER TWENTY-ONE

TRINITY

Trinity's back sank deeply down inside the mattress of Tracy's waterbed as he fell on top of her, the heated water inside the reinforced plastic of the mattress warming their bodies, bouncing them up and down with each aquatic motion.

She quivered nervously under the cool, soft touch of Tracy's hand sliding up her shirt and rubbing her flat stomach. Every time visions of Christian's disappointed face appeared in her mind, Trinity shut it out. She reached down for Tracy's crotch and took hold of it.

When Tracy unbuttoned his pants and let his friendly gesture introduce its bare self to her hand, she gripped it tightly and pulled him even closer to her, kissing him deeper than previously. She guided his hand to the waistband of her sweatpants and tugged at them, freeing herself.

Tracy removed her sweats with his teeth and let them stop at her feet. He crawled back up to her knees and kissed on them both. He placed his hand on her inner thigh and stuck his finger under the lining of her saturated black silk panties. Trinity wiggled her hips until his finger found security within her increasingly hot and bothered body, her crying clit begging to be consoled with a kiss. Seconds later they both were completely unclothed and in dire need of each other's affection.

Tracy lightly licked the closed slit of her goodies, immediately bringing forth cream to the top of Trinity's steaming mug of hazelnut lust, where the overgrowth of hair between her legs captured the moisture.

Her knees locked onto his temples, Trinity released octaves she never knew she could reach, and as he passionately penetrated her, she dug her nails deep into his back and dragged them down his shoulder blades, stopping at the top of his ass. She bit into his shoulder and cried out.

After their session came to an end, while they still lay in bed, Tracy asked Trinity, "How you feel?"

Trinity kissed his cheek. "A little sore, but it's all good."

"If Christian could see us now, he'd be even more pissed at me than he already is. I hate to think what he'd say."

"So, don't think about it, Tracy. It's just you and me in this room, and I don't regret it for an instant, ya dig?"

"Me neither. But you know how your pops can be a not-so-understanding dude when it comes to his daughter."

"Tracy, I'm grown. There wouldn't be too much he could say anyway. But if it makes you feel any better, what went on in here will stay in here."

"Cool."

"It meant a lot. Regardless of what everyone might think about you, you're a real good dude. If these silly chickens don't watch out, I might just steal you from all of them," she said, pinching the skin under his ribcage.

Tracy smiled. "Is that right?"

"Sho ya right," she said, returning a smile, rolling on top of him.

"And just who do you think you are?"

"Trinity Elijah. You better ask somebody."

"You too much. Did you have a good time this evening?" he asked, clutching her buttocks.

"I wouldn't say a good time. But I did enjoy myself very much, and hopefully we'll be able to do this again, soon as my poor little coochie recoups."

"Trinity, you can holla whenever."

"I'ma hold you to that," she said, rolling off of him.

"Do what you gotta. I'm dead-ass. I'm feeling you, ma, and would've holla'd a long time ago. It's just your pops, man. I'd be violating. He'd never go for it. Shit, if the shoe was on the other foot, *I* wouldn't go for it."

"In the meantime, how about this? Why don't we just enjoy what we got going right here, right now?"

Tracy lifted her hand to kiss her wrist. "Sounds like a plan."

"You're sweet."

"So are you." Tracy slid his head between her thighs again and stuck out his tongue.

Christian scolded Tracy for being late. "What took you so long? You were supposed to be here over three hours ago."

"Sorry, man. I was kind of busy. You aren't my only obligation, you know. I got a personal life. What's so important that I had to meet you all the way out here in Manhattan?"

"We need to talk inside my office."

"Naw. What's this all about?"

"I guess it don't matter where we talk at. Tracy, there's two things that are fuckin' with me right now. I mean, really,

really fuckin' with me," Christian said as the garage door hummed open.

"Oh yeah? Like what, huh? Business is going good. Everybody getting shoots. Shit, me being in all this trouble done tripled the sales of your clothes. You looking fresh and smelling like a millionaire. What's the problem?" Tracy shrugged his shoulders as they rode the elevator inside the garage up to the building's roof.

"Step out," Christian said after the elevator stopped on the thirteenth floor and its doors opened. "You a bitch, and I'ma tell you why. Did you think you talking to Michelle Renee about signing a contract with her magazine wouldn't get back to me?"

"So what? I didn't sign anything."

"But you accepted the money from her. Money you told her you wasn't giving back. What type of shit you on? Also, I heard you were running your mouth to Shane's wife about what we really doing. That's some real shit, playa. She left him last night. What is he supposed to do about that? You done fucked up the man's marriage. You got real problems, fuckin' your friends over and ain't even man enough to be real about the shit."

Christian's phone broke up the onslaught. *Riiinnng! Riiinnng!*

"Talk," Christian said into the receiver of the flip. "I'm on the way down." He closed the flip then looked at Tracy. "We about to be out. Let's go."

"Hold up, yo. What you mean, we about to be out? We just got here."

"What? You scared or something, Tracy? You can tell me. That's what big brothers are for. Ain't that what dude said? My big brother was B.I.G.'s brother, that's you and me. Nigga"—Christian chuckled—"I can't even fuckin' believe you not bowing down and humbling yourself yet.

Fuck. Like what's really good? What? I put you on, and you just shock niggas with this lame-ass act you playing. It's bitch shit. You hear that? Let's go," he said, turning his back to him.

Tracy stood his ground, his fist balled up.

"I don't hear your footsteps," Christian said, his back still turned.

Tracy leaped onto Christian's back, just as he was about to turn, and they both hit the ground with an incredible thud, growling at one another. Their arms locked, they took tight-squeezed swings with their intertwined fists, rolling from left to right then breaking free of each other's grasp, and both quickly hopping to their feet.

Tracy quickly reached for his waistline in the back of his black denim Hard Roc jeans.

"What you gonna do, man? You a thug, right? You gonna shoot me? You'll be asking for much trouble, boy," Christian said calmly. "Now we got shit to do, so let's do it. People waiting on us downstairs, so if you not gonna use that"—He nodded over to Tracy's back waist—"then let's go." He turned once again.

Tracy slowly retracted his hand back to his side and watched the door of the garage's elevator as it opened.

Christian walked inside the darkened capsule, only a small fluorescent light above providing illumination. He stood idly with his hands by his side and stared at Tracy. "Let's do it. I'm not asking you anymore. You're the one with the gun. You start feeling unsafe, you the killer. Protect yourself, *B*."

Feeling that Christian had a point, far as him having the gun, Tracy cautiously stepped toward him, stopping before the elevator's open door.

Christian took a step back, and Tracy walked inside, where they faced off, their eyes erratically dancing around.

The door dropped over their profiles and cut the flood of fluorescence running across the rooftop.

Assante and Akinsanya were standing outside the garage when Christian and Tracy reached the bottom floor. A black limousine waited for them on the other side of the street. The African brothers, both dressed in matching black suits, eyed Tracy as he stepped on the sidewalk.

"Tracy," Assante began, "as always, it is my pleasure." He patted Tracy's shoulder. "Come. Let us all step inside my car. Time is of the essence."

As they all got inside the car, Assante said, "Your gun, Tracy, please hand it to my driver."

"Why? What's the problem?" Tracy asked, leaning back on it.

"It is of no cause, other than the security of my mind. So please, Tracy, to my driver. You will receive it back when we reach our destination."

"Christian," Tracy said.

"Be easy," Christian told him. "We got ourselves a real problem."

"Am I supposed to be the problem?" Tracy looked at Assante. "If so, then what makes you think I'd hand over anything to your driver?"

"It is not a request," Assante said just as the limousine's partition rolled down.

A gun aimed to the back of Tracy's head by a man in the passenger seat influenced him to quickly hand over his piece with no further quarrel.

Assante patted Tracy's knee from the other side of the limousine. "Trust me, it will be all right."

"Where we going?"

Christian responded, "How about you wait until we get there?"

CHAPTER TWENTY-TWO

TRACY KANE

Assante's connections at the Seaport had given him un-limited access into one of its many terminals built over the water. He placed his hand on his chauffeur's shoulder after the men reached their destination out in Northern New Jersey. "Thank you." He waved to the driver as he rode off. "We will see."

Assante returned Tracy's gun to him. "Here you are. You see, it is all right." He smiled. "Akinsanya, check ahead. We shall be along soon."

Akinsanya strode ahead toward the manned booths ahead of them. He was given a momentary hassle but then was permitted through the electric chain-linked fence.

"Where's he going?" Tracy asked.

"Yeah, man," Christian said, "you kind of got me trip-ping now. What's going on? You got a new shipment com-ing in? We could've rounded up everybody."

"No. This is how it should be. I sent Shane and Cadillac to do something else. Something very wrong is beginning to tremble me. Something I cannot allow to continue breathing. I am sorry. Come forth," he said, walking toward the fence.

"What's going on, Christian?" Tracy asked.

"Man, I don't know. But what you think can possibly happen out here? People are out working. Ships are docking in. Let's get it." Christian accelerated his stroll behind Assante.

Tracy looked back, then around, before following the two men.

They entered through a steel door and into a long tubular-shaped tunnel where thirty-five watt light bulbs spaced two feet apart and implanted into the cemented ceiling buzzed lightly. Water leaked through the cracks in the yellow-tiled walls of the tunnel, creating a constant flowing stream that ran down the full length of the cement-paved floor in the hallway. The men all tried their best to avoid stepping in the water by walking on the elevated lips of the tunnel's sides.

Tracy's foot slipped off into the stream. "Shit!"

"We're almost there," Assante said.

Christian held on to a brass guardrail protruding from the wall. "You going to tell me what's going on now?"

"Not too much further," Assante said.

A large splash of water dropped from the drain about ten feet away from whence they came, raced up the hallway, and finished by their ankles.

"Shit, Assante!" Tracy shook his feet out of the water. "Where's it at?"

"We are here." Assante walked up four steps then pounded on a door before them.

"All this?" Christian said, infuriated with his enclosed surroundings. "This better be good."

They all walked out on the deck of a large ship, where Akinsanya was holding a prisoner captive, a black hood pulled over his head, and a yellow rope tied around his neck. Waves generated by the forceful winds splashed the bound victim, who coughed and choked, unable to prevent the stinging salt water from soaking through the hood and burning his eyes because his wrists were cuffed to the railing at the front of the ship.

"*Sha-tup!*" Akinsanya hit the man in back of his head.

"AKINSANYA, *ophou*," Assante commanded his brother. "*Ophou*," he repeated, braving the gusts of wind and water as he ran over to him. "You cannot do this yet. Unchain him but leave his hood."

"Who is that?" Tracy asked no one in particular

"Your downfall," Assante quickly answered. "Bring him!"

They walked down into the engine room, and Akinsanya released the prisoner from his hold. He tried walking forward, muffled sounds of terror escaping from his mouth, but Akinsanya pushed him back.

"Hold up," Christian said. "Hold the fuck up. Marcel?" he asked, walking up to the prisoner. "I know this ain't my nigga." Christian looked back at the two brothers. "Marcel?"

Tracy walked over with Christian to free Marcel. "I told you these niggas was crazy."

"What y'all got him like this for?" Christian yelled, untying the hood from around Marcel's head.

Christian carefully pulled off the grey masking tape that was triple-wrapped around his mouth, and left a red mark around his face.

"I didn't do shit!" Marcel exclaimed. "Why you let them do this? I didn't say nothing."

Christian took him by the shoulders and calmly said, "Marcel."

"I didn't say nothing."

"Marcel."

"Come on, man. They're going to kill me."

"MARCEL," Christian yelled, "shut the fuck up and listen. They're not going to kill you."

"How you know?" Tracy asked. "What you doing, Christian? How you know?"

"Come on, Tracy, man. You know me, dawg. Don't let them do this to me. My son is only eight months old. I ain't gonna see him grow up. Please," Marcel said, holding out his arms.

Akinsanya grabbed Tracy's gun from the waistline of his pants and removed the clip.

Christian held up his hands. "Take it easy, Trace. You don't understand what this is about."

"I know what this about. I'm not letting it happen neither," he said, standing by a shook Marcel.

Christian shot back, "Naw, you don't know what this about. Marcel done fucked up. He done fucked up big time. Not only was he running his mouth at some party around muthafuckas he didn't know, but he was dropping names and places too. Good thing one of the security guards working there is part of our team. You could've come and talked to me, Marcel."

"I told you I wasn't with the shit. I said I wasn't down for it."

"So why you run your mouth? What the fuck? We got too much riding on this." Christian shook his head. "Too fuckin' much."

Tracy asked, "So what y'all gonna do? Kill 'im?"

"He has killed himself," Assante answered.

"Naw, naw. It don't have to be like that," Tracy said. "Christian, Marcel like family. What you thinking?"

Christian looked over at the brothers. "It's not my decision."

"That is not all to it, Mister Kane," Assante said. "I will allow Marcel to tell the rest. Let your death not lead with more lies. Die honorably."

"Aw, shit. No, Marcel," Tracy said. "Don't tell me, dawg. No," Tracy said, preparing himself for the already predictable confession. "What else you say? I'm standing here fending for you and shit. What else you done said?"

Marcel bowed his head and closed his eyes.

Assante said, "You see?" He raised his voice at Tracy. "Do you see? He will not even admit his own fault to preserve his honor. If he will not say, then I shall. Marcel made an anonymous call to a detective. I have it here all on this disc." He said to Marcel, "You never talk, because ears you never know of, they hear everything."

"I just didn't want it to get out of hand, y'all. My kids have to grow in this city."

"A snitch?" Tracy said, disappointed. "Did he really mention my name?"

Christian pointed at Tracy. "Yours more than anyone else's."

"You didn't do that, did you, Mar?" Tracy asked.

"How are you going to kill me? The feds will come looking for me."

"How much they pay you, man? Huh?" Christian asked.

"I hope it was enough." Assante snapped his fingers. "Let this be over with."

Members of the Culture walked from behind a thick cloud of steam produced by hot, running engines. Marcel was quickly put into a chokehold then pressed up against a six-foot iron radiator that burned through his shirt and singed his skin, his screams concealed by an emergency foghorn test up above.

Assante reloaded Tracy's gun and handed it back to him.

Tracy looked at the gun then back up at Assante. "Yeah? What you think I'm gonna do with this?"

Assante said, "I also hear that you've been talking. Do you understand where I'm going with this, Mister Kane?"

Tracy looked over to Christian, who turned his head. "You's a real fag, yo," Tracy said to him.

"There's too much money at risk," Christian said. "I'm not letting anybody fuck that up. Not you. And definitely no bitch-ass snitch. Think he your man? He wasn't when he was spraying your name all over the blue wall of silence. Fuck that nigga. He's fuckin' up your money too."

Impatient with all the bitching between Christian and Tracy, Assante decided to take matters into his own hands. He walked right up on a struggling Marcel and stuck a 12-inch fishing blade deep down into the side of his neck.

As the men released Marcel, his body began convulsing before he hit the ground, blood shooting out of his deep wound. Struggling to hold on, he reached up, weakly grabbing at the air. He lay flat on his back while everyone watched him slowly detach from this material world.

Covered and wrapped in black plastic, he gurgled on blood overflowing up his esophagus, and soaking through the black hood and spilling out the holes in the black plastic.

"You making him suffer." Tracy pushed Assante. "Look what you doing."

"Then stop his suffering." Assante pushed him back harder. "Shoot him. Shoot him, if you want your friend's suffering to cease." He folded his arms.

Marcel's convulsions intensified so much, some of the surrounding men had to back away.

"This is real fucked-up, Christian," Tracy said.

"He's already dead, Tracy. You see him? He don't look like he's going to live to me." Christian shrugged his shoulders.

Tracy took three steps toward Marcel's bouncing body and stopped. He looked down, and a tear rolled down his cheek. He looked back at Christian and the brothers.

"I'ma put it to you like this, man," Christian said to him.

"We all got something on us. We all did something. Everybody in here has something on each other, everybody except for you. You know what I'm saying to you? We're not going to feel comfortable if you don't do this. It's not like he walking away from here."

Assante nodded his head toward the members of the Culture. They all pointed their guns at Tracy.

"I wouldn't fuck around if I was you," Christian said. "I think they mean business. Just remember how this all started."

Assante added, "It is either you or him. It makes no matter to me. He will die either which way. The question is, will you be joining him?"

Tracy slowly raised his gun a little above his ribcage and aimed it at Marcel's shaking body.

BOOOOOOONNNNNGGGG! A departing ship's horn drowned out the sound of Tracy's 9mm Glock.

Marcel's body immediately ceased movement.

"I am satisfied." Assante walked over to observe the dead body. He kicked at Marcel with his foot to be sure there was no further movement. "Now we all have something on one another."

CHAPTER TWENTY-THREE

TRACY KANE

"I can't cope no more, man," Tracy confessed to Cadillac as they slummed in Club Phenomenon out in Far Rockaway, Queens.

"You shouldn't have even told me that crazy shit."

Tracy sipped on his drink at their table. "I didn't have a choice. He was suffering. You don't know, man."

A dancer from the stage slid down its shiny brass pole and landed on her hands. She tucked and rolled off the stage, landing on her feet. She walked over to their table, her huge titties bouncing. She threw her leg up on the table and leaned her face over the tip of her toes.

"Not now, ma." Tracy swiped her foot off the table. He got up and walked toward the dance area, "to play the wall."

Cadillac soon followed. "You can't run from it, son. You killed our man. You foul," he said, pointing his finger in Tracy's face.

"He was gonna tell on all of us. Fuckin' conspiracy shit, nigga. I ain't tryin'-a go to jail."

"Damn, Marcel." Cadillac shook his head. "Do his wife know yet?"

"Who the fuck you think would tell her?"

"No. What I mean is, if that nigga truly was talking, then that shit also means he was talking to her too."

"So what is it you trying to say?"

"I'm not trying to say shit. What you think going to happen when that fool don't come home? His bitch gonna go calling the police and whoever the fuck he was in contact with. What you think happen from there?"

"What?" Tracy asked.

"I think you know."

"Let me ask you a question, dawg—What you and Shane went out of town for?"

"You don't want to know."

"What y'all did, man?"

"This money, yo"—Cadillac rubbed his hand over his face—"it's got me acting way out my character. Assante is a callous muthafucka. Understand that."

"What y'all did?

"I don't know if I can trust you, man. I will tell you this, though. Assante pays lovely, but I guess you already know that, don't you?"

"Fuck you!"

Tracy walked off to the middle of the dance floor, and colorful spinning lights from above flashed down on him, as he bopped his head and sipped his drink.

Kanye's hit single dictated the motions of the human beings dancing under the flashing lights.

A young, attractive woman, light-skinned, thin, and short, sipping from a champagne glass, and swaying to the beat of the song approached Tracy. Bearing a smile, she grabbed his hand.

Tracy danced with her, a smirk on his face. He sipped his drink as he grabbed her ass. She immediately pressed her tiny little frame up against his body then passed her drink up to him.

He bent down and asked her, "What's your name, li'l ma?"

"You Tracy Kane, right? Oh my God, I love your ass. You look so good." She grabbed onto his shoulders and gyrated her hips against his hardening penis. "What's going on down here?" she asked, rubbing and grabbing on it.

As her homegirls stood off to the side and cheered her on, she dropped to her knees and pulled down the zipper to his pants. She pulled out his extension with no shame, looked up at him then wrapped her mouth around it. He closed his eyes and leaned his head back.

Once the crowd of entertained freaks realized who Tracy was, they started rooting him on. But after a while, they all began acting like it was routine, and paid the lewd performance no further attention.

Tracy opened his eyes for a brief moment and caught Cadillac slowly shaking his head at him.

The young woman quickly popped an ecstasy pill and stood up. She grabbed her drink from Tracy's hand and gulped it down. Then she tossed the glass on the floor, shattering it. She unbuttoned her blouse and exposed her bare breasts to Tracy. Then she grabbed his hands and placed them there.

CHAPTER TWENTY-FOUR

CHRISTIAN

Trinity opened the front door for Solasse and his wife, Marisol. "Hi, nice to meet you."

Marisol was a beautiful half-black, half-Spanish woman with long, straight, brown hair that touched her elbows. Her eyes were green, and her skin was flawlessly smooth. She had a model's body and a refreshing cover-girl smile.

"The wife, huh?" Trinity smiled.

"I better be." Marisol smiled then looked at Solasse.

"Hey, Solasse," Trinity said. "Well, y'all get on in here. The food's almost done, and my daddy is waiting to meet the great one over here." She tapped Solasse's shoulder.

Marisol looked around as they entered the house. "Wow! This is such a beautiful place your father has here."

"It's just a shell," Trinity humbly responded.

"Your father doing big things." Solasse placed his arm around Marisol's shoulder. "This is beautiful."

"Trinity," Christian called out, "is that our company?"

"Yes, Daddy. We're coming."

"Hey," Christian said as he walked into the den. "Nice to

finally meet you." He shook Solasse's hand. "Hi." He smiled at Marisol. "I'm Christian," he said, kissing her hand. "Welcome to my home."

Marisol smiled. "I feel welcomed already."

"So, my man, Solasse, I hear you want to talk about a revolution?"

"Come again?"

"The protest. I hear you want to speak your mind there, with my daughter nonetheless. It's not going to be no picnic. My boy Tracy got a big mouth, and something's always bound to happen when he's in the picture."

"It's for a good cause, right?"

"Yeah. I just don't want my daughter getting hurt while y'all out there making them crackers upset."

"Isn't that the whole point?"

Christian looked at Trinity. "You better be careful."

"Oh my God!" Marisol said after biting into a butter-garlic sautéed chicken thigh. "This is so good. You make this, Trinity?"

"Not me," she responded, nodding over to her father.

The group all sat at a long rectangular-shaped table in the dining room. Christian sat at the head, while Solasse and Marisol sat off to his right, opposite Trinity.

"Wow! You do a little bit of everything, huh?"

"I guess you can say that. How you like your chicken over there, man?"

"Excellent. You're in the wrong business."

Christian wiped his hands with a napkin. "Trust me, I'm not."

"So, Christian, about your African partners," Marisol said, "will they be there?"

"You know what . . . something's really bothering me. Solasse, where do I know you from?"

"Excuse me?"

"Naw. I'm just saying you look real familiar."

"I don't think we ever met before."

"Yeah. It's just that I never forget a face, you know what I'm saying? But it ain't no thing. So, Marisol"—Christian smiled, placing his hand atop hers—"Pardon me, Solasse— uh, tell me a li'l something about this whole Marcel thing."

"What do you mean?" she said, pulling her hand away.

"What do I mean?" Christian chuckled. "The rumor Marcel spread, you know, that whole gun thing. You remember that?"

"I thought that's just what it was. That is what it is, right? A rumor?"

"Let me ask y'all both something—Who the fuck is you? You who you say you are." Christian pushed his plate to the side.

"Daddy."

"What are you talking about, man? You invite us over for lunch then you start third-degreeing us. My wife doesn't know anything that you're talking about."

"All I wanna know is what you heard him say, that's all. But y'all sitting up here acting really nervous in this muthafucka. Did he say something else?"

Solasse said to Marisol, "Go on and tell him, baby."

"Marcel said you're running guns with those men from Africa."

"Tell him the rest." Solasse nodded. "Go on. It's all right."

"He said y'all are planning on starting a war with the police."

"A war with the police? Who was he talking to?" Christian laughed.

"No one in particular. He was intoxicated."

"What party was this at?"

"Just a little promo party for some up-and-coming rapper. Nothing major."

"What I'm trying to figure out is this—Why in the fuck

would his ass be at some industry party just straight talking out loud? That shit doesn't sound just a little bit strange to you?"

"I'm just telling you what I saw—I mean *heard*."

"Here's the thing, Marisol. You really don't look like the hip-hop type. I mean, like, why would you be at an event like that? You don't look like a video model. You not a producer or director, so what was you doing there?"

"That's enough, Daddy. She already told you what she knows. Why you trippin'?"

"It's all right, Trinity. I understand."

"All right. That's all you heard him saying though?"

"That's all I heard."

Solasse reconfirmed her stand. "It's all she heard."

"I'm sorry y'all. It's just that I don't need that kind of negative publicity. I don't. What I need from you two is not to tell no one else about that lie. That's all it is, a fuckin' lie. And now I know where I remember you from, homie." Christian pointed at Solasse. "You was at the sports bar the night before my dude got married. You came over to the table to shout out Tracy. So, why you sitting here fronting like we ain't met before?"

"That was a while back. You still don't look familiar to me, but I know who you are. You're acting like we're the ones that put your name in the mix. My wife doesn't have anything to do with that. Trinity, my sister, I think it's time we left." Solasse stood. "Thanks for your hospitality. Marisol, we're leaving. You a real gracious host, my man," Solasse said, extending his hand to Christian.

CHAPTER TWENTY-FIVE

TRINITY

Trinity met up with Solasse at The Spot two hours after that nonsense with Christian.

"I didn't think you'd show." Solasse removed his glasses and looked up from a piece of paper he'd been scribbling on at a table then placed his glasses on it.

"Why wouldn't I?" she responded, grabbing a seat and placing her pocketbook down by her feet. "We have our own agenda. That's what we're here for, right?" She rolled a pencil back and forth on the table.

"I just thought that after the thing with your dad and all, you might not have shown."

"I'm not about bullshit. My pops is a real dude. He don't get fazed easily. He just don't like fake people, and neither do I. Guess that's why I'm daddy's little girl."

"Hey, we don't got to be like this. Your father got what he wanted. It wasn't nothing but what he already heard. He needs to be checking for his man. We got absolutely nothing to do with whatever is going on. I don't want this to affect what we're trying to do."

"It won't."

Trinity headed home to have a conversation with her father after wrapping things up with Solasse. Something in her gut wasn't sitting right with these accusations against her father. In her heart, she knew they just couldn't be authentic, yet she felt compelled to question him about it again. She knew that Marcel had recently complained about being released from his contract but didn't think much on it. If she had to, she'd chalk it up as him trying to pull a Tracy Kane move. She really didn't care for him much in the first place, but this here was some real odd shit for her father's name to be caught up in.

Trinity walked in front of the 72-inch projection television screen. "Daddy. I want to know what's going on right now."

"Who you questioning?" Christian stood up out of his recliner. "What you mean, you want to know what's going on?"

"Daddy, why would Marcel say something like that? Did you ask him? Did anybody else say they heard it?"

"I don't like your friend. He gives off a real bad vibe . . . his wife too. I don't want them here anymore."

"That's fine. Are you going to be more direct in answering my question?"

After all this time Trinity still didn't know what Christian and company had going on. She just assumed his clothes sales were doing astoundingly well and the groove was cracking. She truly thought the Africans were investors looking to break off and spread their own Militia 7 clothing line.

Christian figured the less she knew, the safer she'd be.

Assante and his brother were killers and were quick to clog any leak that dripped, so he kept her in the dark.

"Trinity," he said, reaching for her shoulders, "don't go believing none of the rhetoric these fools is kicking. It's all because of one dumb nigga. That's all it is. He ain't down with us no more. He's out. Fuck a contract."

"When you going to see him? This needs to be handled, Daddy. Your name's at stake. This ain't going to be the last you hear of this," she said, tears welling up in her eyes.

Christian rubbed her shoulders then hugged her, squeezing tight. "Stop it, baby. It's going to be all right. I got this."

"I just don't want you to get messed up."

"I got all kinds of lawyers for shit like this. There's nothing going on, so there's nothing to worry about. It's all good."

Trinity just couldn't shake the feeling that her father was hiding something from her. She never in her life thought she'd ever second-guess him on anything he said.

The next day she took it upon herself to check on Marcel. She'd ask him herself why he was trying to shit on her father. She didn't understand why he was taking so long to get at him.

Kaneecha, Marcel's babies' mother, opened the door, holding on to her newborn while her five-year-old daughter held on to her leg.

"Hi, I'm Trinity, Christian Elijah's daughter. I'm looking for Marcel,"

"Yeah? What's up?"

"I need to talk to Marcel."

"Bitch, don't stand there and act like you don't know who I am. You seen me around before."

"I just want to talk to dude about something."

"First off, he ain't home. Secondly, you must be out of your monkey-ass mind. You stay right there."

Kaneecha pushed her daughter aside then walked to the back with the baby. When she returned, she pushed the door open and stepped out. "Now what's the problem?"

"I just need to see Marcel."

"Well, why you gotta come and see him? Why don't Christian come?"

"It's real important. He might be in some trouble."

"What you mean, trouble?"

"I mean, your man can't hold his liquor. Oh, you ain't heard?"

Trinity went on to explain the bullshit Marcel had circulated at the party that night.

For a moment Kaneecha stood in disbelief, folding her arms and frowning. "You going to stand there and act like you don't know what your father's into? Marcel wasn't saying a rumor. You know that. He working with them Africans, selling guns. Got secret codes stitched under the sleeves of shirts and shit."

"What are you talking about?"

"Oh, girl, you all up in the dark, huh? Poor baby. How you think your father can afford to keep you looking so pretty?"

"Where's Marcel?"

"Who knows where the fuck he's at? He comes and goes as he pleases. Fuck it though. I'm in the house, and even if I did know, bitch, I wouldn't tell you anyway. You don't sign his check."

Kaneecha's five-year-old whined, "I want Marcel, Mommy."

"Shut up!" Kaneecha yelled through the screen door. "You about finished wasting your time," she said, walking back toward the screen door.

"You ain't seen him, have you?"

Kaneecha stopped in her tracks and slowly turned around. "I haven't heard from him in two days," she said, looking around. "I don't know if he's dead or if he's cheating."

"Were you serious about what you just told me? About the guns?"

"There's more. Marcel told me everything. Your father wasn't trying to let him bounce."

"All right, I'm listening. Tell me more."

"You wanna come inside? We don't got to be out here like this."

"Naw, I'm a'ight. Let's just enjoy being out here," Trinity replied, a tight, distrusting smirk ripping the seam between her lips.

CHAPTER TWENTY-SIX

THE CULTURE

"Say it loud!" Tracy shouted through a megaphone as she stood on a wooden blue platform behind the chain-linked gate of St. Nicholas Park.

The two hundred plus crowd of protesters, mostly wearing Christian Elijah C.E. 7-7-20 shirts, shouted back, "I'm black and I'm proud!" The young Christian Elijah Culture supporters were tired of the police doing whatever they wanted.

Hip-hop radio stations broadcasted the event over the airwaves, while news cameras rolled, and police stood off behind barricades, their batons out at their sides.

"You see your protectors?" Tracy said, referring to the police. "Do you see them? They see you. You can just look at them and see what they're thinking. So for the sake of everybody's safety, I want all y'all to be easy. We're just here to talk about some things. We have to come up with a plan to stop the mayor and commissioner from allowing cops to shoot niggas in the back. They can't just keep doing what they want to do.

"One of the officers who hopped on my ass a couple of months back is in court for some shit upstate. Yeah. He's being accused of raping a fourteen-year-old girl. How he still walking the street? Three more officers from there are being accused of the same shit. Like, what the fuck is that? Cops coming together to commit crime?"

A disgruntled crowd of young adults ranging from their upper teens into their mid-twenties jeered and threw up middle fingers at the surrounding officers.

"Now they wanna say the girl lying? Everybody's always lying on the poor, innocent police. Every nigga they ever shot, man or woman, had a gun. Allegedly. But ain't no muthafuckin' gun ever recovered. Even after detectives, forensics, and a sniffing fuckin' dog comb the entire area. Why the fuck is that? Because ain't no gun. You get it? Ain't no gun.

"Your mayor and commissioner is saying shoot first and don't bother asking no questions. You know why? A dead nigga can't answer no questions. All a dead nigga can do is just be dead.

"So when I see shit like this happen every day on the regular, how can I ever really give a flying fuck about some Columbine massacre? What about the black massacre? I say take a stand and stop just sitting on your ass complaining. Stop talking about what you're tired of, and do something about it. I mean, let's really kick the ballistics people. Where did complaining really ever got us?"

Christian walked up behind Tracy and whispered something in his ear. He then stepped back next to Assante and his Militia 7 people, all wearing fatigues.

"We have a special guest coming to the stage. Dr. Karlin Ashley from Washington, D.C. Let's give him some New York love." Tracy handed him the megaphone and stepped off to the side after hugging him.

Dr. Ashley wiped sweat from his perspiring forehead.

"You know," he began, "they say the only time black folk come together in peace is at weddings and funerals. Well, I don't see no wedding." He chuckled. "So, we must be here for a funeral. The funerals of so many of our slain black youths by the hands of these murderous racist officers.

"You'd think in this day and time, this would no longer be an issue. But I think we're worse off now than we've ever been. Yes, there are many things that have been abolished, but it's all just an illusion. They'll have you believe that you're free and that you are equal. But let's just be totally honest, young brothers and sisters. Only thing that's free in America is the fact that you believe you truly are.

"You no more free than welfare. Everything costs. Somebody's always paying, whether it's out of pocket or with a life. You got to feel that you're worth more because, if we don't care about us, who will? Not them." He pointed to the police. "Not them." He pointed over to the white news crews. "And surely not us, if we don't start looking out for one another."

"Power!" Assante threw up a fist. "Black power!"

Then the crowd of supporters roared, "Power!"

Christian walked to the front of the platform. "Yeah, that's what I'm talking about. Power. That's what each and every one of us have in common with one another. We can police our own neighborhoods."

"Yeah, that's right," someone in the crowd shouted.

"They think we can't do it, but we can do anything we want. Be whatever it is you want to be and have the power to make a difference. Follow your dreams and don't let anybody tell you that it can't happen. I'm a prime example of that dream. Holla if you know what I'm talking about!" Christian smiled.

The crowd cheered, jumping up and down, rooting like barking dogs.

"Hold on, y'all." Christian laughed, waving his hand to

simmer down the crowd. "Now hold on. We're not done. We're not done."

Assante's small gang of Militia7 soldiers marched back and forth across the stage from opposite sides then met in the middle of the stage. Trinity and Solasse soon joined them and were then left to do their part.

"Peace," Solasse said, walking off to one end of the stage, while Trinity walked to the other.

"Peace, y'all. I'm Trinity. Give yourselves a round of applause for coming out. I have a piece I wrote here dedicated to a friend I lost a while back. She was a strong woman but got caught up in the mix. Feel me? We all get caught in the mix sometimes." She turned back to her father before looking forward again. "Nobody's perfect. Her name was Mya Washington. Killed by the police four years ago after her boyfriend led the police on a high-speed chase, all over a routine traffic stop. When he finally pulled over, there were no questions asked. Six police officers lit his car up with bullets while she sat helplessly strapped into the passenger seat. She was nine months pregnant, but it didn't mean shit to anybody. But people do go through shit sometimes, and you'll never know why they do what they do. It ain't right to judge though.

These trials and tribulations
Bargains in the basement
The exchanging of accusations
Low-price living, crack pipe sensations
Higher learning, walking on sunshine
Balancing on a flat line, stoned off a rocky climb
Kissing death under the full moon, rolling them dice
A life for a life, abortions and suicide
Pro choice, I can still hear your baby cry
It hurts because you're really a killer at heart

Brooklyn garbage bins become coffins in the dark
Embryos have no soul, it does, long as it grows
The howls of innocent infants sucked into a vacuum's
inner flow
One love, one kill,
What you don't do, others will
I'm a woman who's had her fill
Running spines contain chills
Time after time, you will find it
Babies having babies, it keeps rewinding
Over and over, I keep crying
Why, oh why, must our black babies keep dying
They'll make it to Zion, Jah's calling his lions.

The youths cheered and shook the chain-linked fence. Some of the teenage girls in the crowd that could relate wiped tears from their eyes, while their friends consoled them.

Trinity quickly walked off stage past her father and everyone else, the crowd showing concern, looking on with curiosity after her sudden exit. The police behind the barricades began to become agitated as youths and adults began giving them hostile looks.

Christian grabbed the megaphone from Assante and sounded its horn. "Come on, y'all, we're not done. We're not done."

The crowd yelled, "No!"

Solasse took to the front of the stage, and the crowd quieted down. "I'm sorry, y'all," he said, scratching his ear. "I won't be doing no poetry today, but I do want to talk about something with you all real quick. That is if Christian doesn't mind." He looked back.

A stern-faced Christian obliged with a nod of his head.

Solasse looked around at the river of officers guarding the street and scratched his ear again. "My name's Solasse

Barak. I'm too tired to talk about something that I can't react upon. What I mean to say is, me kicking some poetry to a fed up crowd who ain't having it no more would be useless. So we're going to talk about something useful. Something useful, like information.

"Knowing your rights is information. Knowing whom you support, and what they support is information. If a person calls you their friend, but you don't know where they live, that's a lack of information. If the cops stop you, and you don't take down their names and badges, that's a lack of information. I say all that to let you know that if an officer puts his hands on you, you are in your human rights, social rights, individual rights, and whatever other kind of rights, to punch his fuckin' eyes out of his head. No man," he shouted, "doesn't matter who they are, should be able to legally beat on you, tase you, shoot you, belittle you, and disrespect you. I don't have to take it, you don't have to take it, we don't have take it."

The summer heat made the restless, agitated crowd even more bitter toward the police.

Face frowned up, Christian looked up at Assante.

"Do you hear what I said? No man has the right to put his hands on you. ANYTIME! Who the hell is another man, just like you, to tell you that you're under arrest, put you in cuffs, and tell you to shut the *F* up? Peep the science behind that, y'all. Another man like yourself, some of them younger than you, will talk to you like a child in front of your own children. Think you'll still be your little boy's hero after he see you bow down like a bitch?"

"Fuck the police!" a protester chanted.

"Excuse my language. I start getting hype when the truth comes out. But here's where the problem come into play with these goons. They will shoot your black ass in the face if you even grit your teeth wrong. They'll see a silver filling in the back of your mouth and put two in your head then say, 'It looked like he had a gun in his mouth.' It looked like he had a gun in the back of his mouth? Isn't that some stuff? So what do we do? What are we, damned if we do, damned if we don't? Huh?"

Tracy and the rest of the team looked at one another, confused as to why Solasse was wilding out. Christian looked up at him then back at Solasse, and Assante folded his arms and gritted his teeth in anger.

"They don't want to see the niggas go crazy, because the day that the niggas go crazy is the day that we take over. Send all them racist Europeans back to the poorest, most disease-infested, most deplorable places in Africa, and just leave 'em there. Let them live in the mess they made."

Some men from the crowd started climbing the gate and shaking it.

Christian called out, "What you doing, man?"

"Get him," Assante calmly said.

The teens and adults alike began facing off against the police with taunts, threats, and finger-pointing.

Solasse smiled and lifted the megaphone back up to his mouth. "Don't bow down," he said.

Akinsanya quickly dragged Solasse off the stage, pressing his fingers deep inside of his neck, pulling him all the way out the gate.

After the near melee in Harlem, Christian and Tracy were able to calm the crowd down before things really got out of hand. Everyone was trying to figure out why Solasse hadn't stuck to the script.

They took him out to the warehouses for a sit-down, possibly his last.

"Now I remember who this nigga is," Tracy said, snapping his fingers, looking Solasse up and down. "I keep seeing your ass all over the place."

"And I don't think that's no coincidence either," Christian said.

"Who are you?" Assante calmly asked.

Solasse responded, "My identification's in my back pocket. You can check it out."

Assante snapped his fingers, and Akinsanya snatched Solasse's wallet from his back pocket. He flipped through it and came up with two pieces of identification, which he passed to Assante.

Assante looked at the pictures then back at Solasse. He repeated the motion twice then passed them on to Christian.

"I'm tired of seeing you, yo," Tracy said. "What, you some kind of stalking faggot or something?"

"What is this? Y'all kidnap me all the way out to 'west bubble' for what? I thought we was together for a cause."

"I shall be right back." Assante walked away with his ID. "I am going to make a call. You better be who you say you are. You know what happens next, if not."

"What were you thinking, man?" Cadillac said. "You trying to get them kids all wired up? That was a bad move, nigga."

"You stay the fuck away from my daughter. If I see you with her again, I'll kill you."

"You know Trinity?" Tracy asked, surprised.

"Why does it matter?" Christian responded.

"It doesn't. I'm just like, this dick knows Trinity? You everywhere, huh, playa?"

"They met at The Spot. They were supposed to do something together. This bitch is trying to sabotage me. We about to take care of your ass soon as Assante come back. What, you a cop or something?" Christian quickly frisked him.

"Why would I be a cop? You're a legal businessman. Even if I were, I'd never investigate my own people."

"What the hell that got to do with anything?"

Assante came back. "He is who he says he is."

"Yeah?" Christian said. "Who the hell is he?"

"He is of no consequence. My friend at the DMV checked him out thoroughly. He is no one."

Christian asked, "So what now? We just let him go?"

"Free him."

"What the hell do you mean, free him? What you talking? We just kidnapped this man."

"Kidnapped? I was out with my friends all day. I wasn't kidnapped. I was with my boy Tracy." Solasse extended his hand to him. "Right? So you going to tell me why I was dragged out of Harlem by the back of my neck?"

"You was talking real wild," Cadillac told him.

"I thought that whole thing was about protesting. That's what I was doing."

Christian shook his head. "You were saying the wrong things. And that's all you need to know."

"Saying the wrong things?"

"Yeah, Akbar," Tracy said. "You wasn't supposed to say shit but a poem. All that shit you started out there falls on me. And what falls on me falls on this man." He pointed at Christian.

"Isn't the whole Culture and Militia 7 movement all about speaking the truth? It must be. Here you are, this rich, popular clothes designer, and you're out here in the streets getting your hands dirty with the rest of us for your people. I said what I said because your movement inspires me. I like what you stand for, and I thought I was helping. That's all I was trying to do, man. That's my word to Allah. I stress that right now, because the odds are against me and I don't want to die. I don't want to be walking out that door and get shot in the back of my head."

"Should anybody have a reason to wanna shoot you in back of your head?" Christian asked.

CHAPTER TWENTY-SEVEN

TRACY

It was five a.m. when Tracy opened the front door of his condo. He'd been up for twenty-nine hours straight, and his body was begging to make love to his soft bed. It was a day after the so-called protest, which was already beginning to stir up a lot of controversy over the airwaves.

He entered his home with a drunken swagger and was immediately hit from behind. He dropped to the floor and rolled over on his back.

A man standing over him shouted, "Who shot that cop?"

"I don't know," he said, trying to zero in on the voice.

"You're lying." The intruder gave Tracy a kick to his ribs. "You better tell me something, Tracy. I know you fuckin' know something!" He kicked him again. "I know you know, fuckin' piece of shit!" He kicked him twice more. "Don't fuckin' try to look at me." He pushed Tracy's head to the side with his foot. "Now you're going to listen to me real close. Whimper, if we're understanding one another," he said, pressing down on Tracy's head with his shoe.

Tracy maintained his composure and didn't whimper for shit.

"Stay by the windows," the intruder said to his four partners.

"Now let me tell you something, so that you don't think I'm fuckin' your balls." The intruder kneeled down by Tracy and pointed in his face. "You get up on that stand and say anything, I mean anything more about what happened that day, I swear to fuckin' God, I'll be the last thing you ever fuckin' see. You're fuckin' up my upstate trial. I'm not going to jail because of some lying nigger whore that says I raped her, or your sorry ass. And, for the record, you haven't the slightest idea what a real police beating is like. What you got that day was just a tickle. You keep your fuckin' mouth shut, troublemaker." He hit Tracy in the face with the back of his hand. "Let's get out of here, boys. He needs his rest." The intruder laughed as he exited the condo, his boys ahead of him.

Tracy grabbed his side. "Shit, I just can't catch a break."

Detective Dennis Frogger stood over Tracy after walking through the partially cracked door. "You don't look so good. You need a hand?" He reached down. "Come on. That a boy," he said, pulling a bruised Tracy to his feet and guiding him to his couch. "What the hell happened in here?"

"Oh, like you don't know?"

"I know exactly what you know. Absolutely nothing."

"Yeah. This is all bullshit."

"You want to know what's bullshit, Tracy? *You're* bullshit. You embarrassed me in front of my superior, and you made me look like an idiot."

"I didn't make you look like nothing. I'm not feeling all this harassment shit. Your peoples did wrong and don't want to pay the piper now."

"And who's the freaking piper, Tracy? Surely not you, because I'ma tell ya, the tune you playing got nothing but a whole lot of repercussions and consequences following behind you."

"Thank you for your time, detective." Tracy slowly got up off the couch.

"Hey, no problem. Oh, by the way, that was a great performance you and your circus of radical monkeys put on yesterday. You're being watched, buddy. I'm going to find something on you, you mark my words."

Det. Frogger's phone rang, and he answered it on the first ring. He got up and walked over to the window and peeked through the curtains.

"Frogger. What's that? Kaneecha who? I'll be back at the office in about forty-five minutes." He looked back at Tracy.

"What?" Tracy shrugged his shoulders.

Det. Frogger shook his head from side to side as he opened the front door. "I'll just never understand it."

"What won't you understand?

"How you black guys can make all this money and still manage to fuck yourselves over. But that's something me and you'll discuss in the very near future, my friend," he said, closing the door after himself.

"So, yeah," Tracy said, waiting outside Solasse's house in his car, "Christian said to keep this dude close to me. He don't trust him."

"And now that he knows what he does," Cadillac said from the passenger seat, "what makes you think he'll trust you? Or even me, for that matter?"

"It doesn't matter if he does or doesn't. Christian just said to keep him close. Shut up," Tracy said as Solasse jogged down the six steps attached to the porch of the house. "Here he comes."

Solasse leaned down toward the passenger window. "Gentlemen, what's up?" he said, looking around.

"We need you for something, man. You that trustworthy nigga, right?" Tracy said.

Cadillac looked at Tracy. "What you talking about?"

"You coming?"

"I didn't even shower or anything yet."

"You won't need to," Tracy said, looking ahead. "Let's just bounce."

"All right. Let me just lock up real quick."

Solasse ran inside and quickly tossed his cell phone on the couch. He adjusted his shirt around the collar and ran back out.

"You got somewhere special in mind we're going?" Solasse calmly asked, sitting in the backseat of Tracy's new Lexus.

Cadillac turned around. "Yo, just sit back and relax."

"You better tell me something, baby. Where we going?"

"I'm just driving right now, man. I got a lot of shit on my mind. I been thinking about checking on Shane, you know. See how he holding his head after wifey bounced."

"If he wanted to see you, he'd have hollered. You hear from him?"

"Naw, but fuck that. We boys, and I made a mistake. A nigga entitled to one, right?"

"You funny." Solasse laughed. "You said one?" He continued laughing. "Try one million and then some. You don't just make mistakes. You make fuck-me-in-the-ass mistakes. That means your shit hurts." He laughed harder. "From the back and the front," he added, choking and coughing with laughter.

"All that and you still not funny," Tracy said, giving him a shove with his right elbow.

* * *

As they pulled in front of Shane's house, Cadillac said, "Listen, you should let me talk to him first,"

"I'm a man, *B*. I gotta make the shit right."

Shane was just walking out of the house as Tracy took the first step up. He let the front screen door close then stuck his keys in his pocket. He looked past Tracy to Cadillac sitting in the passenger seat, and a stranger sitting in the backseat. He gave Cadillac a nod.

Shane took a step forward toward Tracy. "What you doing here, man?"

"I don't know what to say, man. I'm sorry. I didn't mean to fuck your shit up." Tracy extended his hand.

"You stupid or something?" Shane stepped down and planted a right cross to Tracy's jaw that sent him flying backwards. "You tryin'-a play me or something?"

"Shane!" Cadillac called out. "You see?" Cadillac looked back at Solasse. "I told this nigga not to come to this man's house. Shane!" he called out again, getting out of the car.

Tracy shook off the blow and stood up. "I'ma let that first hit slide 'cause you upset."

"Why you even let this ass even play himself by driving here, Cadillac? Get 'im the fuck off my property. I'm not fuckin' around, nigga. Get the fuck off my property!" Shane rushed toward Tracy.

Cadillac quickly jumped in between the two and pushed them apart. "Y'all just chill out. Look, Shane, the nigga is here to apologize. You don't got to accept it, but you got to respect it. See what I'm saying? His big mouth fucked shit up once again, but you know he ain't say that shit on purpose. We all got to be together in this shit, man. We can't have another nigga walking away."

"Oh? Or what's going to happen?" Shane said, standing alert.

Cadillac placed his hand on Shane's shoulder. "Relax, dude."

Shane flinched and took a step back.

Just then Tracy answered his phone. "Yeah? Yeah, we got him with us now. We're over at Shane's rest . . . A'ight. Hold up, this nigga Christian wanna holla at you." He slowly walked toward Shane.

Shane snatched the phone from Tracy. "Yo. Yeah . . . Nope. I ain't rolling nowhere . . . What job? . . . No, man. No . . . Come on, Christian, man. Naw, I ain't even with that shit. You trippin'." He tossed the phone back at Tracy. "Y'all niggas might as well go on. I'm put," he said, walking to his truck. "Stop coming by here. I'm not fuckin' around." Then he stepped into his truck and drove off.

"SHANE!" Cadillac yelled out, throwing up his hands in the direction of Shane's vehicle as it sped away. "Don't do this, man. You just gonna leave us hanging?"

Tracy parked down the street from Marcel's house, where four police cruisers were parked in the middle of the residential block, with one detective car in the lead. Detective Dennis Frogger was standing on the porch and showing Kaneecha something.

"See that muthafucka right there?" Tracy tapped the windshield of his car. "That's him. The cop that been kicking my ass every chance he get."

"So what are we doing, guys?" Solasse asked.

"Yo, we not here to make friends, baby. Just be easy. That bitch is in there talking, yo. I know she is. Christian said she called crying about Marcel missing, how she ain't seen or heard from him in two weeks."

Cadillac asked, "So we was coming here to do what?"

"Oh, we wasn't gonna do shit. See, Christian don't trust ol' boy right here, so I'm wondering how he gonna prove his loyalty."

Tracy slowly pulled out his gun on Solasse and pushed the muzzle into his shoulder. "Hmm." He raised his brows.

"You didn't hear me, dawg? I said, how you prove your loyalty?"

"Come on, Tracy, put that shit away," Cadillac said. "You stupid or something? The police all out here and everything. We might as well leave, man. There ain't shit we can do now anyway."

"Yeah, I guess you right," Tracy said, retracting his gun from Solasse's shoulder.

Cadillac stared at the spinning sirens of the police vehicles ahead. "Christian's gonna be real tight."

"So what happened?" Christian asked, pacing back and forth in his Manhattan office. "What the fuck happened? I gave you a responsibility. You, and once again you, fucked it up. Again!" He stopped at Tracy's chair.

"I know you not going to stand there and blame me for this," Tracy responded.

"Muthafucka, do you know what we could be facing if they ever was to connect my business to Assante's business? Something much worse than life, my nigga. I could lose everything." Christian kicked in the full-length mirror against the wall. "EVERYTHING!"

"What I'm trying to figure out, Christian, is," Cadillac began, "when did we become killers? What the hell are we thinking?"

"We're supposed to be thinking about the money. The rest don't matter. You pick a fine time to be thinking about any of this shit, after what you and Shane did. Oh yeah. Forgot about that, huh? You stand to lose the same shit that we all do. Maybe even more. Now we don't know exactly what it is Kaneecha may have said, but one thing's for certain, cops or no cops, she's got to go. Y'all hear what I'm saying?"

Christian's secretary called over the intercom, "Mister Elijah, Mister Assante and his brother are here."

"Let them in."

Assante and his brother entered the office stone-faced.

"What's up, Assante?" Christian said, turning his back and walking to his desk. "What's up?"

I know you are no fool," Assante replied. "The girl, Marcel's woman, she has spoken to the police, but they have no proof, so it is nothing. She will be taken care of. We have a bigger problem to worry about now. One of our soldiers killed two officers inside their car early this morning—a message to the police—for raping that little girl in upstate New York. It is not good. The city will soon become agitated. Especially if the accused officer from here gets off. An example must be made. It will soon be time for our soldiers to act."

"It's two thousand and nine," Tracy said. "We not supposed to be nowhere near that for years. What the hell are you talking about? We don't got nothing to do with that mess upstate. You buggin'."

"Take it easy, Tracy," Christian said.

"Naw, man. This fool crazy. He need to get his mind right. Somebody needs to tell him. Shit."

Assante smiled. "Tracy, you are such a fool. You do not think for yourself. You let the money think for you. It is all you care for. That is why we are all here. Now there is a problem that has arisen, and the time has come for challenge. An officer must suffer. Immediately. I will make the call." He looked at his Rolex watch. "Christian . . . the girl . . . take care of it. The responsibility is on you." Then he said to Akinsanya, "Let us go, brother."

"So this is how we do business now? You just let somebody make all of us look like bitches?" Tracy asked.

"Your money's not on the line here," Christian responded. "My shit is."

Cadillac said, "I don't like where this is going no more. I ain't no damn killer."

"But you was when you went out of town, because it was a job, a job you was being paid for. You were taken care of real good, you and Shane both. You don't have to be no killer to be a murderer. Know the difference?"

Cadillac rolled his eyes. "No, Christian,"

"A killer commits the act, but a murderer closes it with no remorse." He turned to Solasse. "This is what it is. You with us or against us?"

"I'm with you."

"Good." Christian pulled a cigar from his desk and sniffed the aroma. "Very, very good."

CHAPTER TWENTY-EIGHT

TRINITY

Trinity walked down the spiral staircase at home and went straight to the kitchen, where Christian was already dressed and waiting for his personal driver to arrive. She poured herself a mug full of steaming green tea.

"I think I'm ready to take that trip down to Florida now, Daddy." She tested the boiling hot water with her top lip. "I just need a li'l rest from the city life. You feel me?"

"Yeah," he said, looking back at her. "Maybe that's a good idea."

"I had a talk with Kaneecha the other day."

Christian continued reading as if she'd never said a thing.

"Did you hear what I said? I had a talk with Kaneecha."

He quickly spun around in his seat. "You put her up to calling the police?"

"You lied to me. You said you didn't know anything that I was talking about."

He slowly repeated, "Did you tell her to call the police?"

"Why would I have someone call the police on my own father? I'd never betray you like that."

"You wouldn't? Then how'd you end up talking to her? What'd y'all talk about? You shouldn't have gone behind my back. You don't know what this is about."

"I do now, Daddy. I know a whole lot now. How could you be involved in any of this?"

"You don't know what you're talking about, Trinity. Stay away from her."

"But why, Daddy? Is it Assante and Akinsanya?"

Christian suddenly stood up and slapped her face, leaving them both in a state of shock. It was the first time he'd ever put his hands on her. His hand froze in place, and his mouth hung wide open.

"Oh no. Oh no, baby," he said, quickly holding her. "You know that's not me." He tightly pressed his lips against her cheek, but she pushed him away and ran up the stairs.

"Trinity." He ran to the edge of the steps. "Trinity."

Her door slammed closed, and music from her stereo exploded through the upstairs hallway and down the steps.

Just then, there was a knock at the front door then two honks from the car of his personal driver. Christian twisted his body back and forth between racing up the stairs and rushing toward the front door. He opted for the front door. Then he yelled up the steps before leaving the house, "We'll talk about this later, baby."

"I can't believe you talked to the police," Trinity said to Kaneecha as she stood on her porch. "I told you I'd talk to him."

"My man is missing. Your father knows where he is. That's fucked up. You should leave. Shit, for all I know, you got something to do with this too. It don't matter though. An investigation is set. The truth will come out."

"Kaneecha, just listen."

"No, you listen. You don't got shit I want to hear, unless you telling me where my kids' father at. If you don't know that, then you just need to step off my porch."

"A'ight. I'm just tryin'-a help you." Trinity turned to walk away.

Detective Frogger's car pulled up to the curb just as Trinity turned around. "Kaneecha," he called out just as she was about to close her front door. He watched as Trinity strolled down the walkway to get into her car.

"Ma'am," he said to Kaneecha, removing his sunglasses.

Trinity sat in her car as the detective walked up the steps to the porch and entered the house. She locked eyes with Kaneecha, who slammed her door shut. Trinity then looked in her rearview mirror at Frogger's car and wrote down the license plate number.

She speed-dialed Tracy. "Tracy, I ain't seen you since the protest. Where ya been hiding?"

"Hey, Trin," he answered. "Everything a'ight?"

"Naw, it's not. I need to see you. Right now."

"I'm at the store. I'll be back at the rest about eight."

After stopping by a few friends and taking care of some business at the bank, Trinity headed straight toward Tracy's home. He was just pulling into the parking space of the condo's lot.

"Hey, stranger," she said, rolling down her window.

"What up?" Tracy rolled down his. "Let me just finish up this call," he said, holding up his cell.

"I'm here." Trinity rolled her window back up then stepped out of her vehicle.

"So what's good?" Tracy said, activating the alarm on his car after he exited it.

"I don't know. I'm hearing a lot of things, Tracy. It involves you, my father, and Cadillac. Shane too."

"You wanna talk inside?"

"Please," she said, walking behind him.

"Do you know where Marcel is?" Trinity asked as she sat on the couch in his living room.

Tracy sat beside her and placed his hand on her knee. "Trinity, leave it alone."

"I can't. My father's involved in this. He's all I got in the world. Tracy, please tell me what's going on."

"You really wanna know? I don't think you do."

"Tracy, I thought we were friends." Trinity turned her head away from him.

"Hey, we are friends." Tracy grabbed her chin and turned her face back toward him. "You hear me? We are." He kissed her lips.

"So tell me something."

"Damn," he said, standing up, "I don't know why you come here doing this." He took a deep breath, walked to the edge of the dining room carpet then returned. He bowed his head. "It's all true. All of it."

"Marcel?" she said in shock. "No, I don't believe you."

"Trinity, you know me. Would I make this up?"

"But why?"

"For the love of money."

"So the shit about the Africans is true?"

"Everything. I fucked up, Trinity. I mean, I fucked up real bad this time."

"Is Marcel dead?"

Tracy walked away again and looked out of the window. He bit on his bottom lip then faced her from afar. He never said a word, but his look of regret was confirmation enough for Trinity to validate her assumptions.

"Where is he? Tracy? If you know, then you can't let Kaneecha be all tripping out. She's worried like crazy."

"Marcel shouldn't have opened his big mouth, and he definitely shouldn't have told Kaneecha shit. You see what's happening now, right? Shit is fucked up, and it's coming to a head real soon. Let me ask you about this dude, Solasse."

"What about him?

"I got a funny feeling about him. I don't think he is who he say he is."

"So who is he then?"

"Don't know. He was checked out, but his vibe still don't feel right to me."

"Outside of the foolishness he pulled at your protest, he an a'ight dude to me. I met his wife and ev'ythang."

"You ain't spoke to Christian about none of this yet or asked him anything?"

"I tried, but he ain't told me nothing."

"Then you know what I'm about to tell you, this stays between us, right?

"Always." She kissed her two fingers and placed them on his lips.

Tracy was a fool for trusting any woman to keep a secret. (Fix your faces.) But he loved Trinity in a way he'd never loved a woman before. In his heart he knew she felt the same for him, because they'd always shared a connection. Not just any old connection, but a "soulful embrace" kind of connection. A mental connection that granted them permission to psychologically link and build on every level of spiritual comprehension. That is, up until now.

"Marcel is dead."

"What?"

"And I killed him," he said, closing his eyes.

"Don't tell me that." Trinity stood up. "What is you thinking?"

Tracy reached out to touch her shoulder, but she jerked away, shouting, "No!"

"I had no choice. He put our names out there. See what it's led to now?"

"Do *you* see what it's led to now?"

"I can't take any of it back now, so fuck it. I mean, with the exception of Marcel, shit, I don't know if I'd even want to."

"You stand all up there at that protest sounding like you all pro-black and mighty. All of this is going on, and I'm the only one in the dark? There ain't no reason in the world you had to do that. You didn't have to kill him."

"He was already dying anyway."

"How did he die, Tracy?"

"Does it really matter?"

"Yes, it does."

"Okay." Tracy shrugged. "I shot him."

"You say it just like the shit ain't affect you none. What does killing him got to do with all the other things popping off? I mean, what's really good? As a matter of fact, don't even worry about it. I'm about to break. This is too much." Trinity grabbed her purse off the couch.

When she attempted to leave, Tracy blocked her path. "Don't leave like this," he said.

She yelled, "Don't leave like what? Huh? Don't leave like what, Tracy? Don't leave knowing you and my father is killers?" She pushed him out of her path and headed for the door. Then she turned around. "You know what, Tracy," she said, wiping tears from her cheeks, "you were right. I didn't want to know."

Trinity's fears of her father's involvement in Marcel's disappearance had been confirmed by Tracy's own admission. She felt as if she'd been played, lied to, and left out of the loop.

She was a block down from Kaneecha's house driving in her car when she slowly approached her street. She didn't know why she'd returned there. It was her intention to just drive by and not stop. It wasn't like she was going to tell Kaneecha anything. That would automatically implicate her father beyond a shadow of a doubt, not to mention, Tracy, whom she loved ever so dearly, on the low. She was feeling guilty, as if she'd pulled the trigger herself. Maybe it was the fact that Marcel's beautiful, innocent children would never see their father again.

"Maybe I'll just stop by and apologize for earlier. Yeah, she'll respect that," she said out loud to herself as she stopped in front of the house. "What the fuck am I doing here?" she said, second-guessing herself as she stepped out of the car and closed the door.

She traveled up the walkway and pondered about-facing. The closer she got to the front door, the more she began to question her real intentions for coming back. She noticed the door was slightly ajar as she went to knock on it.

She heard a baby's wail coming through the partially cracked front door, and a television on maximum volume.

"Hello?" she yelled out through the crack. "Hello?" She knocked. "Kaneecha?" she shouted, "it's Trinity." She held the doorknob.

The neighborhood was unusually silent, with the exception of Trinity's frantic knocks on the door. A moonless black sky enhanced the brightness of flat-screen televisions shining through the windows of surrounding houses.

Her cell phone vibrated, momentarily startling her. She stuck her hand down in her bag and stopped the buzz.

"Kaneecha," she called once more, slowly pushing the door open, "I just need to talk to you. Can I come in?" She cautiously took a step inside, reaching down into her bag and tightly gripping the butt of her .25 automatic.

She crept down the short corridor, her gun hanging by her leg. The loud volume of the television echoed between the walls of the semi-lit hallway. "Kaneecha?" she whispered, standing at the entrance to her bedroom. She stood totally consumed within the illumination of a 75-inch plasma television sitting on a stand, as 50 Cent's "Outta Control" video cast gangsta silhouettes of hip-hop living off the wall.

The baby cried out again, but Trinity stood steady. She looked over to a king-sized bed opposite the flat-screen and saw Kaneecha lying down on her side, her back facing the door.

Trinity whispered again, "Kaneecha?" using the light from the television to guide her to the foot of the bed. She moved toward the left side of the bed to face Kaneecha.

Black satin sheets flowed up to the waist of Kaneecha's still body. The array of vibrant, flashy colors of hi-definition made the sheets occasionally glare purple, and a ceiling fan above slowly spun, rattling loosely. Kaneecha's hands were tied behind her back, her eyes wide open, and her mouth overflowed with foamy saliva.

Trinity stumbled forward over something and fell to the floor. She quickly turned around on her hands and knees to see Kaneecha's five-year-old daughter with an extension cord tied around her neck. She gasped, "Oh God!"

Trinity recomposed herself and tried desperately to free the girl from her bondage, but it was just too late. It'd been much too long. The poor little girl was dead.

Trinity was startled by the cry again. She looked up on the king-sized mattress where Kaneecha's lifeless body lay and saw her eight-month-old son blindly searching for milk from his mother's bare breasts.

Springing to her feet Trinity panted heavily and looked down at the baby. Not knowing what to do next, she began backing away.

The baby began to cry again and shriek. It became so loud, it was scary. It was almost as if he'd finally become aware that his mother's milk had passed its expiration date.

Leaving the baby behind, Trinity ran out of the house

and hopped into her car. As she sped away from the malicious homicide, she nervously dialed 9-1-1.

"Hello, 9-1-1," an operator answered.

"Y-y-yes. Hello," she said frantically.

"Yes. What is your situation?"

"I'd like to report a double murder," she said, turning onto the Long Island Expressway. "And the baby. Please, don't forget about the baby."

"What is your location?" the operator asked.

CHAPTER TWENTY-NINE

TRACY KANE

Tracy sat in the passenger seat of Cadillac's new black SRX truck. They were on their way to Christian's house the very next morning after Trinity's discovery. "Cadillac, man, I think I fucked up, yo. Real bad this time."

"What you done did now?" Cadillac looked at Tracy then back at the screen. "Yo, ain't that Marcel's crib, man?" he said, tapping the screen.

The news and media were reporting live from the front and both sides of Marcel's house, where detectives dusting for fingerprints walked in and out of the house. Police vehicles were parked in the middle of the street and by the curb in front of the house. Flashing spinning lights mounted atop the horse-powered cruisers were magnified each time their red glares kissed the LCD screen attached to Cadillac's dashboard.

"You looking, man? That's Marcel's crib. Look, dude. Oh shit. They bringing out bodies. Dawg, fuckin' look." Cadillac grabbed Tracy's shoulder. "Look at the baby."

Tracy turned away and looked out his window as a female officer walked out from the house and down the steps of the porch.

Cadillac and Tracy's phones both began to ring simultaneously.

Tracy looked at his phone. "It's Christian." He answered, "Yo."

"Who did it?" Christian quickly asked. "Y'all watching the news, right? Who did it? You or Caddy?"

"I don't know what you're talking about, man. I'm just seeing it myself, me and Caddy. We both in shock. Ain't that right?" he said, looking at Cadillac.

"You talk to anybody, Tracy?" Christian asked. "I mean, about anything?"

"Why, every time something happen, am I always the first one to be accused?"

"Because usually you're the one running your fat mouth, nigga. Fuck you mean, why? This particular shit right here is gonna have detectives all over us, so if you know anything, boy, now the time to speak."

"You got anything to do with it?" Tracy shot back as Cadillac pulled up into Christian's driveway.

Cadillac hollered through Tracy's cell, "I don't like all this early-in-the-morning shit."

"I see y'all pulling up. Hurry and get your asses inside." Christian disconnected the call.

"You better talk to me before we go in here." Cadillac put the truck in park, one hand resting on the steering wheel. "You got something to do with all this?" he asked as the screen blanked off when the truck's engine died.

"Not directly. I don't even know if that's because of me."

"I'm stumped, nigga. What's your link in all this?"

"Well," Tracy began with a slight chuckle, "I may have slipped up just a li'l something and put Trinity on to Marcel's untimely demise."

Cadillac, one foot out the driver's door, stared at Tracy and just shook his head. He got out of the truck and slammed the door behind himself. "Hurry up."

Tracy hopped out and followed behind him to the front door. Christian said to the two men after they walked into the kitchen, "We got a serious problem on our hands. The brothers sent some killers out to keep Kaneecha's mouth shut. They didn't even tell me. I just got the call after we got off the phone. This shit is not good." He poured himself a drink.

"She shouldn't have been fuckin' with the police. Watch how all this shit turn out now. Tracy, that detective, Dennis Frogger, the one you said be fuckin' with you, he's the lead detective on the case. That means he'll be paying you a visit real soon. There ain't shit I can do for you, if you open your mouth." He sipped his glass of Henny straight.

"Oh, I think it's already too late for that," Cadillac said, beaming Tracy. Tracy looked at him surprised then tried to telepathically persuade him into not telling Christian what he'd just confessed to when they were outside.

"You my man and all that, but you doing way too much," Cadillac said.

"What I don't understand is why that bitch just suddenly started talking to police out of nowhere." Christian looked through the curtains hanging in front of the kitchen's window.

Christian was a bit on edge because he knew exactly what Kaneecha talked to the detective about. He remembered all too well the intense conversation that he'd had with Trinity. The one where she took it upon herself to investigate Marcel's rumored disappearance by inquiring with his babies' mother, Kaneecha. He himself may have been the very cause of this all. If only he'd just been straight with Trinity when she'd first confronted him.

"I'll tell you how." Cadillac was highly upset and feeling

just a little bit betrayed. "He did it again. He opened his mouth again, and this time, I think he might've told the wrong person." He mushed Tracy's head.

"What's he talking about, Tracy, huh?" Christian walked up on him and grabbed his chin. "What's he talking about?"

Tracy smacked his hand away then took a step back.

"You better tell him or I will."

"Fuck it!" Tracy shrugged. "I told Trinity everything."

"Oh, that's all?" Christian laughed. "Cadillac, you crazy, man," he said, slapping his back. "Ain't he crazy?" He looked at Tracy and laughed even louder.

Cadillac looked at Christian, who held on to his stomach, completely and utterly overwhelmed by the humor in it all.

Soon they all began laughing together. Until one swift, unanticipated motion by Christian made it all stop. He pulled out his gun from the back of his waist and cocked it in Tracy's face. "You . . . you is the biggest dummy I ever met. What the fuck is on your mind? You telling my daughter shit? You got her involved in this now? Huh?" Christian jammed him in the forehead with the nose of his gun. "Don't you know they'll go after her if they find out she got anything to do with this?"

"Christian"—Cadillac cautiously took a step beside him—"come on, man, you can't do this," he said, speaking calmly as he looked down at him.

"Why you keep doing this shit?" Christian shouted, poking him again in the same spot. "You just love fuckin' with people, don't you?" He poked him even harder than before.

Blood began spurting out of a freshly developed wound on Tracy's forehead.

"Christian, man," Cadillac said once more, "put the gun down." He slowly reached for it.

"Get away from me," Christian said, never looking at

him. "I should kill your ass right here, and right fuckin' now." He began tapping Tracy's forehead again, and swiping him across the face.

Cadillac ran behind him to pull him off Tracy, and as they all fell to the floor, Christian fell on top of Tracy.

BLAM! The explosive sound quickly echoed throughout the house and out through the window screen.

Christian and Cadillac both quickly hopped to their feet and looked down at Tracy, bleeding profusely from the left side of his head then going into convulsions, spitting up phlegm and blood. His painful moan was shaky, and his body stuttered as it jumped up and down on the floor.

"Tracy!" Cadillac threw himself on top of Tracy to prevent him from hurting himself. "Look what you did." He looked up at Christian. "Get a towel or something," he screamed, using his hand to block the river of blood crashing through his closed fingers.

"Oh shit! Oh shit! Oh shit!" Christian paced back and forth with his gun by his side. "Is he dead?"

"He needs an ambulance. It didn't go through." Cadillac looked at the side of Tracy's head and held it up. "But the shit did fuck him up."

Tracy's convulsions began to simmer down.

"Call the ambulance," Cadillac said.

"They can't come here. We'll take him to the hospital." Christian went around the house and closed the windows.

"Are you crazy?" Cadillac looked down at his blood-soaked white button-up. "He needs medical attention."

"You wanna go to jail? You know they give life to niggas that was just there too, right? They give your ass life if he dies or not."

Outside, police sirens crowded the driveway.

"Help me move this couch in front of that nigga." Christian looked at the police through the window. "Come on, ain't no time for being no bitch. Let's move the shit. NOW!"

The two quickly moved the couch in front of a semiconscious Tracy, his moans now inaudible.

"Go hide somewhere. You got blood all over yourself. I'll take care of this."

Christian opened the front door before they could ring the bell.

"Mister Elijah?" the officer said, walking toward him.

"Yeah, that's me." Christian smiled. "What's up? What can I do for ya?"

"Some of your neighbors have been calling in complaining about some sort of escalating commotion and gunshots coming from your house. Know anything about that?"

"Officer? What are you, about twenty-eight, twenty-seven? I'm forty-three years old. You see where I live? Around a whole bunch of old and retired white folks. I run my own business. Does it really sound like I have time to be playing cowboys and Indians when I already conquered the horse?"

"So you won't mind if we take a look around inside?"

Christian smirked. "You got a warrant?"

The officer, upset that he wasn't granted the permission, had a look of determination on his face that loudly dictated, *I'll be back!*

"That's what I thought." Christian chuckled, his arms folded. "Well, if that's all for today, I do have other issues I'm dealing with right now. Maybe next time, we'll do donuts."

After the officer left, Christian walked behind the couch, perspiration dripping down his head. "Come on, Cadillac, let's get this muthafucka out of here."

CHAPTER THIRTY

TRINITY

Trinity sat in first class on a non-stop flight to Miami. She leaned her head on the plane's window and looked down to observe the clouds below. The early morning sun debuted off in the distance, carpeting the clouds with its orange rays, as the purple dawn atmosphere faded. The hypnotic metamorphosis temporarily calmed Trinity's tense and uneasy spirit.

After her plane landed around eleven a.m., she caught a cab to the vacation house Christian had purchased some time ago.

"Thank you," she said to the driver as she exited from the rear seat.

Her cell immediately began to ring as she walked up the cement-paved path leading to the front door. She looked down at the display then deeply inhaled. "Hello," she nervously answered.

"Baby girl," Christian said, "where are you at?"

She yelled into the phone, "You lied to me. About EVERY-THING!"

Neighboring senior citizens became startled by Trinity's

sudden outburst in the usually tranquil environment, as they lounged on their beautifully manicured lawns, partially shaded by the swaying leaves of palm trees deeply rooted in the Florida soil.

"Trinity, listen to me," he calmly said. "I want you to come home. Now! Where are you at?"

"I'm in Miami, and I'm not coming home."

"You have no idea what you started. You better get yourself on another flight. Don't play with me."

"Why you want me home? So you can kill me for talking too? Or are you gonna get Tracy to do it? Maybe Cadillac? Shane even? You foul, Daddy."

"I'll see you in the morning, Trinity," Christian said, before hanging up the phone.

CHAPTER THIRTY-ONE

CHRISTIAN

Christian sat in the back of Assante's black Lincoln Continental. He yelled, "That's not the fuckin' point, Assante. This shit don't affect you none. You had the bitch killed and didn't tell me nothing about it. When we start working like that? I got a detective wanting to ask me some questions now." He looked out the window. "The shit is not good."

"Mister Elijah, please be calm. There is no need for arousal. You are not the one who killed her, so why do you worry? You didn't kill Marcel, Tracy did. Where do you see a problem for yourself?"

"I was there when Marcel died, and so were you. Yeah, you were there too. So since this is not such a big problem, maybe when all the questioning starts, I'll just send the detectives your way. My people been doing their part by putting the guns in the street. You got your peoples all out of state doing they damn thing. Why you gotta go and be doing extra shit behind our backs?"

"First, Mister Elijah, it is not I who ran my mouth off at a party. That is what has led to this all. Concerning the woman and her daughter, well, she should have not spoken, or else they'd both still be alive. What is Shane doing? I have not seen him. Is he also planning on leaving us soon? I hear his wife has left him because of a quarrel about guns. Is that right, Mister Elijah? Does the woman know?"

"Why? You want me to find her and shoot her?"

"Only if it is necessary, Mister Elijah. Are you aware that any connection leading back to us can link the guns we sell to all kinds of murders caused by them? Any bodies on any of them will be put on us. So, yes, Mister Elijah, if you truly enjoy life outside of a cage, you will do what you must, to stay free. Or I will. How do we know Tracy will not speak when he awakens?"

Christian directed Assante's driver into the parking lot of a local comedy club out in Southside Jamaica, Queens, where comedian Nasty Mouth Cartel was performing.

When Christian and Assante walked up, Cadillac and Shane were chatting with some young ladies near the entrance.

Assante said to Christian, "I thought you did not know of Shane's whereabouts."

"I didn't tell you anything. I just didn't answer you," he said as he walked past the bouncer at the front door. "Come on, let's go inside. We can't be talking out here."

Nasty Mouth Cartel bopped to the beat of DJ Khaled's club-banging anthem as he stepped out on the stage. It'd been about a good year since the comedian had performed in Queens. "Hello, muthafuckas, hello." He stood on the tips of his toes to salute the audience. "Cut that goddamn music off, nigga," he said to the DJ.

The audience cheered and laughed, anticipating a gut-busting, eye-tearing, laugh-till-it-hurt kind of night.

"A'ight. That's what's up," he said, taking a bow. "Now

sit the fuck down so we can get this started." He turned and picked up a rib-caged plastic bottle of Ciroc and squeezed a stream of it through the pin-sized hole of its green nozzle. He smiled as he scanned the audience. "Look at everybody all up in here looking fly. That's what I miss most about New York—all the beautiful sistas and hood niggas. Y'all go ahead and give yourselves a round of applause. Shit!"

The audience started stomping their feet, rooting for Nasty Mouth.

He asked the audience, "Anybody see Star Jones lately?"

The audience laughed then booed in disgust.

"The bitch done transformed into a bag of bones. Michael Jackson looking to put her up in his exhibit, next to the elephant man's bones. Skin so tight, she looks like some kind of rare leather suitcase and shit. You see her mouth? Shit so wide now, she swallow her ears every time she smile. She always kind of reminded me of a bootleg Oprah Winfrey, except Oprah's weight was more like elevators—up and fuckin' down."

The laughter in the audience began to pick up.

"I don't leave nobody out." Nasty Mouth Cartel walked across the stage to slap the hand of an audience member.

Back up on the balcony Christian and company quietly sat until Shane penetrated the "silence of the lambs." He looked at Assante and Christian. "Star ain't said shit, so nobody got to be paying her no special visits."

"Did anybody say anything about that to you?" Christian asked.

"You didn't have to, nigga. I go by the actions, and I see you finally acted on Tracy's big-mouth ass. You didn't have to shoot him though."

"Did I say I shot him, or you just assuming?"

"Yo, what the fuck you lookin' at, big man?" Shane said

to Assante. "I'm saying, if there's a problem, we can go outside and handle that right now. You don't got me twisted like these niggas here."

"Control him," Assante nonchalantly said to Christian.

"He doesn't control me, and neither do you. I know one thing though—If anything happen to my wife, nigga," he said to Christian, "I'm coming for your ass first."

"You ever had an itch in between your ass crack and couldn't do shit about it because you was in public?" Nasty Mouth Cartel asked.

Once again the audience could not contain their laughter.

"You sitting somewhere going like this." He rubbed his ass back and forth on the wooden stool on stage. "Then try to act like people don't know what you doing. Women are good for that. Men really don't give a shit. We scratch our balls and ass in public all the time, but women . . . shiiit, if there's nowhere for a woman to scratch privately, she'll walk around all day with that anal itch, walking around like this." Nasty Mouth tightened up and stiffly walked across the stage. "Y'all can't front though!" He sipped his drink again.

The crowd all stood and started to applaud and cheer.

"Fellas, when you was a shortie, how many of y'all remember scratching your ass and telling your homeboy, 'Yo, smell this perfume on my fingers'?"

Everyone in the audience roared with laughter, their minds harking back to a time when niggas capitalized on fistfights, not guns.

"Anyway," Christian said, "you're going to stop threatening me!"

"I'm done with this, man." Shane stood up. "And I could give a shit about a contract. You feel you wanna do something, dawg? You and him do what y'all gotta do, yo. Everybody got guns. What you gonna do, nigga?" He looked at Cadillac. "You gonna stay here and let these dudes keep pimping you?"

Cadillac slowly turned his head away from him.

"Just for some fuckin' money, huh?" Shane chuckled. "All the niggas always sell they souls." Shane said, accidentally knocking over his chair as he exited.

As the good times continued to roll on, Nasty Mouth Cartel said, "Who would've thought we'd ever see a black president in our lifetime?"

The audience gave a standing ovation for the first black president in "Amerikkkan" history, cheering and chanting, "Obama! Obama! Obama!"

"A black man in the White House? Goddamn, muthafuckas! Goddamn! There wasn't even a first black man in White Castle. Just yesterday the chances of that was like trying to fit a square into a circle. It just don't fuckin' fit. You know all them rednecks is like, 'Fuck Abraham Lincoln. Fuck 'im for freeing those coons.

"Hey, Hillary? Running for president years after your nationally recognized cheating husband made you look like a fool is not change you can believe in. It's change you can Xerox. When Bill said, 'I did not have any sexual relations with that woman,' I thought he was talking about Hillary. Come to find out, he was talking about Chelsea." Nasty Mouth Cartel laughed.

"What is it with these women over forty, just finding out that their perfect man is really the perfect homo? If your man says he wants to try new things—like sticking your finger in his ass—he's a homo! Why is that so hard to understand? What heterosexual man asks to be penetrated with the index finger?"

CHAPTER THIRTY-TWO

CHRISTIAN

It was late morning the next day when Detective Dennis Frogger slowly walked in Christian's office. His secretary had shouted his name through the intercom sitting on his desk, but the seven officers with Frogger were already rampaging through everything in sight, opening the closet door and pulling down shelves.

They lifted Christian to his feet and thoroughly searched him from head to toe. Then five officers forced his employees twenty-five floors down to the lobby, while the other two stayed inside with Det. Frogger.

Dennis Frogger sat on the edge of Christian's desk and pulled a piece of paper from the inside pocket of his jacket. "Take a look at it," he said to Christian. "That there is a warrant for your arrest."

"Arrest for what?"

"Well, the way I see it, you know where Marcel is, so why not just talk to me now? Maybe we can work something out."

"I don't know where Marcel is."

"You know who killed Kaneecha and that poor little girl?"

"Where you get off asking me? What I got to do with anybody being killed or disappearing?"

"You wanna play games? Good. Then let's play games. You mind if I smoke one of these here?" Frogger reached down into the wooden box of Dunhill cigars. "So," he began after biting the butt of the cigar, "you don't know nothing, right? A child is dead, and you're innocent, huh?"

"Why are you accusing me? You got some proof?"

"Besides the fact that your boy Tracy ended up in the hospital with a gunshot wound to the head? Good thing it was only a graze. Three inches closer and he'd have missed his court date coming up in a couple of months. So the thing I keep asking myself is, Why is everybody in association with you experiencing such an extreme case of bad luck?" Frogger exhaled a thick cloud of London fog.

Christian calmly said, "I didn't catch your name."

"You can call me Detective Frogger. You know, it'll all come out in the end. You're too well-known. Oh, yeah, did I forget to tell you that, the day before Kaneecha was murdered, your daughter paid her a visit?"

"My daughter?"

"Yeah. Trinity, right? Oh shit." Frogger ashed the cigar out on his desk. "My man, your ass is definitely grass. Get him out of here," he said to the two officers.

As Christian walked with the two officers, Det. Frogger banged on the desk. "Hold on," he said. "Gun." He held it up after pulling it from the drawer of Christian's desk.

"I got a permit for that," Christian blurted out. "Find something else."

Dennis said into his radio, "We got him, Captain."

CHAPTER THIRTY-THREE

TRACY KANE

Three weeks later inside of Southside Hospital on Long Island, Tracy awoke from his unconscious state. White gauze softy snaked its way around his head, spawning a bloodstained spot. His eyelids partially eclipsed his pupils, which was probably why he could only see the shoes of the individual standing approximately three feet away from the railed bed he lay on. The officer taking up the trail against Tracy and his partners never seemed to quit.

"Tracy? Wake up." The officer approached the bed. "Wake the hell up." He shook Tracy's foot. "I haven't seen you in a while, buddy. What happened? Somebody try to whack ya?" He walked around the bed to examine the wound to the side of Tracy's head. "Lucky it wasn't me. I wouldn't have missed." He pushed his head off the pillow and said in a raised voice, "Wake your lazy ass."

The room door opened, and another officer stuck his head inside. "Everything all right in here?"

"Everything is fine. Just close the door," the bullying officer responded. "So, are you finally finished fuckin' around yet?"

"I'm done," Tracy wearily answered, saliva dropping from his mouth, and the whites of his eyes turning crimson red. "I can't do this no more. I'll drop all the charges. I don't fuckin' care no more."

"That's about the smartest thing I've heard you say since I first beat your ass. You better leave it the hell alone. You already got enough people uptight with you. You need more problems like you need a hole in your head." He laughed. "Now that was funny—a hole in your head. You get it?" He pushed down on Tracy's knee.

"Aww, man. Yeah. I get it." Tracy weakly pushed his hand away.

"You fuckin' better." The officer exited the room.

He was Tracy's first visitor for the morning, but certainly not his last.

"I was with your wife last night, you asshole." Detective Dennis Frogger was laughing with an officer out in the hallway just before entering Tracy's room.

"Oh shit." Tracy rolled his eyes. "Not you too."

"What? You're not happy to see me? You should be. I may be the only person who can save your life." He lifted the lid to Tracy's breakfast tray.

"What you mean, save my life?"

"Don't you play games with me, Tracy. I'm tryin'-a help you save your own life. Who shot you?"

Tracy turned his head toward the window and sulked.

"Come on, Tracy. I'm not going to beg you. Did Christian shoot you?"

Frogger really didn't care whether Tracy lived or died. All he wanted to do was tie Christian in with Kaneecha and her daughter's murder, along with Marcel's disappearance. He was done playing with Tracy and this runaround nonsense. He knew just how to pull his card. He'd just simply turn his back on him and walk away.

"Frogger," Tracy called, just as the detective had placed his hand on the doorknob. "Hypothetically speaking, what if I told you Christian shot me?"

"Here's the thing, Tracy—No matter what you have on Christian, he got the same thing on you, Cadillac, Shane, and whoever the hell else is involved."

"That's not answering my question, man. What if he did do this?" Tracy pointed to his wound.

"It'd be your word against his, unless a weapon was found. You know that. Look, you gonna continue wasting my time, or did you have something to tell me?"

"Naw. Fuck it. I ain't got shit to say. I don't know who shot me."

"Keep this in mind—He missed by accident." The detective left his card on top of his tray. "Call me when you're ready to talk."

Tracy closed his eyes after the detective departed and never woke up until evening time.

At the foot of his bed was yet another visitor. It was Shane.

"Come to kick a nigga while he down?" Tracy asked.

"Cadillac called me when it happened. How you feeling?"

"Vulnerable."

"Why you keep doing it to yourself? Is this what you wanted? I told you I know Christian a lot better than you. He ain't the father figure you thought he was after all, huh?"

"What am I going to do?"

"You funny. Now you think of that? What in the hell was going on in that crazy head of yours when you decided to tell Trinity everything? You done opened up an official can of worms. You know that man don't fuck around when it come to his daughter. I don't even know how you're going to get out of this one."

"I don't think I am."

"Don't be so overdramatic. I'ma get you out of here right now. That's why I'm here."

"Even after all my shit?"

"Let's not even talk about it. It took me two weeks to convince Star into letting me get you out of here. You didn't have to tell her what we into. Yes. You fucked up. Big time! But you still my dude, and I don't want to see that nigga do you in. Let's go, man. Ain't no time for you to be discharging. We gotta move now."

"I'm ready. Let's bounce." Tracy slowly sat up.

"Tracy, seriously though, state your word you gonna stop all this shit you be doin'. This shit is far from over with you and Christian, so you got to be easy. Cadillac already told me that Christian is going to shoot you in the face next time y'all cross paths. I'ma try to talk to him for you, but I don't know, man. You got the African brothers to worry about. You involved Trinity in this."

"So what am I going to do?"

"I don't know. Star has a cousin down in Miami, this ol' gay cousin of hers named Cee-Cee. He got a li'l bar down there where all the people up in that bitch be fucked up on them *E* pills. You know what I'm saying to you, son? The nigga be dabbling in some felonious shit. You fuckin' move wrong, it won't be very hard for anyone to find you."

"You gonna hole me up with some fag, man?"

"It's either that or the ditch Marcel was dropped into."

As they sped down the expressway in Shane's truck headed to where Star was staying with her mother, Tracy asked Shane, "So are you ever going to tell me what it was you and Cadillac did when y'all went out of state?"

"Why is that so important for you to know? If you was supposed to know, you woulda been there, right?"

"Yeah, man," Tracy said, looking out the window. "Whatever."

"Don't be salty, nigga. Look at the circumstances. Telling you shit is like telling on myself. I got a wife I love. I'm already fuckin' myself, just trying to help your ass."

"Where we going?" Tracy asked nervously. "The airport's in the other direction."

"Calm down. We're going to my mother-in-law's house. You'll be safe there. Your plane leaves at six a.m."

"Something don't feel right about this. It's not making sense."

"It'll all come together real soon, trust me. You good."

"You sure, man?" Tracy was feeling even less secure now.

"Stop being a second-guesser. You're already in the truck. Fuck you gonna do? Jump out? See what that speedometer says?" Shane tapped at the orange dial through its protective plastic window. "Nothing's going to happen. Only reason you nervous is because your conscience reminding you of how foul your ways been."

Shane parked in the driveway of his mother-in-law's house. Two cars, one parked in front of the other, were to the right of them. "Just get out the car."

Tracy nervously followed Shane to the front door of the split-level home. A light above them came on after Shane rang the bell once.

"Come on, nigga," Shane said, standing in the darkened foyer. "Let's go."

Tracy followed closely behind him down a hallway into the dining room.

"Turn on the lights," Shane called out.

When the lights came on, they saw Star standing by the

light switch next to the entrance, and Solasse and his wife sitting at opposite ends of the dinner table.

"What's going on?" Tracy turned to leave.

"Stacy Kane," Marisol called out.

Tracy stopped in his tracks and turned back around. His heartbeat was more than erratic. He'd only come with Shane because he had no other choice. What else was he going to do? He was convinced that someone would get at him if he stayed at the hospital. And a trip to Miami to hide out with some faggot didn't seem like too much of a bad idea, if that would save his life.

"What'd you just say?"

"Stacy Kane. Sound familiar to you?" Marisol put on her reading glasses then pulled some paperwork from a Gucci briefcase.

Tracy looked at Solasse. "What's going on, Shane? What you doing here?"

"Calm down." Solasse stood. "I'm not here to kill you. I don't do what you do, or what he does." He motioned his head to Shane. "You're in some real deep shit, my man. I don't even know what you're going to do. You fucked up."

Solasse's entire vernacular and suave persona had converted noticeably into that of a mole.

"I think you better sit down," Marisol suggested.

"I'm not doing shit until somebody tells me what's going on here."

"You wanna know?" Solasse said. "Here, muthafucka, look!" He quickly pulled his ATF identification from his jacket. "I'm Special Agent Kirk Michael."

Marisol, AKA Special Agent Sanchez, also produced hers.

"You called the police on me?" Tracy told Shane. "And I knew you wasn't right from the very beginning, bitch. I knew your uppity ass wasn't his wife. So, what's this supposed to be? Some kind of setup and shit?" Tracy started backing away.

"Why don't you try sitting your ass down and listen, for a change?" Agent Kirk said.

Shane said to Tracy. "Come on, dude. What we just talk about back at the hospital?"

"Fuck it, right? That's how we do it. What I gots to lose? It's not like I can call on any friends to hold me down." Tracy took a seat. "A'ight. First you then," he said, slapping the table while staring at Special Agent Sanchez. "How you know my momma's name? And why y'all be following me around for the past two years?"

"We know your mother was shot in the head in the middle of the street back in eighty-seven, not too far away from the building you lived in. She was head of a short-lived program in the community called MAD, Mothers Against Drugs."

"So what? Who don't know that? Everybody knows that. This nigga know that." He looked at Shane. "What else you got? Be sure to tell me when I should be impressed."

"Smart ass." Kirk chuckled. "Get ready to be impressed. Yeah, your mother was good at what she did, getting the other mothers together in their community. The attention moved a lot of the dealers to the next street, causing them to clash with the competition."

Tracy shifted in the chair.

Special Agent Sanchez continued, picking up where Solasse, Special Agent Kirk Michael, left off. "Unbeknownst to everyone else, your mother was doing the very drugs she was so against. Go figure." Smiling, she asked Kirk, "You want some more of this?"

Special Agent Kirk Michael smiled. "Mother, may I?"

"Yes, you may." She placed the paperwork back in its folder then slid it across the table to him.

"Fuck you!"

Kirk said, "You do a much better job fuckin' yourself, Tracy. Let me move on with this—You ever saw any of the pictures from your mother's murder scene?"

Tracy blurted out as if he didn't hear the agent's question, "If you're ATF, why the hell you exposing yourself to me? Why not Christian?"

"We don't just want Christian right now," Kirk told him.

Star intervened, "Hold on, Solasse. Now that's not what you said earlier. My husband is not taking the fall with everybody else. We got Tracy here for you. We just want the trouble to be over." She hugged Shane.

"We weren't trying to set you up, Trace," Shane said, "but all this bullshit has got to cease. Too many people are dying. It ain't worth the money."

"Let me see these pictures you got of my mother," Tracy demanded of Kirk.

"You sure? Because it's not pretty. Let's give him a moment." Kirk stood after sliding the envelope to Tracy and asked Star, "Do you got somewhere else we can sit while he looks those over?"

Tracy stared at the envelope for about five minutes before pulling out five pictures of his mother laid out on the hood of a silver BMW, a single gunshot to the face. Bits and pieces of bone and fragments of her teeth, nose, and jaw lay on the hood and windshield. All this did was bring back haunting memories of the last day he saw her. Unfortunately it was the same day she was killed. He still had no idea, amongst everyone else who cared, why she had to die in such a heinous manner. He lay his head on the picture and let his teardrops fall on his mother's face. He pounded the table twice with his fist and released a cry of outrage.

Kirk slowly walked back into the dining room alone. He placed his hand on Tracy's shoulder. "We can help you,

Tracy, but you've got to help us. I know the kind of man Christian is, but we really are after the brothers. Christian's next. Far as your mother goes, what if I told you I know who killed her?"

"What information you know about my mother's murder that no one else does?"

"I'll tell you like this. The same way I was able to come into all your lives and just rock is the same way a man you've known for years could be the man who kills you next week. And the shit wouldn't even bother him the next day. He'd go to your funeral and everything. Kiss your family. Give them his condolences and rob all their houses blind while they're at your burial. You get what I'm saying?"

"Why you need my help? You know what's going on. You seen shit." Tracy shrugged his shoulders.

Special Agent Kirk inhaled deeply, scratching behind the collar of his button-down shirt. "Let's talk outside. It's getting kind of warm in here."

Outside, Kirk told Tracy, "So this is what it is really all about. Now, once I tell you this, there is no, I mean, absolutely no turning back. I'm serious, Tracy. We can make things happen to you that wouldn't even require you going to no court, because you'd never make it there. If everything goes according to plan, we can place you in a witness protection program. You'll be able to pick where you want to live."

"What do I have to do?"

"I don't know how you're going to do it, but you need to be there for Assante's next big shipment, you and Shane both. We can get that guy. All you have to do is wear a wire. We have a video cam and all. You wouldn't even have to say anything. It's going to be the biggest shipment of artillery Assante's ever had delivered, and I want to know where it's coming from and when, specifically."

"So what? I'm just supposed to jump up and do your job for you? Christian wants me dead. What makes you think Assante don't want the same thing for me? Anybody he think is snitching gets put underneath."

"We've been watching Assante the past five years. There are some real powerful people assisting him. You can help prove that, and this'll all be over."

"I don't know, yo. I think it'd be a lot easier on everybody if I just stepped."

"What are you, stupid or naive? Assante is a murderer and will eventually find you and kill you when you're found. You can't go running. Out of all people, you need to stay the furthest away from him. I'm sure, by now he's already convinced you're a snitch." He poked Tracy in the chest. "You're next on his list.

"Yeah, my man. I bet he told all of you some far-fetched story about a revolution in two thousand twenty. That he's fighting a war against the police because he's tired of how they treat black people. Did he tell you about all the men he has waiting on standby all throughout the States? It was all bullshit, Tracy, and all of you had to be some real dumbass muthafuckas to fall for that shit. I mean anybody that thought there was the slightest possibility of it being true should stop reading and thinking for themselves."

"So why he make all that up then?"

"So your boy Christian could continue funding his gunrunning operation. He didn't just start bootlegging his clothes for no reason. It was only a matter of time before Christian found out, but you had to go and fuck up the whole operation by acting out that day in Manhattan." Kirk offered Tracy a cigarette after lighting his own. "You want one?"

"Naw, man. I don't smoke."

"Things were not supposed to work out this way, Tracy. They weren't, and I'm sorry. But, right now, you are caught up in the most awkward position of your life." Kirk exhaled a transparent mist of non-menthol smoke through his nostrils. "Take this." He handed Tracy an odd-looking silver coin. "Hopefully it'll bring you some luck."

Tracy dropped the odd-looking silver coin down into his pocket. "I don't know about this, man," he said, leaving his hand in his pocket. "Y'all standing behind Assante one thousand percent and don't have the slightest idea what the fuck is going on. Are you out of your mind? Assante and his brother are mercenaries. They have a lot of money invested in what they do. Why he ain't been busted a long time ago, since he doing it like that?"

"Because," he exasperatedly responded, looking up at the small blinking lights of a charter plane flying above, "he's not only being funded by Christian, but he's also being secretly funded by the CIA. They're funding him because they need him to place more guns in the hands of black youths. It's that serious. They need more of them to be in jail, more of them dead.

"Primarily, here's the real shit. You keep all of these guns circulating in the street, right? Let's assume about three niggers are shot to death this month, two more are caught with guns then arrested, and one more, some weak son of a bitch, shoots himself in the head because life's too hard. That's six guns and six niggers in six situations.

"But the guns, they just get recycled back into the hands of Assante and the CIA. You're probably asking yourself, How do they get the guns back after they're already checked into ballistics? Who the fuck you think brings all the guns into the country so the police can have them? Niggers are stupid and think basically common. Logic is out of their grasp. Anything is possible with the government. Better start widening your horizon."

"Who killed my mother? You said you know who killed my mother, right? Who did it, muthafucka, huh? Mister ATF."

"Christian." Kirk focused on Tracy's facial expression as best as he could in the dark.

Tracy's head momentarily began to spin. He leaned against the front door then stood alert.

"Remember the story I was telling you earlier about people coming in to your life? You have to watch everybody."

"I don't know if I believe all that, but entertain my uneducated ass anyway."

"Let's just be up front. Your mother was a junkie activist. Don't know how she pulled that one off, but God bless her heart anyway. Your mother was stopping somebody's money from generating the way it had been before she came on the scene. She protested and rallied so much, it forced the police commissioner to put more police on the block so the community kids would be safe. I know you remember. You was there growing up in the middle of it all."

"Are you getting to a point? It's getting a li'l chilly out here."

"Your mother got a big-timer's entire operation shut down and got him put away for two hundred and thirty years. His name was Blue, and at that time he and Christian Elijah were best friends. Partners. So when things had to be handled, Christian did what he had to do for his man. Christian was sent out to kill her for talking. What you think about that?"

Tracy was speechless.

"And what's even more, asshole, all this time you been under the impression he found you by coincidence. All those years you thought you had a friend, he was only trying to see what you knew. He has you thinking he loves you like the son he never had. Everybody calls him your father. Feels good, doesn't it? He made you feel like you still had family. He was playing you the whole time through, Tracy! How does that make you feel?

"You're what an FBI profile would classify as a puppet, but it seems that Christian done cut your strings. Now look at you. You can't even stand by yourself." The agent was using his degree in criminal psychology to mentally break Tracy down.

"Remember what I said about people coming into your life? You don't know every fuckin' body. Remember the thugs at the mall in Jersey?"

"How you know about that?"

"Agents from the FBI. Everybody knows what's going on, Tracy. You do this with me, and you can start life all over again. You won't have to perform no more. You get the chance to just be you all over again."

"Do you have proof Christian really did it?"

"Back at my office. I can show you in the morning when you're activated."

"Activated? Anyway, I won't be here in the morning. I'm heading out for a minute. It's too hot for me up here."

"Don't leave, Tracy. You won't come back."

"One more question. If there's this proof about Christian pulling that trigger, then why is he still walking the streets?"

"Because he gave them something on Blue that led to the arrest of a small Mexican cartel that he was getting his product from. That's how it works, baby. No matter what your crime is, if you can give the government something bigger than what they're presently working on, and it leads to an arrest and conviction, especially when it comes to drugs and guns, they'll buy you a new life. That's what's on the table, my man. You staying for dinner, or you leaving hungry?" Kirk extended his hand.

Tracy stared down at Kirk's hand and laughed. "Get the fuck outta here," he said, slapping his hand away. Then he walked back inside the house.

CHAPTER THIRTY-FOUR

CHRISTIAN

Christian and Assante stood quietly side by side, both staring out of the large-framed window of Christian's twenty-fifth floor penthouse office suite. Early-morning grey skies and dark, threatening clouds gave way to whipping gusts of howling winds and horizontal rainfall. Consistent blue flashes of pure electricity that cut across the sky spawned thunderous explosions that rattled the windows. The powerful and spontaneous storm dimmed the office lights and disrupted the frequency of Hot 97's morning show, not to mention the bitter, contemptuous mood held by both men.

Assante looked down at Christian. "When were you going to tell me of your daughter's involvement with the detective?"

"She has absolutely nothing to do with this," Christian responded, still looking out of the window.

"There is too much at stake. You do not understand, or maybe you do. Do you understand?"

Christian quickly spun his head around. "What the hell is your problem? Why you always so nervous?"

"The problem is, I am beginning to suspect that you can no longer be trusted, Mister Elijah. Why is it that I feel such a way?"

"Well, that's a good muthafuckin' question, and I could ask you the same thing, nigga. See what I'm saying? This is one of those situations where the potentiality of a business relationship is about to be dissolved. You feel what I'm saying? The way you been doing business lately is not what we agreed upon. So, what I'm thinking is, maybe you got an ulterior motive. Maybe you're planning to have someone killed again."

"Mister Elijah, please do not talk to me of an ulterior motive because, then, you would have to think back on when you killed Tracy Kane's mother. I will tell you of ulterior motive. I needed you to make this work, your money, your name, and your insurmountable greed to drown and die in the cold ocean of materialism. I sought you out and knew your profile because you were explained to me. Remember earlier on what I say? I know you, Mister Elijah. Oh yes, I know you very well."

"What? This some kind of setup?" Christian quickly frisked Assante.

"Back away, little man." Assante shoved him back. "Where is Tracy?"

Christian, looking across the room at Assante, ran around to his desk to pull out his gun.

"Come now, Mister Elijah. For that, there is no need. You'd never get the opportunity to tell the story tomorrow, so please sit. I am not armed." Assante lifted his shirt then turned around in place.

"You a damn fool." Christian reached in the drawer anyway, pulled out his thang and cocked it, then sat on the edge of his desk. "Go ahead," he said, the gun resting on his lap. "Talk, nigga."

"So petty." Assante smiled. "This is where we are at right now. Think of dissolving nothing. This is a partnership you are bound to. If you ever tried to leave or sue me, you would lose in court because, then, the real truth would come out. You'd lose everything. You and your daughter would become poverty-stricken victims of Section Two, which, to my understanding, is a very far cry from Section Eight."

"What you mean, the real truth? Stop with all that Tracy shit too. I didn't have shit to do with that."

"I want to know where everyone is. Why does it seem they are all in hiding? Where is your daughter?"

"You better begin walking away now, Assante." Christian aimed his gun at him. "Five seconds."

"It does not matter if it is one second. I do not fear death. I am a warrior, Mister Elijah. Warriors do not beg another man to spare their life. I am at war always and am prepared to face the benefits of becoming a spiritual king. Shoot!" Assante closed his eyes and slowly mouthed a prayer.

"Two."

Assante had committed a no-no, asking for Trinity in a threatening manner. It didn't matter who it was, or the consequences he'd face later on down the line. No one was going to ever get in the way of what he was feeling. No one. He'd die for her, just as she would for him, no matter what issues they were going through.

"One."

Standing erect as possible, Assante slowly opened his eyes. Even Christian had to respect Assante's gangsta. Here he was facing the imminent possibility of getting his head blown off, yet he remained cool, calm, and confident.

"All right." Christian retracted his gun from arm's length. "You don't mention my daughter. I don't want to hear anything about her come out your mouth again, or next time, nigga, I'll shoot your fuckin' face off. You understand that, Assante? Because if you don't, then nigga—" He raised his gun up again. "Now you had something to tell me in the beginning? I'm listening." He rested his gun back on his lap.

CHAPTER THIRTY-FIVE

TRACY KANE

Tracy's plane touched down at Miami International Airport approximately 8:35 the next morning. The only things he had with him were his guilty conscience and the clothes he'd worn the night before.

While sitting on the three-hour flight into Miami from New York's LaGuardia Airport, he had ample time to reminisce on all the disruptiveness he'd brought not only into his life, but the lives of those surrounding him. At one point he'd even pondered the possibility of his flight experiencing engine troubles and plummeting 33,000 feet from the sky and killing the two hundred and something passengers aboard. Then he dismissed the thought.

While Tracy waited on Star's cousin, Cee-Cee, outside the sliding doors of the busy airport, white Town Cars and yellow taxicabs trailed slowly behind one another, horns beeping, their drivers shouting out profanities. And the hellacious Miami heat drew perspiration to the foreheads of tourists in their straw hats and Hawaiian short sets, as they were graciously welcomed into the powerful spotlight of the sun with hugs, kisses, and smiles up and down the airport's front, heavily congested with parking, double-parking, pick-ups, and deliveries.

On the other side of the street a stern-faced man stared dead at Tracy through the crowd of frantic business executives marching to and fro. Tracy locked eyes with the man then casually crossed the lot over toward him after the man acknowledged him.

As Tracy got closer to the gleaming black Maybach, Trick Daddy's bass-propelled platinum hit single "Shut Up!" vibrated throughout his lungs. Some people were astounded by the expensive luxury car, but others turned their heads away, splenetic from the bombardment of hip-hop music.

"Cee-Cee, right?" Tracy asked.

"Welcome to Miami." Cee-Cee bit the tip of his long pinkie nail.

Cee-Cee, born in Brooklyn, New York, was around Tracy's age. Brown-complexioned and 5 foot 7, his hair was naturally curly and had a part that ran straight down the middle of his head. Cee-Cee was into a little bit of everything, but his primary source of income was selling new identities, an operation he'd been running after suddenly leaving Arizona four years ago.

Cee-Cee had moved out of his mother's apartment when he was sixteen. She couldn't afford him anymore, and Section 8 just wasn't cutting it. He'd lived on and off with different friends and family until he turned eighteen. His father was locked up in prison for the rest of his natural life. In a way, Cee-Cee felt as if he was doing the same life sentence, seeing that his father wasn't there to raise him, and often used that as the excuse for crossing over to the bend in the road.

"So you're the incomparable Mister Kane, huh? Mm-hmm." He looked Tracy up and down. "You is just way too fine to be in so much trouble." Cee-Cee slid his Gucci sunglasses over his eyes.

A platinum ring with black diamonds set in it glistened on Cee-Cee's middle finger as he lifted his hand to catch a spontaneous sneeze. "Pardon me," he said, pulling a hand sanitizer packet from inside his car door. "Before we go anywhere, you're gonna tell me what you about. I can't be having no trouble down here with you."

"Yo, man, I ain't about shit. I just wanna kick back and chill until things cool off back home. That's it. Case closed."

"Ooh. You a li'l fiery muthafucka, huh." Cee-Cee smiled, fanning himself with his hand. "I like that. I'm sure they done told you about my preference. Don't worry about it though. It don't mean anything. I'm not after you. I don't want you, and you don't want anything to do with fuckin' me over. You're down here as a favor to my family. With all that being said, hop on in on the other side and let's ride." Cee-Cee closed the door as he stepped into the driver's seat.

"So how you wind up getting yourself in so much trouble up there in New York?" Cee-Cee stuck his mirror back at the cars beeping behind him.

"Stupid muthafuckas," he said, sitting forward and driving out the airport exit.

Tracy's phone rang just as Cee-Cee headed toward downtown Miami. "Yo," he said, looking at Cee-Cee. He pointed toward the radio, so Cee-Cee could turn it down. "Yo," he repeated.

"Yo. It's me. Shane. You make it there all right?" he asked through the storm of static interference.

"I'm here. What's good?"

"You with son now?"

"Yeah. Why?"

"Yo, he cool and everything, but watch him."

"What I'm supposed to be watching?"

"Just be safe, and I'm sorry it had to happen this way."

"Tell me what else I need to know."

"You just better think real hard on what Sol—I mean Agent Kirk—said. You not the only one caught up in this. You know it'd be a lot easier on Assante and Christian if you were just dead. I'ma do my part up here and make sure I hold Christian off as long as possible, but you do need to get up with Assante."

CHAPTER THIRTY-SIX

CHRISTIAN

It'd been two days since Tracy's departure, and things had been quiet, and just a little too tight for Christian, who stood on Shane's front porch at six in the morning. "So, Shane, what's good, baby? Why don't you come and take a ride with me? I want to talk about your contract, you know, shit like that."

Cadillac, sitting in the passenger seat of Christian's car, yawned then nodded his head at Shane.

"It's like six in the morning, Christian. Why you here?"

Christian gave a slight chuckle then walked up a step closer to Shane. "What the fuck you think I'm here for? Don't play stupid with me. Not today, man. How you think I wouldn't find out you took Tracy out the hospital, huh? You tryin'-a play me? This shit ain't got nothing to do with you, but you must want it to be, huh? You want something to do with this?" he asked, gritting his teeth. "Where the fuck is he at?"

"I don't know what you're talking about, Christian. I haven't spoken to Tracy since that last time he was here and I was beefing about not rolling out with him. So, I don't know where you getting all of this I-took-him-from-the-hospital jazz."

Christian sniffled the mucus in his runny nose. "You know what, Shane, when none of y'all niggas was shit, what I did? I turned around and made you shit. I gave you shit. I gave you a life, nigga. If it wasn't for me, y-y-you wouldn't have half the shit you have now. And this is how you repay me? By letting some bitch-ass nigga tear down what we all built together? You ain't the same Shane I used to know." Christian shook his head.

"But you still the same Christian."

"And what's that supposed to mean?"

"Fuck you, Christian! Fuck your contract! Fuck everything you do! What? You think I'm scared of you or something? I know you know people that can get shit done to anybody. So what? I'm not under pressure, dukes. You know what I'm saying? Get the fuck off my porch, man. You cut." Shane sliced his hand across his throat.

Christian began laughing as he took a step down. He pointed his finger up at Shane. "You don't know nothing about being a gangster. I'll be back here in about three hours. If you don't know where Tracy's at, you better find out. Don't fuck with me, Shane. Go 'head on inside. Your wife peeking through the curtains like she nervous." Christian waved at Star through the bay window.

"So, what happens next?" Cadillac asked Christian as they drove away from Shane's house.

"We got loose ends to tie up here right now. We got to pay Solasse a visit. I ain't seen or heard from him ever since Tracy disappeared. I don't like that. He might know something. Assante wants him dead. He's a paranoid freak. He doesn't want Solasse to be down no more."

"Just tell me something, man," Cadillac said, looking at

him. "I'm here with you and everything, but just answer me this. None of this shit really affect you? Like niggas is your peoples and—"

"Ain't no *and*. I'm already working with some real corrupt niggas. I don't need corrupt niggas working for me. That's why Marcel got fired. Tracy's definitely fired, and if Shane doesn't come up with some answers real quick, he'll be fired too. Shit." Christian pulled over to the far left lane of flowing traffic on the parkway. "You ready to hand in your letter of resignation or something?"

"Naw, man."

"My man." Christian patted Cadillac's leg. "When the money really start piling up, you'll be glad we did what we did to get it."

It was still early in the morning when Christian and Cadillac showed up at Solasse's house unexpectedly.

"All we want to see for right now is if he knows where Tracy is. Go on up there and knock on his door. I need to make a private call." Christian flipped his phone open.

Cadillac got out of the car. "What I'm supposed to say, dawg? You want me to just grab him up and drag him over here?"

"Stop being crazy, nigga. Just go knock."

Christian turned his attention to his outgoing call. Since last they'd spoken, he'd been trying Trinity's phone at least six times a day. He felt secure in the fact that he knew she was safe at the vacation house, but he just wanted to hear her voice. The only reason he hadn't gone down to Miami after her was because he didn't know who was watching.

It was no longer a secret to anyone that Trinity was wanted for questioning in connection with Kaneecha's murder. The call she'd made from her cell phone that night was traced back to her Sprint account by Detective

Dennis Frogger, who came up with a name, address, and an accusation from a neighbor placing her at the scene. If she came back up, Christian knew Assante would have her killed, thinking she'd talk and mess everything up, so it was better she stayed where she was at.

"Trinity," Christian calmly said to her voicemail after the seventh ring, "you need to call me. It's serious. The police want to question you about that night at Kaneecha's. You called the police, Trinity. What were you thinking?" He cut the call off as Cadillac began his stroll back toward the car.

"Nobody answering?" Christian looked at the front door through the passenger window. He got out of the car and started walking toward the front door.

"What you doing, man? Nobody home. No cars is here anyway, yo."

"No cars got to be here. You see that window up there on the side of the house?" Christian pointed up at the second-floor window.

"Yeah. What about it?"

"The steam, nigga. See how that's the only fogged-up window in the house?"

"So?"

"Somebody just got out the shower recently. Somebody in there." Christian jogged up the steps then banged on the door. "Solasse!" he shouted, banging on the door even harder.

Cadillac looked around as the neighborhood dogs barked in unison. "That's too much noise."

"Shut up," Christian responded after hearing the door unlock.

Marisol, AKA Special Agent Sanchez, slowly opened the door in a pair of sweatpants and a T-shirt. Guarded by a secondary glass-plated door with a lock, she looked at the two men.

"Sorry to bother you so early, Marisol. It's Marisol, right?" Christian asked, standing as close to the glass door as possible. "I'm looking for your husband."

"He's not in at the moment. He should be home from work sometime this afternoon."

"Is that so?"

"It is. I'll be sure to let him know you stopped by."

"You do that. Tell him it's very, very imperative that he gets back to me."

Marisol stared at an edgy Cadillac. "What's this all about?"

"This all started with you, you know," Christian said, ignoring her question.

"That whole thing with Marcel, you mean. Well, it's his fault for talking, but you got it circulating. So that sort of makes you responsible."

A red Ford Explorer pulled up to the curb and stopped right behind Christian's car, and Agent Kirk, AKA Solasse, exited the vehicle.

"Gentlemen," Solasse said, activating the alarm on his truck and walking toward them. He looked at Marisol. "Go on and close the door, hon."

Marisol, fearful for her partner's safety, hesitated before obliging.

Solasse looked at his watch. "Now, gentlemen, how can I be of service?"

"Yo, you seen Tracy, man?" Cadillac asked impatiently.

"Why would I have seen Tracy? Only time I was ever with him is when I was with you."

"Here's where the problem comes into play, Solasse," Christian told him. "You'd be the last guy anybody would have expected Tracy to run to. You know why? Because nobody liked him anymore, and he never liked you, so—"

"So that means I know where he's at? I don't like being all involved in this, Christian, not if it's going to be all about Tracy. Don't put that on me. I have nothing to do with him."

"Why your wife was acting so nervous?"

"Well, Christian, it's six-thirty in the morning. I think she's warranted in feeling nervous."

Christian looked directly into Solasse's eyes. "You didn't hear anything from him?"

"No. I'm here to do whatever you want me to do. That doesn't include withholding detrimental information from you."

"I don't need to hear all that. You ain't seen him, right?"

"No."

"Then that's it. Let's go, Cadillac." Christian started walking away then stopped and turned around. "If I have to come back, you and girlfriend in there is dead. I better not find our you're lying!"

CHAPTER THIRTY-SEVEN

CHRISTIAN

Assante, Akinsanya, Christian, and Cadillac were having drinks inside Illicit Behavior, a Soho club.

Assante said, "Everyone who was with us from the beginning must be there for the conclusion. It is just as simple as that."

The four gentlemen sat at a cube-shaped crystal table behind a two-thousand-dollar bottle of chilled champagne. Red lights dully shined throughout the entire loft, and "screw music" slowly drove its powerful yet dreary body-banging bass through the *E* pill–induced individuals constructing a rave on the dance floor.

"My friends," Assante continued, "things have not gone in the direction I plan. There has been dishonor, trickery, and lies. It is not what I thought would occur. So with that, it is over between us all." He stood up. "We pick up the last shipment and we part ways. We all have things on each other. What I also want is Tracy here the night of. Someone track him. If he blows this, each and every one of you and your families are accountable. That goes for

Shane and his wife also. You let him know that he is in this too. If he does not appear, then I will assume he has been a traitor, and he will be dead."

Christian was angered by the disrespect. "See, this was a good idea for you to pick a public setting. Am I hearing you right?" he said, cupping his ear. "It's over? You don't get to say it's over until I say it's over. We got a contract."

"A simple thing to be vanquished. Do you not understand that, Mister Elijah? It is for the best in each of our interests to be separated. There will be more than enough money in the upcoming package."

"And when this package supposed to come, man?" Cadillac looked at Christian. "I'm getting tired of all this, man."

"Yeah, Assante," Christian said, "when's it coming?"

"Pardon me, please." Akinsanya pulled his phone from his pocket and stuck the finger of his free hand into his ear to block out the loud voices and music. He walked through the crowd and under a sign that read MEN'S LAB, its letters brightly emphasized by electric blue lights shining behind them.

"I will let you know when. It will all be over soon. Get Tracy from wherever he is at. If one of us falls, we will all fall together. Not just some of us while the rest hide under a rock. I do not care as of right now what beefs you or I have with him. He must be there. Your daughter also." Assante mentioned Christian's daughter, in spite of what Christian had told him earlier.

Christian shot up from his seat. "Now I done—"

"It is either one way or the other," Assante calmly said. "Bring them all out."

Akinsanya returned with a cold stare in his eyes as he leaned down to whisper something into Assante's ear.

Assante began slowly mouthing something in his native tongue, staring at Christian and Cadillac.

"What, man?" Cadillac said.

Assante said, "Mister Elijah, it seems we have a serious problem."

"Oh yeah? Like what?"

"The man, Tracy's friend. His name is not Solasse Barak. It is Agent Kirk Michael."

"What you mean *agent*? I thought you checked him out. Aw, fuck, man. This shit here is on you." Christian banged on the table. "What is he? FBI?"

"I'm afraid he is ATF. His wife also. She is Special Agent Sanchez."

"We going to that muthafucka's house right now." Christian pushed back his chair so he could stand up. "Let's go, Assante. This is your mess to clean. We are going to pop that nigga in the head, and that will be that. We take them both out for a little ride and end it. I'm tired of this shit." He walked toward the open mouth of the loft's elevator. "Let's go!" he yelled out to the three men.

Instead of having Assante's driver take them to Solasse's house to have a talk, Christian went over to Shane's house first. The high-beam floodlight attached to Shane's garage came on as they pulled up in the driveway.

"Yo, tell me if I'm seeing things. Isn't that Solasse's car parked out front there?" Christian pointed at the vehicle parked in front of the house.

"Yeah, that's that muthafucka's car," Cadillac said.

"Do you think that he knows?" Assante asked.

"We going to run up in that bitch and get to the bottom of everything. Come on," Christian said, walking up to Shane's front door, his gun exposed.

Shane opened the door before turning on the porch light and was hit in the head by the nose of Christian's gun.

"Shut up!" Christian said closely in his ear. "Where's he

at?" He grabbed Shane tightly by the collar of his shirt and aimed the gun at his head. "Come on, man, where's he at?" He pushed him toward the only room with a light on in the darkened house.

The other three men quickly rushed in together, their guns drawn. Christian pushed Shane to the entrance of what appeared to be a den, and all four men stepped forward as Shane stood with his hands up.

Star quickly stepped forward. "What's wrong, baby?"

"I'm what's wrong," Christian said, his gun pointed at Shane's head. "What's up, Solasse? Marisol. Don't even try it," he warned Solasse, who made a slight gesture for his weapon. "Both of y'all, toss those things over here. Take the clip out first. Real slow," he said to them. "Real nice and easy. That's right. Now toss those over here first and empty that extra one out the chamber."

"You don't know what you're getting yourself into, Christian," Agent Kirk said.

"No. *You* don't know what you done got yourself into. Send both them bitches over here. Shane, you get your ass over there," he said, mushing his head.

Shane stumbled over to Agent Kirk but managed to maintain his balance and avoid falling.

"Now, I don't give a fuck which one of y'all it is, but one of you is going to tell me where Tracy's at, or I'm killing both these bitches right now. Three seconds." Christian aimed his gun at Star.

Assante pointed his in Special Agent Sanchez's face.

"You can't kill government officials, Christian," Special Agent Sanchez said. "You'd never get away with it."

"Two," Christian said, almost wishing they'd accept his challenge.

Experiencing more than a slight anxiety attack, Shane yelled out, "NO!" throwing his hands up in the air. "Just chill out. I'll tell you what you want to know."

"No, Shane, you'll blow everything," Special Agent Sanchez said.

"One." Christian, his finger wrapped around the trigger, flashed the gun in Special Agent Sanchez's face.

Shane then blurted out what Christian and Assante had been waiting to hear. "He's in downtown Miami staying with Star's family until shit cool down. The dude he staying with, his name is Cee-Cee."

"Oh. Y'all all in on this?" Christian chuckled. He asked Shane, "You've been working with these people? Now everybody's trying to hide Tracy?"

"They cannot live." Assante looked at the two agents. "If they are allowed to leave, you will forever spend your life in prison. Myself? I shall go back home and cope."

Cadillac gripped the handle of his gun tightly. "This some leery shit, Chris."

"He's in downtown Miami?" Christian automatically thought of Trinity. "You call whoever it is you got to call. I want to speak with that muthafucka."

"Speak to who?" Shane asked.

"Cee-Cee. You call him and let him know there is a proposition on the table for him."

"What proposition is that, Mister Elijah?" Assante asked.

"The one where Tracy doesn't make it back to New York."

CHAPTER THIRTY-EIGHT

TRACY

"Hello?" Cee-Cee said, answering the phone inside his luxurious downtown Miami apartment overlooking the beach. "What's up, Star?" He leaned over a black granite countertop. "Why you sounding all funny? What's wrong?" he asked his nervous-sounding cousin.

Tracy was sitting on a black leather lounge chair in Cee-Cee's living room. He didn't feel safe at all. He was 1288 miles away from New York and still felt as if this was to be his final destination. Between Christian and Assante's connections with out-of-state goons on standby, he knew it wouldn't be long before word got back up top where he was bottomed out at. It was a good thing Cee-Cee had some "willie" in the house because Tracy needed it more than ever before.

"Oh yeah?" Cee-Cee puffed on a Black & Mild, looking at the back of Tracy's head. "That's what he's talking? I think I can make that happen. Just tap my jack when you ready for me to make that happen, hon."

Just as Cee-Cee hung up the phone, another call came in. He activated the speakerphone. "Yeah?"

"What's up, boy?" Cee-Cee's father asked. "How things going?"

"It ain't time yet. Why you calling me?"

Ever since Cee-Cee's father got his hands on a cell phone while serving his lifetime sentence at Morton State Prison, he'd been calling just a little bit more than usual.

"Look here, prison or no prison, I'm still your father, so get your mind right and listen. I know I ain't been there for you the way I should've when you was coming up, but that's over now. I fucked up leaving somebody else in charge to hold y'all down. We all suffered for a minute, but you not suffering now, so all this disrespect and whatnot every time I call needs to stop. Get over the shit, Cedric."

"What you want, man? I'm in a rush. I got some real important shit to take care of."

"I'ma get to that. Look, boy, shit happening in the street don't take long to circulate in here. You know that. It's high-profile shit."

"I'm lost. What are you talking about?" Cee-Cee shook his head from side to side slowly, still keeping his eyes directly focused on an oblivious Tracy.

"Why you playing with me, boy? Huh? Don't I treat you good? You know if it wasn't for my name and my juice, the streets would drink you. You're a faggot, and you gets no respect unless I say so. You get that bitch Tracy to get in touch with Christian." And he hung up the phone.

CHAPTER THIRTY-NINE

TRACY KANE

After shopping for new clothes and getting a fresh haircut, Tracy began to feel like his old self again.

Fully clothed, he walked out of the bathroom and up the hallway when he was done showering. "Yo, Cee," he said, going into the kitchen. "Yo." He went back down the hallway. He walked back up the hallway into the living room with its glossy white painted walls. He opened the single sliding glass door of the balcony and stuck his head outside to see if Cee-Cee was out there and saw no one.

The loud ringing phone hanging on the wall in the kitchen made him quickly jerk his head around. The voice mail picked up after the fourth ring.

"*Ay, look, boy, I want you to call me back soon as you get this. I told that bitch Christian I'd catch up with his ass one day.*"

Tracy had no clue that it was Cee-Cee's father who'd just left a message. He stood silently before speaking out loud to himself. "What?" He walked over to the machine and played the message again. He fast-forwarded to the focal point of the threat then pushed play.

Beeeep. "I told that bitch Christian I'd catch up with him one day."

Beeeep. "I told that bitch Christian I'd catch up with him one day."

Beeeep.

Tracy stopped the machine then immediately began heading toward the front door. Just as he opened it, Cee-Cee and two big bouncer-sized men wearing sweat pants and tight T-shirts were standing at the entrance.

"Do these gentlemen got to grab you up, or you gonna come quietly?" Cee-Cee pulled his door closed and locked it. "You a stupid muthafucka. I would have never gone anywhere to hide out with some nigga I don't know. Now you got some prices on your head." He gave him a little shove in between the hulking hoods.

"Are you going to at least let me know what's going on?" Tracy said as he was forcibly pressured into entering Club Blue, a gentlemen's sports bar.

They walked down a dim, red-lit aisle in between two purple velvet ropes that divided the left and right sides of the lobby. The walls were draped with velvet purple curtains and golden tassels that sprouted at their ends.

Thumping music escaped through the soundproof door ahead, where another massive-framed bouncer looked down at Tracy then to Cee-Cee before opening it.

"Keep an eye on this fool until we get back," Cee-Cee said, bumping his hip against Tracy's. "Don't let him out of your sight. He's worth something."

All Tracy could think of as he ran back down the long aisle back toward the way he entered was, how long would it take for him to storm right through it?

"Shoot his ass," one of the bouncers yelled as the other ran in pursuit of Tracy.

A gunshot whizzed by Cee-Cee's ear and shattered the glass door of the lobby as Tracy jumped through what was left of it.

"Not in here," Cee-Cee shouted.

With glass on his face, Tracy took a right turn up the crowded, brightly lit Miami street. He didn't know where he was running to; he just ran, dipping and dodging between people. Even after he no longer heard the stomping feet of the bouncers chasing him down, he continued running.

Suddenly he stopped and attempted to cross the street with its steady-moving cars. He stood patiently then took off, but tripped in the middle of the street into the path of an oncoming car. Tires screeching, the car swerved to avoid running Tracy over, who rolled over in the opposite direction.

As pedestrians and cars immediately stopped their flow to observe the near-fatal accident, Tracy quickly rose to his feet and looked over toward the open passenger window at one ticked-off female driver. He then stared back down the street to see if he was still being followed.

The woman got out of her car. "Are you out of your freaking mind or something?"

"I'm sorry," Tracy said, panting heavily, taking a second to make out the familiar face in the light.

"Oh my God!" Trinity screamed in shock. "Tracy?"

"Please," he said to her, "please, let's go, ma. We gotta go now." And he limped over to the passenger side of her rent-a-car.

CHAPTER FORTY

CHRISTIAN

Agent Kirk Michael asked, "So this is what it's going to come down to, Christian?"

Agent Kirk Michael, Sanchez, Shane, Star, and even her mother were all stripped completely naked in the basement of Star's mother's house. Each sat tied to chairs, their hands behind their backs, their ankles tied to the chair legs.

Agent Kirk Michael looked Assante's way. "You'll never get away with it, Assante. You're a done deal sooner or later. Why don't you tell Christian all about how there's not going to be no racial war? What kind of idiot believes that?" Then he said to Christian, "Assante been playing you for a fool since day one."

Akinsanya quickly walked over to Kirk and kicked him in the chest, and Kirk fell backward and hit his head on the cement floor with a loud thud. When Star's mother screamed out, Assante slapped her into submissive quietness.

Star tried to protest the excessive brutal force imposed upon her mother, but Christian gagged her with duct tape.

"Yeah. You're going to get the chair when they catch you. *Pato!*" Sanchez spat phlegm on Christian.

"You'll never find out about it. I can guarantee you that." Christian stroked his hand through her hair. "What you got? Some Jennifer Lopez in you? You was all up in the spotlight that night with Marcel, like you was down."

"You're going to kill me for doing my job?" Special Agent Sanchez asked. "Think, Christian."

Christian told her, "This is the role you wanted to play, so don't be trying to psych me out with all your little governmental, reverse psychological bullshit, because it ain't going to work. You are going to die."

"Christian, man," Shane pleaded, "yo, why you doing this, man? Nobody did nothing to you."

"Shut up. All of y'all been running behind my back being fake. Tracy's time is limited. Yours is about to be too, right now, nigga. You understand? In my day, you'd have been dead long ago." Christian turned his attention to the floor, where a half-conscious Agent Michael painfully lifted his head and moaned. "Oh, you awake again?" He frowned—"Nigga, go back to sleep."—and stomped his face. Hard!

"They cannot all die," Assante said. "Two must be there with us. After such, there is no need to spare lives any longer."

"Why can't they? We don't need any witnesses. All them people you got on the payroll, we don't need them." Christian nodded over to the petrified group bound to their chairs.

"This is your situation," Assante told him. "You pick who is to go and who is to stay." He started pulling on a pair of black leather gloves.

Shane said, "Come on, Christian, the women don't got nothing to do with this."

Christian pointed to Star's petite mother. "Her first."

Star's mother's tears increased in flow as Assante approached her. Assante carefully wrapped his large hands around her frail neck and slowly pressed his thumbs down on her larynx.

"What you getting ready to do?" Shane asked.

Star tried to free herself from her bondage then looked over to Shane, but he was just as helpless. She bounced up and down in her chair, bruising her wrists trying to escape.

As Assante squeezed the life out of his mother-in-law, Shane cried, "I can't do nothing, baby. I can't do nothing." He looked into Star's eyes. "There ain't nothing I can do."

Star's mother struggled as Assante began to apply maximum pressure, gagging as her air supply was cut off.

"Shhh, momma," Assante quietly whispered, releasing one hand to stroke her long hair. "Come, momma. Stop it. Don't fight. It is almost over."

Hot, smelly piss began traveling down her legs, forming a puddle at her feet.

Assante then applied one last great heave of pressure, and her head tilted off to her left shoulder then rolled onto her chest. "And that is that." He bent down to kiss her forehead. "Do not fear," he said, standing erect. "Allah will soon welcome her."

Star hysterically bawled out of control.

Special Agent Sanchez yelled at Assante, "*Cabrón.*"

"Sha-tup, woman!" Akinsanya walked over to her and slapped her face.

"Christian, man," Shane said through his tears, "what the hell you doing this for? This is my family."

"You turned on me, so that's that. No more talking, just reactions from now on."

Christian, while looking down at Agent Michael, said to the brothers, "Wake his ass up!" Then he added, "Give me your knife, Akinsanya."

Christian walked behind Shane, and as he cut the tape off his wrists and ankles, Akinsanya aimed his gun at Shane, just in case he attempted to play hero.

"Put your clothes on," Christian said to Shane, flipping him forward out of his chair.

Shane quickly turned to Star and thrust his arms around her, kissing all over her face, but Akinsanya suddenly pulled him back by the neck.

Christian walked around from the back of the fallen chair, staring at a semi-conscious Agent Michael, standing wearily in point-blank range of Assante's black-and-silver Ruger handgun.

"Put your clothes on," Christian calmly said to Shane's face. "Last time I'm telling you."

"Christian." Shane fell to his knees. "My wife, man," he said, extending his arm out to her. "She's my life. I can't live without her. Come on, man." He slapped the hard, cold floor.

"Stop being a bitch." Christian quickly spun around and shot Star in the head. Her head jerked back, and her body hit the floor, blood pouring from her eyes and ears.

"Oh shit!" Shane jumped to his feet then dropped back to his knees.

Christian's hand-held persuasion was now pointed at Shane's head.

"You're not going to get away with this!" Special Agent Sanchez hollered out.

"Awwww, nooooo," Shane cried in a high pitch, like someone was crushing his testicles. "Nooooo." And he fell face first to the floor.

"Now I done told your ass to get dressed."

Special Agent Sanchez stared at Christian. "I hope you burn in hell."

"You know what?" Christian rushed over to her. "You talk way too fuckin' much." He forced her mouth open with the nose of his gun and tried shoving it down her throat, causing her to gag. "You gonna shut the fuck up?" He jammed the gun farther into her mouth then grabbed a handful of her long hair with his free hand. "You gonna shut the fuck up?" he asked her again, forcibly bobbing her head up and down. "That's a good girl." He slowly removed the gun from her mouth. "All right, everybody, let's roll out." He said to Shane, "Grab your clothes, bitch."

Walking closely behind a nude Shane, Assante asked of Special Agent Sanchez, "What about her?"

"Take care of her, Akinsanya," Christian said, steering Agent Kirk Michael forward, his hands raised to the sky.

As the four men walked up the stairs, leaving Akinsanya behind to handle her, Special Agent Sanchez pleaded, "Wait a minute. You can't do this."

Akinsanya put on his black leather gloves and slowly took two steps toward Special Agent Sanchez. With no warning at all, he punched her directly in the forehead with his right hand. Her eyes rolled to the top of her head, and her face fell forward.

"Awaken," he said, lifting her chin up with his foot and drawing his gun on her. "I want for you to see this."

Nervous as the doomed agent was, she refused to provide him with the fearful outcry he was waiting to hear. Instead, she slowly lifted her head and gave him a hateful glare. "Do it," she said and closed her eyes.

"*Beetch*!" Akinsanya said, spitting on her and shooting her in the head at point-blank range. "And that is that, agent." He wiped her blood from the side of her face with his hand then licked it from between his fingers.

Akinsanya knelt down beside her dead body and kissed

on what was left of her lips. He stood up, lifted her, and carried her bloodied body to a nearby couch. Then he removed the cushions and laid them over her, and smashed all of the overhead basement lights before jogging up the steps.

CHAPTER FORTY-ONE

TRACY

Tracy slept uncomfortably, tossing and turning on the couch in the living room of Christian's Miami home. His head unconsciously shifted from left to right, and he uttered near inaudible whispers of distress.

"Tracy!" shouted a voice without a face.

Tracy ran up a narrow, darkened alley leading to nowhere, his heart two seconds away from exploding out of his chest. Loud, sporadic gunfire bullied the silence.

"Tracy!" the voice yelled again off in the distance behind him. "I know you hear me, muthafucka!"

Tracy looked back while running but never saw a face.

Suddenly two pairs of footsteps chasing him turned into four, then six. Before he knew it, the entire alley was filled with killers pursuing him. Then a light ahead of him came on.

He looked back one more time, but the men had disap-

peared just as suddenly as they'd appeared. He sighed in relief and turned to walk into the light. He took one step and was immediately greeted by a face he could see.

"What's up, big mouth?" Christian aimed his gun straight at Tracy's head then pulled the trigger. BLAM!

"Ahhhh!" Tracy yelled out, almost falling off the couch. He quickly looked around, inhaling and exhaling heavily.

It was all a dream, but it had felt so real. He sat up on the couch and felt for the reminder that Christian had left on the side of his head.

Trinity walked up the hallway. "Tracy, are you all right? I thought I heard you yell out."

"Come here, Trinity," he said, standing off his painful injured leg. "You saved my life." He embraced her when she approached him.

"What are you doing down here?" she asked after he released her.

Tracy pointed to his scar. "Your father tried to kill me."

"He did this to you?" she asked, feeling on it. "What did you do, Tracy? Why would he do this?" She sat on the couch.

"I told him that I told you everything, and he flipped. Now the police are looking for Kaneecha's killers and Marcel. Why'd you say anything to Christian about what I told you, Trinity? I confided in you."

"I was only trying to help my father. That's all."

"Shit is worse now. I can't go back to New York anytime soon."

"You know you can't stay here for long. I know Daddy. He'll be down here to make me come back home with him. I've been away for almost a month now, so when he does come, he's not going to let me know he's coming."

"I need to get in touch with Shane. He gets me to come

down here and lay low with some faggot-ass cousin of Star's, and the dude tried to kill me. Then, while I'm over at his condo, some dude left a voicemail talking about your father. Don't know who it was, but he sounded pissed."

"Anybody else know you're here?"

"I hope not."

"I don't even want to think of this anymore right now. I'm just happy you're alive."

"I hope you didn't stop loving me."

"I never once even stopped thinking about you, Tracy." Trinity kissed his lips. "Not once."

Tracy and Trinity's knees sank deep inside the soft mattress of her king-sized bed. They kissed naked under the influence of genuine love and romantic music. Wet, lip-smacking kisses and back-rubbing affection gave way to a missionary position of mutuality. They both stared into one another's eyes while Tracy slowly moved in between her legs then quickly slid down to her navel, circling his tongue inside of it and lightly nibbling around it.

Still looking into her eyes, he ventured farther down and watched her eyelids slowly flutter after placing his lips on her Georgia peach. Her knees were bent upright, but soon fell apart and widened.

Tracy licked all around the edges of her wings then took hold of her transmitter in between his top lip and tongue. She moistened as he pulled her down by the hips deep into his mouth. He sucked on it like a miniature pacifier, and she wailed like a helpless baby, flapping her arms, and opening and closing her knees around his head.

Tracy dropped his head a bit and stuck his tongue up into her hot, willing asshole.

Trinity slid her body up and down on the bed, moaning loudly. Her toes curled and cracked under the sexual pressure. She pulled at the wrinkled sheets, and the elastic slung from the top two corners of the mattress. Her love began shooting out love signals all over the bed. She screamed, sighed, cursed, and split her ass apart with both hands.

Tracy slowly inserted his hardness inside of her tight, thoroughly juice-filled pitcher of love, and her satisfied walls of satin immediately collapsed around his head then gripped him with a firm, silky softness, popping each time he pulled out.

"Tracy, Tracy," she yelled out, digging her nails into his ass, while having her back twisted out on cum-soaked sheets.

Perspiration poured down Tracy's body and dripped onto Trinity's as he began swirling around the walls of her cherry-scented inner flesh.

She followed in sync with his rough rotational movements, creaming, and the hot butter of her churn ran down her thick thighs. She cried, "I love you, baby," her multiple orgasms saturating Tracy's entire body with her storm.

"Thank you for saving my life." Tracy wrapped his mouth around hers.

Trinity sat up and reached around his neck while he remained in position. She put one leg around his back then the other. She lifted herself under his chest with him still inside of her and began slowly swinging herself on and off his dick.

"Oh damn, Trini. Damn, ma." Tracy closed his eyes, sucking in spit. "Did you hear me?" he asked, a strained look on his face.

"I heard you, crazy," she responded, getting wetter by the second.

Tracy sat in the middle of the bed and pulled her on top of him. "You know I love you, right?"

"I love you too," she said, snaking her body.

"This right here is something I will never forget, and if I ever get out of all this shit alive, I want you to be my wife. I don't got nobody else."

"It's going to be all right, Tracy." Trinity grabbed on to his shoulders, hugging him and patting his back. "You know what I'm saying? It's going to be good, boo. You'll see. Trust me." Then she leaned her head on his shoulder.

CHAPTER FORTY-TWO

DETECTIVE FROGGER

"There was no sign of forced entry," Detective Frogger said to his captain as he sat before him at his desk. "But we have fingerprints and the name of the caller who reported the call that night."

"And? Who was it?"

"You're not going to believe this—Trinity Elijah, of Cherrywood, New Jersey."

"Elijah," the captain said, repeatedly snapping his fingers.

"That's right, Trinity Elijah. Christian Elijah's daughter."

"What the hell was she doing there?"

"I don't know, Captain, but there's more to this than just Tracy Kane."

"What are you still doing here then, Detective? Bring her in. Bring Christian in. Bring Tracy in. Bring in that whole crew."

Detective Frogger was about to exit his captain's office when the phone on his desk rang.

"Captain Ronald," the captain answered, annoyed with

the whole situation. The more he kept the phone to his ear, the more his thick eyebrows lowered and thin lips tightened.

"What's wrong?" Detective Frogger asked.

"This is not good." Captain Ronald covered the receiver of the phone. "Yes, sir. Yes, sir," he said slowly as he put down the phone.

"What happened? What's wrong?" the detective asked, his hand on the knob of the office door.

"I'll explain to you on the way." The captain secured his gun in its holster. "Let's go."

Detective Frogger and Captain Ronald stayed concealed within the shadows of the overhead tree branches as they stepped across the front lawn of Star's mother's home. A squadron of backup officers stayed at the edge of the lawn, while others secured the perimeter of the house.

The detective took the lead before reaching the front door then quickly turned around. He and Captain Ronald both stood on either side of the front door and stared at one another, their backs against the house.

Frogger quietly pulled the screen door open then signaled to the first officer, leading six others behind him. He counted down from three on his fingers then quickly kicked the front door in. He and the captain rushed inside the dark house and took to the nearest wall opposite each other.

The seven officers ran in behind them and were met in the middle of the living room by five officers who'd simultaneously barged through the back door. Captain Ronald led some of the officers toward the second level of the house.

Detective Frogger took off toward a door that appeared to lead to the basement. He slowly pulled it open and felt on the wall for a switch. He flicked it on and off to no avail. Sending two officers down into the dungeon first, Detective Frogger followed, four officers in the back of him.

High-powered beams from the flashlights held by the officers downstairs in the basement battled for superiority, each searching for anything that might provide them with a clue.

"Hold up." Detective Frogger snatched a flashlight from one of the officers. "You," he shouted to an officer near him carrying a flashlight, "shine that over here."

The light first presented itself upon the dead body of Star, while another beam of light focused on her mother.

"Detective," an officer frantically said, "this one here is still breathing." He felt on the side of her neck for a pulse. Star's mother, her breathing ever so shallow, was still alive. Barely.

"Captain," the detective called through his radio, "you better get down here. "Call for an ambulance. NOW!" He lifted Star's mother's head. "Ma'am, can you hear me? Who did this? Who did this to you?"

"Detective, look over here," another officer said. His beam of light focused on a pair of bare feet sticking out from under the cushions of a nearby couch. The officer cautiously walked over to the couch and lifted the cushion, his other hand locked around the handle of his gun. It was Special Agent Sanchez. The young rookie officer turned around and vomited all over his shoes.

"Get outta the way." Detective Frogger rushed over to the murder victim. "Somebody flash a light over here. I can hardly see shit. Too many bodies." The detective checked Special Agent Sanchez's neck for a pulse.

EMT workers' radios beeped and crossed frequencies as they rushed past the officers upstairs.

Captain Ronald walked down the steps and stopped in

front of Star's body. Her mother sat on a couch nearby in a catatonic state, slowly rocking back and forth, staring at her murdered daughter.

"Christian," Star's mother whispered.

Detective Frogger spun around. "What'd she just say?"

One of the EMT workers taking her blood pressure said, "She's delusional, sir."

"No. What'd she just say?" Frogger walked over to her. "You know who did this to you? You know who did this to your daughter? Come on, do you know who did this?" He pointed at Star, who was being zipped into a black body bag.

"Christian," she whispered again.

"Who?" He yelled, moving closer to her again.

She screamed out, "Christian!" as loud as her weak body allowed.

"Okay, you did good. These men are going to take care of you now," he said of the EMT workers. "We're going to bring him to justice, ma'am. Don't you worry. He's going to pay for all of this."

The tires of Detective Frogger's car tore into the well-maintained front lawn of Christian Elijah's home, Captain Ronald riding shotgun. The red light spinning on the dashboard was left on as both men quickly jumped out of the car and ran straight toward the front door.

Detective cars and squad cars barricaded both corners of Christian's street, others obstructed the exit to the driveway. Soon after, the rotors of low-flying police helicopters circling rumbled, shaking the foundations of all the houses and bringing out the neighbors in their robes and pajamas to complain about the early-morning disturbance.

After thoroughly scouring Christian's house the officers concluded that Christian and his daughter were not inside, and confiscated files, clothing, computers, and two luxury cars parked in the garage.

Detective Frogger stood on the porch, his hands on his waist. He said to Captain Ronald, "This fuckin' guy is going down. You hear that? You son of a bitch!" he shouted, looking around. "I got your number muthafucka! You"— He pulled an officer off to the side—"I want reports on all outgoing and incoming flights, arrival and departure of train and bus schedules, and also any recent car rental service transactions." He lit a cigarette before reaching for his ringing cell phone.

"Yeah, Frogger here. What do you mean, you can't find him?" He covered the mouthpiece of his phone and told Captain Ronald, "Tracy's nowhere to be found. Okay. Captain, I want some officers to stay here, just in case Christian catches wind that his house has been raided."

CHAPTER FORTY-THREE

CHRISTIAN

Christian handed Shane his cell phone. "Call Star's cousin."

Christian and company had taken Shane and Agent Kirk Michael to the warehouse in West New York to wait on a shipment of guns set to dock in just three days, which was the only reason their lives had been spared, at least for the time being.

Assante, Akinsanya, and Christian encircled the two kidnapped victims, who sat freely back to back on the floor.

Shane looked up at Christian. "You might as well kill me now, Christian. I'm not calling anybody for you. I'm out." Looking away, he added, "Do what you gotta do."

Akinsanya kicked Shane on the shoulder, knocking him over.

"We have no time for this," Assante said. "Tracy can be dealt with further on. Agent Michael, quickly tell us all that your men know and it can all be over."

"Assante," Christian intervened, "we gotta find Tracy. Understand? This is not a case of your shit being more important than my shit. It doesn't work that way. You get what you need to get out of him." He looked at Agent Kirk Michael. "And I'll get what I need from you." He pulled out his gun on Shane.

"I told you already, man." Shane slowly sat up. "Do it. What else I got to live for? You done murdered my family. The only thing I had left in this world. What I got to live for? Huh? Huh, killer Chris? What? So you go ahead and pull it."

Agent Kirk Michael said from the floor, "Shane, stop being stupid. Just call him."

"You better listen to him, snitch," Christian said. "It might save your life. Unless you want me to let loose the dog again." He motioned his head toward Akinsanya, who was standing behind him. "Now here, call him." He shoved the phone to Shane's ear.

Cee-Cee answered on the first ring. "Hey. Cee-Cee here. Holla."

"Cee, it's Shane. I need to know where Tracy is. He's not picking up his phone."

"Your guess is as good as mine, hon. He just up and left one night. Didn't leave no note or nothing."

From the corner of his right eye, Shane stared down the barrel of Christian's gun. "Look, playa, this is a matter of life and death. How you let him out your sight?"

"What you mean, out of his sight? Gimme this." Christian snatched the phone from Shane's hand and pushed him away. "Sit down!" Then he said to Cee-Cee, "Yo, this Christian. You know where Tracy at, you better say something. You don't want to be involved, trust me."

"Hold up. Who you is?"

Christian responded to the man with the girly voice,

"Christian. That's right, the official clothing line. You know where my boy at?"

"What's he worth to you?"

"What's he worth?" Christian responded angrily.

After discussing some numbers, the two came to an agreement.

"I like the sound of that," Cee-Cee said. "What if I told you that I already know something?"

"I'd say you're about to be a hell of a lot richer."

"Here's the thing, though, Christian. I'm having just a wee li'l problem with those figures you talking."

"Oh yeah?"

"Eighty Gs and you got your man. You gonna have to come down and get him, though, if you want him alive."

Christian flipped the door on his phone then looked down at Shane.

"So that's what's been going on? Y'all associating with faggots now?" He turned toward Assante. "Tell me again why these two bitches are still alive?" he asked, referring to Shane and Special Agent Kirk Michael.

Before Assante could respond, his cell phone rang. "Yes," he answered, looking around the room. "What is it?"

Not only did the caller ID display screen read private, but the call appeared to drop instantly the moment he spoke. Assante swung the phone around for a better signal. "Hello."

Christian's phone rang next.

Then Akinsanya's.

Caller ID display screen on both phones said private, like the call Assante had just received.

"What is going on here?" Assante looked at Special Agent Kirk Michael. "Do you know of this?"

"Your time is coming," Special Agent Kirk Michael said. "Why would you think they would not be looking for me by now? The bodies of all the victims have been discovered. You can do what you want to me, but it's all over, Assante. We know when your guns are coming in and where."

"You only believe that you do. It is not here where the guns will arrive."

Special Agent Kirk Michael said, "Let me ask you this, Assante. Why are we still alive?"

Just as Assante was about to respond, all three phones began ringing simultaneously. They all answered their phones, to no avail, which only enraged Assante further.

"Who is this that call our phones? Speak or die where you sit." Assante slowly pulled out his gun. "Let us all go outside in the back. Come." He jerked the weakened agent off the floor by his arm. "You want to act as if you do not know what this is about? Are we fools to you? Go!" He pushed the agent in front of him, toward the back door.

"Wait, brother," Akinsanya said. "What about this one?" He snatched Shane off the floor by his arm also.

"The more I think about it, Assante . . . why are they still breathing?" Christian shook his head from side to side. "We don't need them. I mean, for what?"

"Everything has a purpose, Mister Elijah. We go outside and maybe make things clearer to Special Agent Kirk Michael."

As the men walked outside behind the warehouse, Shane began to vomit. He knew death was closing in.

"You changing your mind yet?" Christian handed Shane the phone again.

Shane stopped in his tracks and took the phone, and Assante and Akinsanya stopped with Special Agent Kirk Michael in between them both.

Tracy's phone rang and rang then went to voicemail. Shane, looking into Christian's hard, cold stare, left a message. "Tracy," he said nervously, "look, it's real important that you get back to me, man. We need to talk."

"Yeah," Christian said into the phone after snatching it out of Shane's hand, "we all need to talk. Make yourself available. Bitch!"

CHAPTER FORTY-FOUR

TRACY

Tracy pressed the number nine on the keypad of his cell, so it could save Christian's taunt on file. He and Trinity were refueling her car at a Shell gas station when the call came in, and he refused to answer it when he recognized Shane's number.

"We're going to have to get you out of here." Trinity placed the gas nozzle back in its holder. "What are you going to do? You know that Daddy was with him, right?"

"I know." Frustrated, Tracy rubbed his irritated eyes. He smiled then placed his hands on the roof of the car. He looked over at Trinity, tapped the roof, and chuckled.

Trinity chuckled too. "What's so funny?"

"Naw. I'm just laughing because I remember how much I used to love the smell of gas. Everybody always said it stunk, but I always loved it. Even now. Ain't it funny how we hold on to childhood memories?" he asked, wide-eyed.

"You all right, Tracy? Come on, baby, get in the car before somebody sees you." Trinity stepped inside the driver's seat then turned the ignition. "Come on, Tracy," she said, rolling down the automatic passenger window.

Tracy turned around for a brief moment on the gas station's island and faced the Daytona-like westbound evening traffic of Miami.

"Tracy, let's go," Trinity called again out of the window. She quickly answered her vibrating phone, "Hello," without looking at the display screen.

Christian's commanding voice thundered into her Bluetooth earpiece, "Trinity, don't you dare hang up! Just listen. You had your little vacation, and now it's time to come back home. I'm not upset with you, but I will be, if I have to come down there and get you myself."

The phone dropped from her hand, and she shut off the power. "Tracy, man, come on," she yelled, looking around.

Two westbound vehicles, green Suburban trucks, sped into the parking lot of the gas station and blocked Tracy on either side. Doors flung open, and five men jumped out, including Cee-Cee and two bouncers from Club Blue.

One of the bouncers ran over to the driver's window of Trinity's car. "Uh-uh, miss."

When he stuck his hand inside and reached for the keys, Trinity quickly sank her teeth into his hand and pierced his skin, causing him to punch her in the left side of her face.

Meanwhile, as the other men tossed Tracy all through the parking lot, the Arab owner of the gas station said, "You leave. You leave now. I'm going to call the police."

One of the other thugs tried opening the passenger door of Trinity's car by sticking his hand through the passenger window. Still stunned by the bouncer's sucker punch, Trinity stepped on the accelerator and took off with both men holding on and jogging with the car, until their legs began to drag across the jagged pavement. She quickly swerved into traffic, erratically dipping and wildly turning up the straightaway.

"She doesn't matter none." Cee-Cee sucked his teeth. "Just get his ass in the truck."

They flung Tracy into the backseat of the truck, and the two bouncers sat beside him, blocking his exit.

Cee-Cee said from the passenger seat, "Man, I had no idea you was the most wanted nigga in America. You got a price on your head, cutie, and guess who's collecting?"

"So y'all just gonna kidnap me right in public, right? Real smart."

"Heard about your slick-ass mouth too," Cee-Cee said. "Somebody make 'im shut up. He's making me carsick."

Cee-Cee and his men took Tracy back to his father's club, into an upper office. The walls of the large office were covered with long mirrors all around that reflected even the slightest of movements.

Tracy sat in a black leather chair, looking around at the bouncers surrounding him, not blinking for even a second.

Cee-Cee, drink in hand, said to him, "Now we gonna only go through this one time, muthafucka."

"Yo, man, whatever y'all got going on down here ain't any of my business. I don't give a shit. Just let me be out. I ain't gonna say nothing to nobody."

"I know you not. You're in some serious shit, boy. Shane ain't tell me everything you got going on. Your big mouth is the cause of all this, though. I remember your ass from when we was younger, living in Brooklyn. Your mother got killed for the same shit, right? Having a big mouth?"

Not even for a second did Tracy think that he'd once known Cee-Cee. Tracy stared at him long and hard before realizing he was Blue's son.

"Yeah." Cee-Cee laughed. "Look a little harder. You remember me now? Blue's son?"

Tracy leaned back in the seat. "All I want to know is if Shane knew who you was before he sent me down here."

"He ain't know that shit. What it matter anyway? You're here now, but not for long. Christian's coming down here for you. There's a eighty-thousand-dollar bounty on your head." Cee-Cee tossed back his cognac drink. "Think I'd pass that up?"

"So that message I heard on your answering machine earlier was Blue, your father? The one who gave the order to have my moms killed?"

Tracy quickly sprang out of his seat, but the bouncers grabbed him and forced him back down.

"All that you doing right there, honey, is a lost cause, sweetie." Cee-Cee chuckled as his men securely weighed down on Tracy. "That hopping-up shit. I ain't the one you should be tight with. Your bossman Christian the one who killed your moms. My father only gave the order. You know what else? My father just gave another order. Know what it is? He wants Christian and you dead. And if you really want to know, Star let me know who you was before you got here. Surprise, nigga! You're gon' die because my daddy said so. Who's the girl you were with?"

CHAPTER FORTY-FIVE

Detective Frogger

"I can't believe it. Look at this asshole," Dennis said, sliding down in the driver's seat of his car. He was parked down the street from Cadillac's house for the past two days, only going home to shower and change clothes. He'd heard through a reliable informant that Cadillac had been observed slipping in and out of his home late at night and in the wee hours of the morning. He was the only chance Dennis had of finding out where everyone was hiding.

Cadillac stood inside the foyer of his house and stuck his head out.

"Look at this fuckin' guy. He thinks he is so slick. What time you got?"

"It's five a.m. on the dot," Captain Ronald told him.

"Something's got to give. It's either now or later. Let's go get this guy. Tell the backup to get ready."

Cadillac, in a robe and boxers and slippers, slowly crept out of the house carrying what appeared to be two bags of garbage to the can by the side of the house, the belt of his burgundy robe dragging across the ground as he made his way there. He lifted the top of the green plastic can and looked around once more before dropping his garbage in.

"I'm going." Dennis quietly opened the driver's door. He stayed kneeled down as he exited the car and closed the door lightly. He lifted his chin over the hood of the car and slowly began moving around to the front of it.

Cadillac quickly turned around, and Dennis ducked even faster. Cadillac closed his robe then walked to the edge of his lawn to pick up the morning paper, never taking his eyes off his surroundings.

Just as Dennis was rising from behind the car, two barking pit bulls ran down the gated driveway of the house behind him.

Cadillac turned around and began jogging toward his front door.

"Cadillac, hold up. I just want to ask you some questions." Dennis ran after him. "Everybody, move in now!" he yelled, pulling out his gun as he reached the curb. "Stop running, or I'll shoot."

Cadillac reached the top step of his porch and stopped in his tracks, his hands up.

"Don't make me have to tase you." Dennis placed his gun back in its holster in exchange for his stun gun.

The streets filled with red and blue lights, screeching police tires, and wailing sirens, not to mention the howling of neighborhood dogs.

Cadillac dropped the newspaper. "Don't shoot."

"Don't you move," Dennis said, cautiously moving in on the tall, muscular model.

Other officers began crowding the lawn, slowly moving forward with their guns aimed.

Cadillac slowly turned around. "Look, I know what

you're here for, and I can tell you whatever it is you want to know." He noticed an opening in the barricade of officers standing on the lawn, and in one quick motion he jumped off the porch and ran toward the break in the circle of cops.

Dennis fired his Taser, and the charge flew past Cadillac's left ear as he made it to the sidewalk. The officers, Dennis, and Captain Ronald immediately followed behind Cadillac, his long legs extending as he ran up the street.

A police cruiser speeding toward Cadillac stopped and swerved to the side, knocking him over the hood. Cadillac rolled across it, landed on his feet, and continued running.

"You better stop!" Dennis yelled as he and the fleet of officers continued their pursuit.

A nearby German shepherd off his leash, confused by all the commotion, chased after Cadillac and tugged at the belt on his robe, growling and snarling, before finally latching on to his leg.

"Augggh!" Cadillac screamed, grabbing his leg.

The dog bit down into his wrist and wildly pulled him toward the ground then started biting at his exposed skin.

"Auuuggh! Get him off me!" Cadillac kept swinging at the dog.

"All right, boy," Dennis said.

The dog turned and snarled after Dennis stopped behind him so suddenly.

"It's all right, boy." Dennis smiled and held his hands up, using his experience with dogs back when he worked for the K-9 unit. "That's right, boy. It's all right."

The dog began to simmer down, panting and jumping up on his hind legs, his tongue flapping and licking Dennis all over the face.

Dennis patted the dog. "Anybody got any biscuits for

the hero?" He looked over at Cadillac, who was examining his bite marks and torn robe. "Get this asshole in cuffs."

Detective Dennis Frogger, his head down, leaned against the wall of the interrogation room, where Cadillac sat in a chair at a rectangular-shaped table. "That was stupid, you know? You didn't have to run. Why did you run? You ran because you know you're in big trouble. Where's everybody at, huh?" Dennis asked, his arms folded. "Where's Christian? Marcel? Tracy? Shane? Christian's daughter, Trinity? Do I have to go on?"

"I'm thirsty," Cadillac said, his head down.

Dennis cupped his ear sarcastically. "What's that?"

"I said I'm thirsty." Cadillac slowly lifted his head.

"You're thirsty." Dennis laughed. "You know what? I'll get you something to drink. You hungry too?" He secured Cadillac's wrist inside the grasp of his silver bracelet. "I'll be right back. It's not that I don't trust you or anything like that, but I'm going to have to cuff you. You're a runner."

"Pepsi, if they have it." Cadillac looked down at the ring his cuffed wrist was locked through.

"Don't go anywhere." Dennis laughed, as he let the office door close by itself and walked out.

Dennis went down the hallway and into a room with a one-way mirror, where Captain Ronald, sipping a mug of steaming coffee, stood staring at Cadillac. Fishing through his pocket for change, he told the captain, "He wants something to drink."

"He looks exhausted. He'll talk soon."

"He better." Dennis slid a crisp dollar bill into the soda machine, pushed the wide Pepsi tab, and an ice cold can of soda dropped down to the bottom of the machine with a thunk. He grabbed two white insulated foam cups from a small table holding a coffee pot and filled them both.

"I want him to talk, so don't be your usual self, all right?"

"He's going to talk." Dennis spat in Cadillac's cup and calmly walked back toward the interrogation room. He re-entered, popped the can of soda, and placed it on the table in front of Cadillac. Then he pulled up a chair, turned it around, and placed his feet firmly on the floor.

Cadillac downed the icy drink in about four huge gulps then released a belch.

"Finished?"

"Are you going to take these cuffs back off?"

"Sure." Dennis unlocked the cuffs and removed them from around his wrist. "Now is there anything else I can do to make your stay here more pleasurable?"

Cadillac rubbed his wrist. "I'm good."

"Okay. So . . . now that we're done fuckin' around, we can get down to business. Everyone is in trouble. You understand what I'm saying to you? And if you don't answer every single question that I ask you correctly, I mean, if what you're telling me even smells anything remotely like bullshit, you'll just be making it harder on yourself."

"I don't know what you want to know. You ask and I'll answer."

"I don't have to ask. You already know what I want from you. See, you want to sit up there like your little homeboy Tracy. Well, let me tell you something." He moved closer to Cadillac's face. "It's not going to get you anywhere."

"I stopped hanging with Christian about two weeks ago. That's why I been creeping. The nigga is crazy. I think he plotting to kill me. That's why I been hiding out. He got them Africans with him, and they got like so many people rolling with them."

"Why do you think he'd want to kill you? Is he a killer? Did you ever see him kill anyone?"

Cadillac stood up, walked over to the iron-gated window of the fifth-story office and stuck his fingers in between its links. He looked down through it and rested his head against its cold metal. "Why you making me do this, man?" He exhaled loudly.

"The only way you're going to get out of this alive is if you tell me everything. From the beginning." Dennis produced an audio recorder, which he placed on the table.

"Before you push record, I want it in writing what you'll do for me, if I tell you these things that'll get me killed. I want it in writing and on tape that you're going to protect me." Cadillac turned around, releasing his hold on the window's gate. "You promise me that, and then we can talk."

"I'm not going to bullshit you, Cadillac. If it is as deep as you say, then I can't promise you that. But I tell you what: you help me and I'll do my best to make sure you're put in a safe place."

Cadillac sat down and began slowly. "It all started when me and Tracy got arrested in Manhattan." He cleared his throat. "You think I can get another one of them sodas?"

"No." Dennis shook his head. "Not at all. Start talking." He pressed the red button on the digital audio recorder.

Five hours later Detective Dennis Frogger and Cadillac were both exhausted from the very lengthy confession. Dennis's eyes were red and heavy, while Cadillac's dry, pasty mouth caused his breath to stink worse than the decision he'd made to save his own ass. Just a quarter of the information Cadillac had divulged on record was enough to qualify him for the death penalty.

Dennis looked at the mirror, trying to imagine the expression on Captain Ronald's face as he listened to the shocking confession, which consisted of multiple counts of murder, extortion, kidnapping, and fraud, among other things. He stood to stretch his legs, and walked over to Cadillac. He placed his hand on his shoulder.

"You did good, kid. Real good." He opened the door to the room. "Hey, I'm going to bring back some sandwiches and drinks, okay. I'll see if I can find you a shirt to put on."

Cadillac didn't respond. He sat wondering if Dennis would remain true to his word and keep him out of harm's way.

Dennis now knew where to find everyone, including Marcel's body and the young kid that murdered the rookie officer way back when. He walked back into the room where Captain Ronald was observing Cadillac.

"We got a confession, Captain. Alert the authorities in downtown Miami. Trinity Elijah is down there, and Cadillac's going to show us where Marcel's body is, and the kid who killed John."

"I heard it all." Captain Ronald shook his head as he stared through the window at Cadillac. "You know there's nothing we can really do for him, right?"

"I know." Dennis laughed. "Boy, do I know." He looked at a nervous Cadillac through the mirror.

Captain Ronald's phone rang in the middle of Dennis's laughter. "I'm on the way," he answered, quickly opening the door.

"What's wrong?"

"We have two missing ATF agents that were sent into Christian's organization to follow those African brothers Cadillac was talking about. They haven't reported to their superior in days."

"The girl," Dennis said, fired up.

"What? What girl?"

"The girl from the house. I'm going to kick this kid's ass. He's playing us."

Dennis rushed back into the room where Cadillac was and grabbed him by the collar of his robe. He yelled into Cadillac's face, "You think I'm fuckin' around with you?

Tell me where those agents are. Government agents, you fucker. Did you pull the trigger?" He pushed him over from his chair and fell on top of him.

Cadillac held his hands up to block Dennis's furious swinging.

Captain Ronald ran into the office with some detectives behind him. He grabbed Dennis and tugged at his shoulder. "That's enough, Dennis," he said. "Let him up."

"You don't play games with me." Dennis smacked Cadillac's face as he climbed off his chest. "Did you know that the girl was working undercover?" he yelled. He pulled Cadillac to his feet and slammed him against the wall.

Cadillac yelled, "I didn't know."

"You did know!" Dennis swung him around and slammed him into another wall. "Don't you lie to me, you fuck!"

"I told you before, I wasn't down there when she got killed. She was alive when I saw her last."

"Come here," he snarled, grabbing Cadillac by his robe. "Sit down." He forced him on to another chair in the office. "Do you know what happens to people that kill federal agents? Do you?" He pushed Cadillac's head to the side. "There's another agent missing. I'm only asking you one time—Where the fuck is he at?"

"Where's who?"

"Stop fuckin' with me!" He grabbed Cadillac around the neck and took him to the floor once again. "Where is he? Where is he?" he repeated, choking him, banging the back of his head on the floor.

Captain Ronald and the other detectives waited a while before restraining Dennis.

Cadillac gagged and struggled for air after Dennis released his death grip. He backed up against the wall, terrorized by the thought of what may have transpired next, in a room full of men just like Assante and Akinsanya, except these men wore badges.

"I'll talk, I swear," Cadillac cried. "I'll tell the shit." He tried to think quickly. "I'll tell you where a shipment is coming in."

Captain Ronald calmly asked him, "Where is the other agent?"

"Last I saw, he was with Shane, Assante, Akinsanya, and Christian." Cadillac used the wall for support to slide up off the floor with his back.

"What's his name?" Dennis growled.

"I don't remember, but I know where they have him at. The same place Marcel is at. In the back of Assante's warehouse out in West New York."

Captain Ronald stared at Dennis. "Detective?"

"I'm on it." Detective Frogger secured his gun in its holster. "If I find out you're lying about this," he said to Cadillac, "I'll be sure to let Christian know how much of a rat you are. Then I'll make sure you both share the same cell."

CHAPTER FORTY-SIX

TRINITY

Trinity made sure to lock all the doors and close all the windows. She sat near the headboard in her bedroom, the phone pressed to her ear. "Daddy, it's me. Can you please come and get me? I'm scared."

"What happened?" he said loudly.

"Tracy," she responded crying. "Somebody took him."

"Tracy? You've been with him all this time?"

"No," she yelled, slapping her leg. "Just since last week. He's in trouble. They pulled him right off the street."

Christian knew it was Cee-Cee and his people. What he didn't know was that Cee-Cee was Blue's son.

"Did they hurt you? Touch you?"

"They just tried to scare me. Stuck their hands in my car and tried to take the keys." Trinity looked through the blinds at the darkening skies.

"You stay put. I'll be down there soon as I can. Keep all the lights out and do not go anywhere. Stay put."

"I hear you, Daddy."

"I love you, baby. Everything's going to be fine. We'll

straighten everything out with the police when you get back. Don't worry about nothing. Give me a kiss." He blew her one over the phone.

Five minutes later there was a knock at the front door. Without thinking Trinity automatically assumed it was Tracy. By the time she came to her senses, her hand was already on the knob of the front door. Before she could push it back closed, it was kicked open, and she stumbled backwards.

"You can thank your father for this. Get up, bitch." Cee-Cee pulled her up by her hair, while two of his bouncers stood by his green SUV parked in the driveway. "Now don't you start up no shit. You just get your ass out there into the truck and act normal."

Cee-Cee wrapped his arm around Trinity's shoulder after they exited the house, to make it appear to the neighbors as if they had a lover's quarrel. Matter of fact, Cee-Cee even kissed on her cheek while waving to them.

When Trinity tried to pull away, Cee-Cee jerked her back into his embrace. "Get on in the back," he said, opening the rear door to the truck. He slid in beside her, and the two bouncers took to the front.

As the truck sped off down the street honking its powerful horn, Cee-Cee waved farewell to the nosy neighbors. "Have a good evening, y'all."

CHAPTER FORTY-SEVEN

CHRISTIAN

Assante and Christian stood out on the roof of the West New York warehouse overlooking the Atlantic Ocean. Assante asked him, "Do you regret this all?"

"I can say this much." Christian, his arms crossed, looked up at Assante. "None of this would've ever happened if Woody would've just gone straight to the police." He chuckled, reminiscing on a line from a cartoon. "What the fuck you think? Yeah, I regret the shit. I regret a lot of shit I did."

"Like killing Tracy's mother?" Assante kept looking at the water.

"Why does that concern you? You seem to be focused on that very much. How I know you not another Solasse? Huh?"

"You do not, but this is the path you choose to walk. This is why I say we must part ways. You are very untrusting, and that may someday be the very thing that hinders my operation."

"Yeah. Well, forget all that. How you know about Tracy's mother? You want to talk about trust, right?"

Assante turned and looked down on Christian.

"Right?" Christian took a step to his right. "Who gave you the information?"

"Oh. It is a known fact you are her killer, Mister Elijah. That is without question. What you fail to understand is the information is out there, if you know the right people. I will never reveal to you the nature of my source, but I will tell you this—There is more to this kind of life we live than just cops and robbers."

"I feel that. Tell me this, though." He stared back into Assante's eyes. "Are you the cop or the robber?"

Akinsanya walked onto the roof. "Brother, it is time." He looked at the approaching storm on the horizon.

Christian turned to Akinsanya as he neared them. "Time?"

"Time, Mister Elijah," Assante said, as a helicopter raced through whipping winds toward the roof.

Christian covered his eyes from the flying debris generated by the helicopter. "What is that for?"

"I have taken care of them, Assante," Akinsanya said of Agent Kirk Michael and Shane. "They have been left as you say to leave them."

"What was the sense in bringing them along just to kill them here?" Christian asked Assante.

The hovering helicopter tipped forward and backward then landed softly on the wet warehouse roof.

"I'm not getting on that!" Christian yelled over the loud, spinning blades of the black chopper as rain saturated his clothes.

"There is not much time!" Assante stepped into the aircraft, his brother right behind him. "Look behind you, Mister Elijah! Get in!"

Christian ran to the edge of the roof on the other side

and looked down into the distant city street. Red flashing lights in dramatic numbers sped in their direction. He quickly spun his head back around and ran back to the helicopter. He looked back once more and stepped in with one leg before stopping. "Are you sure they're both dead?" he asked Akinsanya before being pulled inside by the two brothers.

CHAPTER FORTY-EIGHT

Dennis Frogger

Dennis's vehicle was the first to reach the long stretch of closed garages at the warehouse. Detective cars and squad cars alike kicked up mud and skidded across the pavement as they screeched to a halt, bumper to bumper. The officers all set up behind their cars and aimed their guns at the closed doors and garages of the warehouse.

"Shoot anybody that moves funny," Dennis said to the officers.

Dennis, his cheeks turned red under the frigid November downpour, almost slipped as he climbed atop the roof of his car. He then turned toward a nearby officer and signaled for him to pass the megaphone.

He yelled, "You know what, Christian? You're dumb, and I'm smart. Why, out of all places, would you come here? I thought you'd be off on a plane far out of town by now. Look, do yourself a favor. Just come out with your hands up. Tell your little Ethiopians in there that I'm here for them too. I'm going to give you three seconds then I'm coming in. One!" He dropped the megaphone and hopped off his car. He cocked his gun and charged the entrance door.

Detectives and officers quickly followed behind him. With all the detectives' and officers' guns trained on the green door, Dennis pulled at the rusting handle. It opened, and he took a step back. He turned and put his finger in the air then pointed inside the opening. The small army rushed inside, with Dennis in the lead, and scoured the lower level. The men carefully combed through each section of the five-story warehouse.

Dennis stared at a single door toward the back of the warehouse. He said to some officers, "Hey, anybody check that room?" He boldly stepped toward the first-floor room.

Dennis, three detectives, and five officers entered the large, cold room to a strong draft, which tossed sawdust spread out across the floor. The wind whistled wildly through the crack of an open door.

"Where's that draft coming from?" Dennis shook sawdust from the tip of his shiny black shoe.

"I think it's coming from over there, sir," an officer said, pointing toward a vertical crack way off in the corner of the semi-dark, windowless room.

"That's the outside, isn't it?" Dennis looked back as he cautiously proceeded forward. Droplets of rain attacked his face through the partially cracked door. He placed his hand on the door and slowly pushed it open. "Don't make me have to shoot you."

Without the protection of the door's shielding, Dennis was immediately immersed under the torrential teardrops of earth's global-warming effect. He neared the ditch Cadillac had told him of previously.

Dennis's fleet of backup officers soon followed behind him after donning orange raincoats, shotguns, and bringing in their dog. The dog barked ferociously, dragging its human counterpart toward the pit. Everyone stood around the ten-foot-deep hole and looked down. The dog continued barking and jerking toward the pit below, filled with broken pieces of wood, garbage, and frenzied seagulls battling for morsels of discarded food. All the while the men covered their mouths and noses because of the stench.

"It stinks," Dennis said. "There's a body down there. Call it in."

A detective called from inside the warehouse, "Detective Frogger, I really think you better come quick."

"What's up?" Dennis wiped rainwater off his face.

"You're not going to like this."

They rode an elevator to the fifth floor, where they exited and walked down a hallway.

The detective took a right turn into a dirty bathroom. "It's right here. Watch your feet." The detective extended his arm toward the open door of a stall, where a nearby urinal flooded the floor.

Dennis looked back at the detective then stepped in front of the stall. Dirty water rushed out of the clogged porcelain bowl and washed over Dennis's shoes. There, Agent Kirk Michael sat nude on an overflowing toilet, his back up against the square-tiled wall, his government identification hanging around his neck by a beaded chain, and his golden needlepointed badge plunged deep down in his forehead.

But that wasn't what killed him. Upon further inspection, Dennis discovered the massive trauma he'd sustained to the back of his head. He compared Agent Kirk Michael's face to the picture inside the protective plastic. "This is our man," he said, his feet splashing water as he took a step back. "They didn't have to do this to you."

"I'm afraid that's not all."

"Why did he bring him back here to do this?" Dennis pulled the door closed. He inhaled deeply then watched as the detective pushed open the adjacent stall door.

"Shane." Dennis looked at his dead body lying in a pool of blood and water. "Why'd they bring them back here?" Dennis pondered out loud, counting the bulletholes in Shane's back.

Dennis may have not known why the two men were brought back to the warehouse to be executed, but he damn sure knew what all this really was about.

He wasn't going to let on, though. His career would surely be on the line, if he ever admitted to all that he really knew.

His phone suddenly rang as he knelt down to examine the bullet wounds that had taken Shane's life. He answered, as he usually did, without checking the caller ID. "Yeah."

"Detective," Assante asked, "how do you like my artwork?"

CHAPTER FORTY-NINE

TRACY

Tracy was trapped in Cee-Cee's office by a locked door and no windows. He scanned the room, but there was nothing in sight to break the doorknob off. No phone. No computer. *How did it all come to this*? The disengagement of three security locks on the door gained his attention.

"Got some company for you, honey." Cee-Cee, his arm around Trinity, walked in behind his stooges. "Does Christian know you fuckin' his daughter?" He pushed Trinity into the office. "I guess y'all can discuss it when he gets here. This is such a surprise," he said, clapping his hands.

Trinity ran over to Tracy and held on to him tightly. She'd thought he was either dead or badly hurt.

"What you mean, when he gets here?" Tracy asked.

"What I mean, sexy, is that Christian wants your head, and he's paying me to hold your ass until he gets here. This little hottie right here is just some insurance. It gets even better. Ready for more?" Cee-Cee smiled. "Sit down, bitch." He pushed Trinity to the couch. "Don't be looking at me neither." He sucked his teeth. "I'm much too pretty for you to be staring at."

"You all right, Trin?" Tracy asked her.

"Nobody hurt her. Yet!" Cee-Cee laughed. "Hello?" he said, answering his cell phone.

"This is Detective Frogger," Dennis said.

Cee-Cee stared at Tracy. "Hey. What you want? I'm busy right now."

"You know what I want. I hear that your father's been in contact with you several times this month. I know why and I want in. There's a lot of shit going on up here right now. Your father reneged on our deal after I made life in prison easy for him. I don't like backstabbers."

"I can't talk right now. Call me back in ten minutes."

"You better not be pulling my balls. Ten minutes."

Cee-Cee quickly ended the call. "Whatever."

"Troubles?" Tracy asked sarcastically.

"Did I ask you to be all up in my business?" He smacked Tracy across the face. "React if you want to. These fine gentlemen in here will beat your ass."

"Tracy, just stop it."

"Better listen to Ms. Elijah and watch your mouth," Cee-Cee told him. "Wow, Trinity, you sure grew up. At first I didn't recognize who you was at the gas station, until Rico over here"—Cee-Cee patted the hulking bouncer's shoulder—"remembered you from a magazine, and I was like, 'Well, kiss my ass and lick the hole.' You do know why you here, right?"

Trinity sniffled. "No."

"You're here because your father is a backstabbing thief, and when he gets down here, I got a surprise for his ass too. My father is doing life, and I ain't seen him once since he went in. Fucked up, right?"

"What that got to do with her?" Tracy said. "She's not the one who put him away.

"Nigga, didn't I just tell you to shut up? Shit." Cee-Cee rolled his eyes at Tracy. "Now, to answer his question," he said, directing his attention back to Trinity, "your daddy owe out hella money, and he's gonna pay, uh-huh."

CHAPTER FIFTY

CHRISTIAN

"All right. Good looking, my man." Christian flipped his phone closed.

After his and the African brothers' Hollywood-like escape, they hooked up with one of Assante's convenient connections out in Clinton, Connecticut.

Their names were blasted all over the radio and their pictures posted on television.

Trinity was wanted in connection with Kaneecha's and her daughter's murder. Marcel's body was discovered under all the garbage way down in the belly of the ten-foot depression. Tracy was wanted for not only failing to appear in court but also the association he shared with Agent Kirk Michael before he was killed. Shane was dead, as was Special Agent Sanchez.

And all the while Christian was concocting a plan to have Cadillac killed for spilling the beans about everything he knew. He should've made him come in the house that day when they all went to Shane's house, instead of telling him to wait in the truck.

Worst of all, Star's mother didn't die. She should've been shot in the head like everyone else. That way she wouldn't have been able to give an accurate description of everyone.

Assante sat on a plane in disguise. He pulled down the shade to his window seat. "Your friends are *bullsheet*!" he said, gritting his teeth.

"You fucked up. The lady didn't die. So *you* are *bullsheet*!" Christian said in a low voice, mimicking Assante's accent.

"It is because of your friends."

"You really kill me." Christian chuckled. "You can't even kill a frail old lady. Fuck you! Let's just get down to where we got to go and depart ways. Don't even talk to me when we touch the sky."

As Christian stood up to change his seat, to move away from Assante, Akinsanya spread his legs so that Christian could remove himself from the three-seated row of comfortable reclining chairs.

Assante had anticipated his shipment of guns being intercepted because of a "leaky faucet" and quickly changed the point of delivery to Miami, where, coincidentally, Christian needed to be.

"Why you not tell me about this sooner?" Assante said to Christian as they stood on the balcony of the Chateau-Bleau Hotel.

"It was none of your business, but I have to get her now that we're already here."

"Isn't your daughter part of the reason why we are in the position we are in? To dissolve our relationship humbly, I shall assist you. But first the shipment then we will deal."

"I don't know why I ever hooked up with you."

"It is for the same reason America suffers from a recession, Mister Elijah, your lust for power and money. Your government has taught you all very well."

Christian answered his phone, "Hello," and turned his back on Assante.

"Yeah, Christian. This is Cee-Cee. I got somebody who you may wanna holla at."

Christian immediately recognized Cee-Cee's faggot-ass voice. "Oh yeah? Who might that be?"

"Hold on, sexy." Cee-Cee laughed. "Hold on."

"Daddy," Trinity cried, "they said they're gonna kill me."

"That's enough," Cee-Cee said, apparently snatching the phone back from her. "You hear that, Christian? This bitch will die if you don't come up with the dollars. I know you got the shit. You got to the end of the week, and you better not call the police. Oh yeah, my father said to tell you hello."

"Your father? Put my daughter back on the phone. I swear to God, if you harm her, I'll take you and your whole family out."

"Oh, I think you already did that, muthafucka. Does the name *Blue* ring a bell? I thought it might. Call me before you leave New York."

After Cee-Cee disconnected the call, Christian speed-dialed the number. "Come on," he said, dialing it again after getting Cee-Cee's voicemail.

"Is there a problem, Mister Elijah?" Assante asked.

CHAPTER FIFTY-ONE

Dennis Frogger

Dennis sat at the small circular dinner table in the kitchen of his one-bedroom apartment, sulking in the bottom of a bottle of cheap vodka, his gun sitting on the table in its holster. He knew of a lot of things that went down in the street. Matter of fact, there wasn't much that ever went down without him knowing about it first. Dennis was making a lot of money outside of the law. And Captain Ronald was involved just as much.

1987

"Yeah," Blue said over his phone, "she's making things bad for us both."

Sergeant Frank Ronald said, "This is how it works. Take care of her. Tonight."

"Hopefully we can resume our business without your officers fuckin' it up for me?" Blue asked.

"Get it done first."

* * *

Stacy Kane had just gotten some papers from her church and had stopped by the corner store to pick up a carton of milk for her son Tracy. It was a little brisk out that night, so she accelerated her footsteps.

Startled by an unfamiliar face quickly approaching her, she stopped, thinking he would pass, and turned her shoulder to the side, but he turned with her and backed her up against the side of a silver BMW parked in front of a NO STANDING ANYTIME sign under a blown out lamppost high above.

She shuddered, one arm wrapped around her bundle of papers. "Look, I don't have any money on me. I'm just trying to get home to my son."

Without uttering a single word, Christian took three steps back and shot her in the face. Her papers flew in the air, and she fell backwards on the hood of the BMW. Christian ran up the block and hopped into the passenger seat of an awaiting vehicle.

Meanwhile, an off-duty Sergeant Frank Ronald and Officer Dennis Frogger observed from afar in an unmarked car. They sped past the scene and confirmed the hit when they both saw Stacy's brains splattered across the hood of the BMW.

"She's gone," Dennis said, looking out the passenger window of the car.

That was twenty-something years ago, and karma was finally about to make its rounds.

A knock on Dennis' apartment door broke him out of his pitiful drunken trance.

"It's open."

Captain Ronald entered and slowly closed the door behind him. He looked around at the sink full of dirty dishes and crushed beer cans on the kitchen counter. Even though Dennis owned a home on Westhampton, Long Island, he used this trashy apartment as a cover-up, since he'd never be able to explain how he was able to afford such an expensive home based on his salary.

"I've been calling you. Why haven't you been picking up? Don't go falling apart on me now. I need you." Captain Ronald checked the half-empty bottle of vodka Dennis had been sipping the entire night.

"This is not the way it was supposed to go, Captain."

"Christian has to go. He will tell it all when the time comes. I've contacted the warden at the state prison. Blue will see us."

"What do you mean, he will see us? You set him up for murder, and Christian's running free."

"It was the only way, you know that. I wouldn't be where I am at today if Blue didn't go down, and neither would you, Detective. Christian was nobody, and Blue was somebody. A somebody that killed a lot of innocent people and destroyed a lot of families with his drugs."

"And what do you think we did?" Dennis reached for the bottle of vodka.

"You mean what *you* did, don't you?" Captain Ronald quietly patted Dennis down for a wire.

"What are you doing? You think I'd ever rat you out?"

"Cops don't rat on other cops, Dennis. Always remember that." Captain Ronald poured the rest of Dennis's drink down the sink.

"What are you doing?" Dennis slurred, standing sluggishly.

"Don't let this be the mirror to your career." Captain Ronald shook the bottle of vodka free of its contents. "Get yourself together. There's not a lot of time."

"You got a lot of nerve coming here," Blue said to Captain Ronald and Detective Dennis Frogger through the holes of the Plexiglas window. "The both of you." He pointed at Captain Ronald. "You fucked me."

"We need some information from you," Dennis said.

"You want me to help you? Man, fuck you."

"Fuck me? No! Fuck you. Do you think that cell phones in prison are free? It comes out of my pocket to keep you in touch with your son."

"My son. The son you took me away from? You made a commitment and did me dirty."

"Blue," Captain Ronald said, "what's done is done."

"It sure is. Christian deserted my family, and you are all protecting him now. Why am I the only one here? I didn't pull the trigger."

"You're such a fool, Blue. It was never about the murder. It was always about the drugs. You thought you were stringing Christian along, but he was playing you the whole time."

"You cut me out of our agreed-upon terms," Captain Ronald reminded Blue. "You tried to be slick."

"So, what are you doing here then? You said if I took care of that business, things would be better for us all. Only shit I see things done got better for is you, you, and Christian. Nice stripes," he said, referring to Captain Ronald's uniform. "You used me to work your way up the ranks. Good shit!" Blue chuckled, his head bowed. "Christian did the same thing, but it's all right. Good job. Now I'm already doing life. What else you want from me?"

"How would you like to get even with Christian?" Captain Ronald asked.

"I think I'll pass on any more deals you got for me. You already fucked me with the deal of the century."

"Let me ask you something," Dennis said to Blue. "You've been locked up now for about, what, a little over twenty years, right?"

"Get to the point. I need to go and eat before lunch is over."

"If you want to keep living like a king in this animal

house, you'd better cooperate with us. Which part of Miami is Christian going to?"

"I don't know what you're talking about."

"Cee-Cee told me everything."

"I don't know what you're talking about." Blue stood to walk away. "Guard!"

"Christian will kill your son on the spot when sees him," Dennis said through the glass partition.

Blue continued walking until he met the two guards, who took hold of him and placed him back in his silver restraints.

Strange enough, Blue returned five minutes later without the restraints and lifted the phone to his mouth. "Pick it up," he said to Dennis.

"Talk."

"Not with him in here." Blue looked over at Captain Ronald. "Get him the fuck out or the conversation's over. I don't trust him one little bit."

"Captain, let me see what the dumb fuck has for us."

"Do it right, or things will never be the same for you again." Captain Ronald stood. "Are we clear on that?" he asked, walking away.

Captain Ronald showed his badge to the officers at the gate so that they'd open it, and carried on down the long corridor, occasionally looking back as the gate buzzed closed.

The inmates at the overcrowded facility screamed and shook the demoralizing cages above, while the footsteps of others could be heard on the second tier, stomping for freedom.

"Talk fast," Dennis said, after seeing Captain Ronald disappear.

"Officer Frogger." Blue smiled after sitting down. "My main nigga. That's a pretty good front you put on in front of your captain there. He's a real bitch, you know."

"Did you tell your son to kill Christian?"

"Hell yeah. His ass is gone. His daughter and Tracy too. And it's too late for you to do anything about it. So that's that."

"Did you just say 'his daughter'? Whose daughter?"

A smiling Blue stretched his legs out in the chair then clasped his hands behind his head.

Dennis punched the window. "Whose daughter?"

"Christian's daughter. I am superior to that nigga, even behind bars, and whoever's in the crossfire of his bullshit is getting it too."

"So that's that, huh? Just like that?"

"Nigga, it's just like with a wave of my hand. Just like when I waved my hand and got you to come work for me after that bullshit you and your captain pulled. All along y'all was playing me to move up in the ranks."

"Weren't you doing the same thing? Trying to move up in the ranks? You're still making money, so you should stop complaining. I told you I'd take care of business. Now, fuck. I know these ain't the best conditions in here, and yeah, we may have shitted on you, but you was breaking the law." Dennis smiled.

Blue spat on the window. "Fuck you!"

"Christian and his people killed two ATF agents. He's running around with those two crazy Africans, doing a whole lot of killing for nothing."

Dennis looked left and right then hung up the phone. He moved his face toward the holes in the partition, and Blue met him halfway.

"How the fuck did the ATF get involved? If they get to those brothers before we do, the whole shit will be fucked. It'll all come out that it was you who supplied the funding for the Africans to bootleg Christian's clothing line."

"That's not all that'll come out. When your captain finds

out you're working for me, selling my shit in the street with your homeboys, now that'll really be some fucked-up shit. And you're buying guns from the Africans to sell undercover to niggas in the street. I bet Christian don't know about that one. Do he?"

Dennis flared his nostrils. "You better watch what you say in here."

"Christian fucked this all up. We can't afford for anybody to talk. You need to do whatever it is you need to do and take care of everybody associated with him. You're not going to fuck up my money for a second time, or the time you see me waving my hand will be when I'm spreading rose petals across the top of your casket."

"You threatening me?"

Blue, confident he had the upper hand, said, "You take it how you want to. Also, I know a way to get out of here, but I need your help."

"Are you kidding me?"

"Does it look like I'm kidding? I want you to get me a pardon. I've been hearing and seeing a lot of shit in here, and if we can make it look like Christian is running those guns, with the right information, of course, and he's convicted, shit, I'll be free, and that nigga will be here. Or dead. I want to be there, so I can see the expression on his face when he sees that I told on him."

"Do you really think I can get you out of here that soon?"

"Better make it happen, or nothing is happening at all. Guard!"

CHAPTER FIFTY-TWO

CHRISTIAN

Christian flipped his phone closed. He'd been trying to reach Trinity for the past three days. He was almost in tears at the thought of what might have happened to her, as he paced back and forth in the hotel room in the dark. Assante and Akinsanya were off somewhere handling business. He needed a drink and was going to take a cab over to Club Blue. He'd thought that just maybe a couple of drinks and loud music would block images of his daughter lying in a canal somewhere, tossed in as alligator food.

His phone rang before he opened the door. "Hello," he answered quickly.

"Hey, boo. It's me. The one and only Cee-Cee," he said with a lisp.

"Where's my daughter, muthafucka?"

"Oh my. You is just too harsh. She a'ight, crazy." Cee-Cee laughed. "I was just calling to check in. You got that paper yet? You're already three days past due. I'm only being nice here because I think you are so handsome. Otherwise, I would've blown this stupid bitch brains out a long time ago." He shouted, "Don't fuck with me, bitch. I want my money," then disconnected the phone.

As long as Cee-Cee thought he was going to get that money, Trinity would be all right. With that attitude, Christian took a cab to Club Blue.

Thunderous explosions of mega bass ripped through the souls of those with happy feet, causing their bodies to shake in sync, like harmonic convulsions. Constant flashes of blue strobe light lasers sliced through, highlighting the perspiration on the bodies of the flamboyantly exquisite.

Christian pulled his white Kangol over his eyes and walked over to the female bartender.

The pretty, young Asian girl yelled over the music, "Hey, sexy. What can I get for you?"

"Let me get a scotch on the rocks with a lime twist." Christian pointed at the glass shelf in front of the mirror.

She stood on a stool to reach the bottle. "Spending big tonight, playa?"

"What is this, some kind of fag club or something?"

"Gay night. You here by yourself?" she asked, joking.

"Real funny," he said, watching his back for those that got too close.

"Hey, I know you. You're Christian Elijah. Hey, look, I just started tonight and already don't like this place. I'd move to New York if I could work for you." She smiled.

Christian totally ignored her and turned his back. He got up and walked to a lone table and cushioned bench, where an array of lights shifted into different shades and hues of blue. He sat and leaned back into the comfortable bench.

He thought about how fast he was going to shoot Cee-Cee when he saw him, then Tracy, if he wasn't dead already. He lifted his drink and sipped it with his head leaned back.

"Excuse me, is there room for two?" a beautiful young black woman asked, pulling at one of the curls in her long, curly hair.

"What?" Christian quickly sat up, astounded by her beauty. "I'm sorry. Uh, yeah. Sure. There's always room for two."

"This place is so loud. Look how close I have to get, just so that you can hear me," she said, moving closer to him.

Christian couldn't help looking at the top of her breasts bulging out her blouse.

"You lose something?" She put her hand over her breasts and moved away.

"Apologies." Christian extended his hand. "Christian. What's your name?"

"Mia," she said, gently shaking his hand. "So, tell me, Christian, are you waiting on someone?" She surveyed the ratio of males to females in the club.

"You've gotta be kidding me. The bartender just asked me the same thing."

"You're a very good-looking man." Mia ran her hand through her hair. "I'd think you'd be at home with your wife, not here at the boys' club on gay night. Let me find out that you be saying, 'I'm not only a client, but I'm also the president.'" Mia laughed.

"You're just too funny. I like that. But, no, cut that out. I'm not from here and didn't know about this fag-night shit."

"So you stayed after the fact?"

"Just for a drink then I'm gone. Let me ask you a question. How old are you?"

"I'll be twenty-two next month."

"Cool. So can I get you a drink?"

"I don't know. Can you?"

"What's your flavor, neighbor?"

"Huh?" the young woman said, confused by the old-school phrase.

"What you drinking?"

"Uhhhh. I'll let you decide, since you the one paying for it."

"Naw. You go ahead, sweetheart. Get whatever you want. It's not a problem."

Several drinks later, the two made an immediate exit for the door. They were attracted to one another and wanted to prove it.

"Come on," Mia said, walking to the back parking lot for her car. She activated the alarm of her two-toned black-and-platinum Chrysler.

She fell into Christian's arms and began kissing him. "You want to drive?" she asked. "I'm twisted."

"Yeah, I got you. Just tell me how to get there."

"So are you from here?" Christian asked as he drove through the Miami streets searching for a hotel open at two a.m.

"I've been here for a couple of days. I don't like it, so I'll be leaving soon."

"So where you from?"

"Brooklyn."

Christian and Mia checked into a suite at Riverside Hotel in downtown Miami. Christian didn't care about the expense, knowing he was about to increase his revenue after parting ways with Assante.

The thought of Trinity dying was no longer on his mind, mostly because he was drunk inside of some tight, young, shaven pussy.

Christian pushed his liquor-hard dick deeper and deeper inside of Mia.

"Oh shit! Oh shit!" Mia screamed out, holding on to the

headboard of the soft bed, squeezing the back of his thigh with her free hand.

When she dropped her hands on the bed and stuck her ass up, Christian stood up and positioned himself behind her. Bending at the knees, he grabbed her by the hips and immediately slid right back into her burning volcano, where boiling lava was just waiting to erupt.

A highly aroused Mia looked back at him and bit down on her bottom lip, her long hair bouncing off her shoulders with every stroke, her clit standing out much farther and longer than its usual five-second lookout session.

Christian grunted, "Give me this pussy," and slammed his hips into hers from an upright, slanted kind of angle. Each time he pulled his dick out, the head throbbed then swelled before he could re-enter.

After they came simultaneously—she'd already come five times—Christian rubbed cum all over her apple-shaped ass then slapped it.

"Oh, you just one of them ol' nasty men, huh?" Mia rubbed her stinging ass. "I know you're not finished." She turned over on her back and spread her legs open.

"I like that. You aggressive."

"Come here." Mia stuck her tongue out at him and cupped her breasts. "Why you not sucking on these titties?"

"Because," he said, slowly thrusting himself inside of her, "this ain't intimate, this is *fuckin'*. Ya feel me?" Then he quickly increased the pace.

Christian's phone rang just as he was about to nut. It was Assante's emergency ring. "Let me get that." He reached over her to grab his phone from the nightstand.

"No!" Mia grabbed him around the waist. "Don't stop!"

Christian shoved her away. "Stop!" he yelled.

When Christian started putting his clothes on, Mia followed suit. He looked down at the phone. "I gotta go. Can you drive me back?"

"Whatever!"

"It was nice meeting you," Christian said to Mia. "Don't kill 'em out there. You got the goods, baby." He got out of her car and headed for Assante's.

Assante waited for a moment before pulling off. He stared at Christian through his sunglasses.

Just then Christian heard a man with a feminine voice call out to Mia, "Where you been, girl? Don't be acting grown, sis. I don't care if you is older."

"Act grown? Shut up, punk." Mia opened the door to her car.

Christian turned his head back to Assante, who was still staring at him. "Are you going to pull off or sit here like a fuckin' dummy? Let's move."

"Mister Elijah, what have you been up to? I have not heard from you. Are you making new friends?"

"Look, let's just take care of business and fuck all this. I don't need your help getting my daughter. Just drive, nigga."

Assante smiled as he slowly drove off. "This experience has been most entertaining, Mister Elijah. There is much to go over before tonight."

CHAPTER FIFTY-THREE

TRACY

Tracy and Trinity had been held captive for almost a week now and hadn't been permitted to wash. And the Miami heat caused their bodies to wade in a pool of their own sweat. All week the two had been transferred to different locations, until the night of the exchange was to occur. And tonight was the night.

Cee-Cee gave Trinity the evil eye. "You stink, bitch. Is that your nasty-ass coochie smelling like that? Phew! You need to put an Alka-Seltzer in that cesspool. Get in the fuckin' car." He pinched his nose and rolled his eyes before pushing her, bound and gagged, into the trunk of a '73 station wagon.

Tracy sat in the passenger seat of the Suburban, while Cee-Cee sat behind him, the nose of his gun pushed into the back of Tracy's neck. And the station wagon with Trinity trailed the two green Suburbans packed with thugs.

They were on their way to meet with Christian when Cee-Cee's phone rang.

"Yoo-hoo," Cee-Cee answered after looking down at the

caller ID. "Uh-huh. Okay. What's up? Shut up!" he said laughing, his gun still pressed to Tracy's neck. He cut the call off.

He said to Tracy, "You better not be trying anything funny. I don't think your boy gonna be happy to see you." Then he said to the driver, "Rico, there's been a change in plans."

Tracy said, "Cee-Cee, man, this don't make no kinda sense."

"It makes perfect since to me, sweetie. I get paid for you and her. What? You want me to let you go? This is only business, not personal. Tell you what, though. Maybe in your next life you can come and model for me. In a pair of pink boy shorts." Cee-Cee laughed along with his thugs.

CHAPTER FIFTY-FOUR

CHRISTIAN

Christian, Assante, and Akinsanya were headed to their big shipment and the exchange of one million dollars for Trinity.

Christian said, gun in hand, "When I say I'm going to kill that faggot-ass-sounding bitch, I'ma blow his head smooth off."

Assante, one hand on the wheel and the other on his weapon, drove slowly through an open-gate entrance of an enormous trucking yard by the water, where, in the silvery midnight moonlight, boats wobbled from the rippling effect caused by the waves off in the distance.

Left and right, two rows of diesel engine Mack trucks facing each other stretched four hundred feet. Their exhaust clouded the long set of headlights approaching them from afar.

"Okay. So what? You got the shit coming in the water? I don't see a big ship coming in anywhere. I don't hear no foghorn. How in the fuck you get this hooked up so fast anyway?"

Assante stopped the vehicle and gripped his gun.

"What you stopping for?" Christian snapped.

"Look ahead, Mister Elijah." Assante tapped the windshield once with his gun.

The headlights unnoticed earlier became quite apparent now. Thumping bass from the nearing vehicles echoed off the steel and iron trailers on the back of the trucks.

"This nigga stupid." Christian angrily opened the door and stepped out.

Assante stepped out too and placed his handgun on the roof of the car. Akinsanya stayed in the back with two guns on his lap.

Christian's phone rang, but he ignored it. It rang again and again.

The African brothers' phones began to ring also.

"What is this?" Assante said in a fit of rage. He quickly ran around to the trunk and hit it. "Aki," he said to his brother.

When Akinsanya popped the trunk, Assante reached down inside and came up with a .38 Magnum.

Christian looked at the deadly weapon with a scope atop it. "Goddamn!"

"This will end," Assante said.

Akinsanya stepped out of the car quietly with both guns in hand and stood behind Christian.

The lights of the vehicles ahead, from Cee-Cee and his men, were turned off, and they stopped thirty feet away from Christian, Assante, and Akinsanya.

Cee-Cee made Tracy get out first.

"Wait a minute." Cee-Cee grabbed Tracy by the arm as he held the gun under his ribs and said, "This is for good luck"—and thrust his tongue into Tracy's mouth.

Tracy immediately pulled back and punched Cee-Cee in the jaw, then the forehead. But then the thugs in the backseat started beating on Tracy's head.

After Cee-Cee regained his composure, he yelled, "Get the fuck out!" He jabbed his gun into Tracy's cheek. "Hurry up." He opened the passenger door then pushed him out on the gravel-filled lot. "Walk, bitch, until I tell you to stop."

Tracy painfully rose to his feet and looked back at the station wagon Trinity was in. Cee-Cee's hoods crawled out the backseats of the vehicles and stood by, waiting for action. Even in the dark, Tracy, as he turned around, could see the hateful expression on Christian's face. There were guns behind him, guns next to him, and guns ahead of him.

He cautiously walked forward with his hands raised and stopped exactly six feet away from Christian. The click-clack of Assante's and Akinsanya's guns simultaneously echoed inside his eardrums.

"I got this," Christian said to the brothers. He walked toward Tracy.

"I want to see the money," Cee-Cee said.

"I want to see my daughter."

Cee-Cee told one of his thugs, "Go get the bitch."

Seconds later, a gagged Trinity was pushed next to Cee-Cee.

"Let it all go smooth, hon. She all right. Ain't you, stinky?" Cee-Cee pushed her back into the grasp of his thugs. "All right, you saw her. Where that money?" he said, leaning on the grill of his truck.

Christian turned around to Akinsanya. "Throw me the briefcase." Then he directed Tracy back toward Cee-Cee and company. "Let's go. You're doing this with me."

Cee-Cee asked Christian, "All the money in there?" as he and Tracy approached.

"You want to count it?"

"You know I do." Cee-Cee smiled and reached for the handle of the Gucci suitcase.

"Not so fast, muthafucka." Christian snatched the case

from Cee-Cee's clutch. "My daughter first. Untie her and give her to me."

Cee-Cee laughed. "Push the bitch back over here." He pulled a fishing knife from under his pants leg.

Straightaway, Christian aimed his gun at Cee-Cee, but Cee-Cee's men all put their guns on Christian.

"You said you want her untied, right? That's duct tape around her wrist. I gots to cut it off," he said innocently, cutting through the thick, grey tape in just two strokes.

Trinity stared at her father. Then they both broke down crying.

Christian said to Tracy, "This is all your fault."

Trinity ran over to Christian, and they momentarily spun around in a circle. She squeezed her arms around his neck so tight, she almost broke her wrists.

"Go ahead and walk, Trinity." Christian motioned his head toward the African brothers. "It'll be all right."

When she turned to look at Tracy, Christian gave her a slight shove. "Go on now."

Trinity carefully walked over the mixed gravel. The Africans silently guarded her approach as she looked back at her father.

Christian turned to face Cee-Cee. "You want to kill this kid, or should I?"

"That nigga your problem." Cee-Cee looked at Tracy. "Let me ask you this, though, Christian—How many fools you think it take to make moonshine?"

"I don't got time for riddles."

"Just answer it, silly. Then we can conclude this business." Cee-Cee waved his hand at Assante.

BLAM!

An explosion from Assante's handgun was followed by a sudden scream from Trinity, whose life was cut short by a piercing bullet to her heart.

Christian and Tracy spun around simultaneously, only to see Trinity become a fallen angel.

"Nooooooooooo!" Christian hollered out, screaming and pissing his pants.

"Trinity!" Tracy raced toward her.

No sooner had Christian taken his first step toward Trinity, when Cee-Cee took a step back behind him and, as if almost in slow motion, raised the gun to the back of Christian's head and squeezed the trigger, causing his blood to splatter all over Cee-Cee's face and clothing.

Oblivious to the murder scene behind him, Tracy continued running forth.

Assante and Akinsanya both stood in front of their vehicle and took aim.

Cee-Cee and his crew began marching toward Tracy, who stopped and looked in both directions as both sets of men began closing in on him.

"Mister Assante," Cee-Cee sang with a smile.

Both sets of men stood five feet apart on each side of Tracy. And all he could do was spin around and around on the frenzied carousel of panic.

Sirens surrounded both entrances of the trucking yard then rolled in at full speed. Police and news choppers paraded around the sky, projecting their technologically advanced searchlights to flood the murder scene down below. And the Miami police and detectives kicked up gravel as they closed in.

A commander shouted, "*This is the Miami PD. Put down your weapons immediately, or you will be shot where you stand. There are no negotiations.*"

Another car, not associated with Miami's finest, careened through the lot with a spinning red siren in the window. The driver, badge hanging down around his neck, quickly hopped out, while a man in the passenger seat stayed hidden within the shadows.

Everyone dropped their weapons and lay on the ground and was immediately tackled and cuffed.

Tracy lay face down on the ground crying. Footsteps walking toward him kicked a small rock past his head. He slowly lifted his head, dirt all round his face, the tears leaving wet lines on his grey facial mix.

Dennis laughed. "I told you I'd get ya." He stuck his hand down to pull Tracy up.

Tracy took his hand and rose to his feet. He began storming back toward Trinity's body as she was being bagged up.

Dennis followed him. "There's nothing you can do for her."

"Trinity, I'm sorry. Trin." Tracy lifted her body out of the bag. He cried by her side until his vision became blurry.

A lump in his throat and a hole in his heart compelled him to throw in the towel. He was tired of running and not knowing why. And, to make things worse, he'd just lost his future life. What other reason was there for him to live? He always said he'd never marry, because he didn't want a wife. What he wanted was a life, but now she was gone.

Detective Dennis Frogger said, "Let's go, Tracy. We have to leave now."

"I'm not leaving her," Tracy said, still holding her in his arms.

EMT workers held the door open for the coroner, but Tracy wouldn't let go.

"There's nothing you can do for her, man," an EMT worker said.

"Tracy," Detective Dennis Frogger said, "let's go. Unless you want to spend the rest of your life in prison down here, you better make a move."

"You're not helping her," the EMT worker said.

Tracy stood with Trinity's blood on his face and stared Detective Dennis Frogger in the eyes. "What do you want from me, man? Huh? I ain't do shit."

"There's a way for you to end all of this," the detective said.

Helicopter lights continued running across the ground and ocean, searching for any remaining culprits. The lights flashed by the faces of the detective and Tracy every five seconds.

"Man, do you see what the fuck just happened out here? My girlfriend is dead."

"Yeah. And so is your father, Christian."

"Yo, stop calling him my father."

"You acted like his son the whole time along, so why not? Anyway, get over it. Now it's time to think about your own ass." Dennis lit a cigarette. "So what are you going to do? You coming or you staying?" He started walking toward his car.

"Hey, you," an officer said to Tracy.

Dennis had a few words with the officer and relayed them to his superior.

Tracy cautiously followed behind the detective, not knowing if this was a setup or not. The man got out of the front passenger seat of the detective's car and into the back.

"Who's that?" Tracy stopped, about to turn around.

Dennis tossed his cigarette. "Let's go!"

Tracy watched as the coroner took Trinity's body away. Then he stepped into the passenger seat, all the while looking back.

Detective Dennis Frogger drove out toward the exit and stopped where Cee-Cee and his thugs, Assante, and Akinsanya were all cuffed together on the ground, locked by the ankles.

Assante looked up toward the detective's window and gave a wink as his headlight passed his face.

"What was that?" Tracy looked at the stranger in the back.

"What was what?"

"Assante. He just winked at you."

"Assan who?"

"He winked at you. I saw the shit. Yo, let me up out of here." Tracy frantically reached for the lock on the door.

The stranger from the backseat said, "Stop being a bitch and just wait a minute."

CHAPTER FIFTY-FIVE

TRACY

After Tracy had been moved to an upscale part of Miami, he and Detective Dennis Frogger stood on the back deck of a house by the water, where a speedboat, *Need For Speed*, was tied to its post.

"Why won't y'all just let me go home?" Tracy asked.

"You got yourself into this, buddy. How do you go from socking an immigrant in the face to being set up to be killed? Because I'm sure you do know by now that Christian was going to murder you, right? So, don't you ask about home. You messed up a real good thing for a lot of people, you li'l fuck."

Tracy sucked his teeth. "I knew you was dirty."

"Yeah, but you also knew that I was the only one that could save your ass."

"So I'm not going back home is what you're saying?"

"You help me, I'll help you. Tell me about Marcel, from the beginning. Then continue going down the line until you get to that ATF agent. I want to know everything he knew, saw, and said to you."

Tracy divulged everything that he knew, and also his role.

Dennis sat down in deep thought, massaging his temples.

Tracy continued, "But by the time I found out he was ATF, it was too late. I was just trying to get up out of dodge. I didn't know about him being dead until just now."

"How does it feel, Tracy?" Detective Dennis Frogger growled. "How does it feel to know that this is all your fault? Everything!" The detective pounded on a table behind him.

"No way. You can't put this all on me."

"I can put anything I want on you."

The stranger from the backseat said, "He sure can." He had walked through the front door and straight back to the patio and through the deck's sliding glass door. "God." The bulky but muscular man stretched his arms then stepped outside. "It's a good day to be free." He smiled at Tracy.

Detective Dennis Frogger asked the man, "Where are they?"

"Slow it," the man said, referring to the detective's quick temper. "They're coming inside now. Tracy, my main man, what's up?" He extended his hand.

Tracy looked at both men and began to step backwards, bumping into a steel banister that secured the deck.

"You know who I am?" Blue withdrew his hand. "I'm sorry your girlfriend died. She wasn't in the plans. My stupid-ass son took it upon himself to get her involved."

"Your son?"

"Cee-Cee," Blue answered. "He was only supposed to kill Christian."

"You a bitch." Tracy lunged at the detective but Blue quickly subdued him, pushing him back into the banister.

"Now you better chill if you ever want to get out of this alive," Blue said. "Don't get it twisted, though, Tracy. You, on the other hand, were supposed to die, but because you lost your girl, I'ma give you a pardon. You are going to help us though."

"Is it true?" Tracy asked.

Blue said, "Is what true? Is what true?"

"Did you—" Tracy choked up. Reminiscing on his mother's tragic death only enhanced the hi-definition image of Trinity being killed. "Did you give the order to have my mother killed?"

"Is that what you've been hearing?"

"From the beginning."

"So now you know. If it's a problem, then we can solve it right here."

Tracy slowly rose to his feet. "All I want to know is why?"

"Your mother was a troublemaker an—"

Before Blue could say another word, Tracy swiftly jumped forward and grabbed him around his neck, and they both fell hard on the deck, tussling and wrestling.

Detective Dennis Frogger jumped over them both as they rolled to the other side of the deck. "OK!" He shot his gun off in the air. "That's enough! It stops now, or I'm going to put one in the both of yous."

Blue and Tracy then retired to separate corners.

A crying Tracy yelled to Blue, "You didn't have to kill her."

"There is nothing I can do to make that up. She's gone and that's that. Your mother was a good woman with a good heart, but she just wouldn't shut the fuck up. I personally warned her many times."

"What you doing out of prison? Ain't you supposed to be locked up for life?" Tracy looked at Dennis Frogger.

"What he doing down here with you?" Then he lifted himself up on the banister.

"This has gone far enough." Detective Dennis Frogger, his hand on his trigger, ordered Tracy, "Get your ass down from there! You try to jump in that water, I'll put a bullet in you before you hit it. Now get the fuck down!"

Persuaded by Frogger's directive, Tracy came off the banister.

"Now tonight is showtime, kid." Detective Dennis Frogger jerked Tracy inside the house by the collar of his shirt. "Sit down," he said, forcing him to a chair in the guestroom.

Blue grabbed an apple off the table. He asked Frogger, "You ready to tell him the rest of the story?"

"Why not? It's not like he'll be getting out of this alive anyway. To make a long story short, Tracy"—Frogger rubbed the top of his head—"you're a good boy, but you're fucked." He smiled. "You're going to take the fall for everybody because you're the only one left." He lit a cigarette. "You see, Blue and the Africans go way back."

"The Africans. Them niggas is wild, ain't they, boy?" Blue slapped down his hand on Tracy's shoulder. "A while back, around the time when your deceased homeboy made his dramatic re-appearance, there was this African dude I met while I was locked up. We shared the same cell and shit. The nigga kept talking about this gun connection he had. He could get guns anytime. He said he and his two brothers were making money selling guns and bootlegging clothes as a front for the deliveries." Blue circled the table as he talked. Now he was facing Tracy. "He said that they was using the money from the clothes to buy more guns. The shit didn't sound right to me. I got ol' Frogger here to invest some of my money into sabotaging Christian's business, once I found out it was him they was bootlegging.

But I really wanted in on the gun business. I got word to Frogger, he made a call, and the rest is history."

"You knew the Africans was behind this the whole time?" Tracy asked.

"Don't you dare judge," Detective Dennis Frogger told him. "You killed your best friend."

Blue looked at his watch. "They should've called by now."

And, right on cue, Detective Dennis Frogger's phone rang.

To be continued ...